To Alice,

x

Ginger

A Family Saga

Irene Lebeter

Other Titles by Irene Lebeter -

Vina's Quest

Maddie

The Clock Chimed Midnight

Who Were You?

ISBN: 9798415446346:

In memory of Ian and Rene Lebeter,

forever grateful for their kindness to me.

For Alma

Dear Reader

Authorway first published my work back in 2014 and I'm delighted to have all five of my novels now in print under their auspices. Because my I.T. skills are extremely basic, without their help you would not be reading this book. Thank you Gerry and Elaine from Authorway.

In her book *'The Mills Family of Long Melford, Suffolk, England – The Journey to Hobart Town, Tasmania, Australia'* detailing the history of her convict ancestors, Christina Callinan has given me valuable insight into the cruelty my character, Ginger, would have suffered during his time in a penal colony. Thank you, Christina.

The cover picture of Port Arthur Penal Colony is thought to have been taken around 1870 and is believed to be the oldest known picture of this establishment. Picture provided by

Photo © www.BeattiesStudio.com and used with kind permission of John Stephenson.

Alma Ross gave me assistance in planning Lily's journey in 1880 from Dubbo to Melbourne. Lily used a horse-drawn carriage for part of the way, changing to the train on stretches where railway lines had been laid by then.

Of course in 1880 such a long trip would have involved Lily in staying overnight at inns on the way. Alma has also shown great patience in answering my frequent questions about Australian flora. Thank you dear friend.

I am indebted to my good friend Patricia Hutchinson for so willingly spending many hours in proofreading the story and offering excellent suggestions for changes. She also laid out the two Family Trees in the story, giving them a much more professional appearance than I could have. You know how grateful I am Patricia.

Thanks to Paula Andrews (author of teen novel *'Oranges and Lemons'*) for helping me create the scene of Lily's birth in 1861. As an ex-midwife, Paula's advice was most useful.

Helen Hodge provided helpful information in the section of the book that was set in Longniddry. Thank you Helen and I hope you like the way I have described the house in Kitchener Crescent.

I am grateful to Jo Love for providing the author picture on back cover. The photograph was taken in Rutherglen library. Thanks Jo.

I've received invaluable feedback from my fellow members of Kelvingrove Writers' – *Linda Bell, Pat Feehan, Madeleine Gorham, Patricia Hutchinson, Eilidh Maclaine, the late and sorely missed Theresa O'Hare and Lorraine Smith.* Thanks so much folks.

The wonderful writing produced by my fellow members of Strathkelvin Writers' - *too many to name individually* - has inspired and motivated me to try and make this fictional tale as believable as possible. Thanks everyone and I hope I have succeeded.

Finally I hope you, the reader, will find the story as enjoyable as I did when creating it. I would be delighted to have your feedback on the website – *Author on Amazon Irene Lebeter.*

Kind regards from

Speirs Family Tree

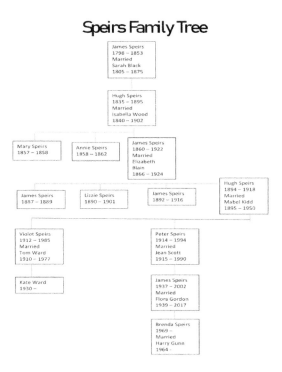

James Speirs
1798 – 1853
Married
Sarah Black
1805 – 1875

Hugh Speirs
1835 – 1895
Married
Isabella Wood
1840 – 1902

Mary Speirs
1857 – 1858

Annie Speirs
1858 – 1862

James Speirs
1860 – 1922
Married
Elizabeth
Blain
1866 – 1924

James Speirs
1887 – 1889

Lizzie Speirs
1890 – 1901

James Speirs
1892 – 1916

Hugh Speirs
1894 – 1918
Married
Mabel Kidd
1895 – 1950

Violet Speirs
1912 – 1985
Married
Tom Ward
1910 – 1977

Peter Speirs
1914 – 1994
Married
Jean Scott
1915 – 1990

Kate Ward
1930 –

James Speirs
1937 – 2002
Married
Flora Gordon
1939 – 2017

Brenda Speirs
1969 –
Married
Harry Gunn
1964 -

Wemyss Cemetery, Longniddry, Scotland
August 2019

The young woman rested under the copse in the shadow of its leafy branches until her breathing returned to normal. It had been an uphill slog, with the sun beating down on her bare shoulders. She sat on a nearby bench and applied some more sunscreen.

The grave looked neglected; the angel on top of the stone had been beheaded, and the wording was badly worn and encrusted with dank greenery. She scraped away as much moss as she could until the names slowly became visible.

First was James Speirs, who'd died in 1853. She read down, and stopped when she came to four siblings, their ages ranging from 18 months to 25 years. Two had died as young children and the other two sons had lost their lives in the First World War; she knew from the tracing she'd done via Ancestry that only one son, Hugh, had married and produced heirs, before being killed in action.

A frisson of excitement pulsed through her as she studied the notes she'd made about the earlier generations of her family. She stood in front of the grave, trying to sort out who was who. It had been difficult getting this information pieced together, especially with the names James and Hugh featuring so regularly down the generations. Since the first Census had taken place in 1841, she'd been forced to resort to old church records when tracing the earlier members of the Speirs family.

Emotion swept through her as she knelt down on the grass in front of the headstone and took her phone out of her handbag. As she pressed the camera button, the distant hum of a lawnmower cut through the still air. A tiny sparrow landed on the top of the headstone and chirped at her before flying off.

After a few moments of reflection, she got to her feet. It was only then that she spied something written near the bottom of the stone, partially hidden by the long grass growing around its base. The name wasn't engraved on the stone but looked like it had been scratched on by a nail file or a pair of scissors. She hadn't come across it during her family research, and she'd used both the Ancestry and Genes Reunited sites. How odd. Who would have done that and who was this mystery man on her ancestors' gravestone?

Her curiosity was aroused and she'd definitely do some further research. She trampled down the long grass with her foot and took a picture of the new inscription. She'd ask Aunt Kate if she knew anything about him. At nearly 90, Aunt Kate might have been told something when she was younger.

The question still ran through her mind as she carefully made her way down the steep slope, back to the massive iron cemetery gates.

CHAPTER ONE

On board 'Waverley' in the Indian Ocean
September 1847

Surrounded by the snores of his fellow convicts, Ginger wrestled with fear. The memory of his earlier flogging weighed heavily on his mind. Sweat drenched his face and neck and he clenched his knuckles so tightly it felt as though his fingers would snap. In the dim light, he could barely see someone kneeling beside his mattress.

'Drink this, laddie.'

Recognising Tom's voice, he gratefully drank the rum, which brought some fire back into his belly. 'Ta,' he said, and handed the bottle back. He and Tom, along with Jack and Will, had formed a band of four since boarding the vessel, in irons, from their prison van.

'Noo, try and get some sleep.'

Ginger felt Tom's hand brush over his arm, before his friend returned to his own mattress. Despite the rum, sleep eluded him that night. He ran his fingers over the unsightly birthmark on the side of his neck, something he often did when he was worried or nervous.

Two pinpricks of light glinted at him in the darkness; the giant rat frequented their quarters to forage for morsels lying on the floorboards. Ginger listened to the creaking of the mainsail up above and felt the vessel tossing from side to side as it fought its way through the treacherous waves.

Dawn was breaking when he was brought up under heavy guard. His fellow prisoners, silent and brooding, were lined along the deck. His hands were tied to the mast and, from where he hung, Ginger saw only the black-shod feet of his aggressor, the silver buckles on his shoes glinting in the first glimpse of early morning sunshine. Second Officer Fraser had taken a dislike to Ginger from the moment he'd boarded Waverley, and picked on him with little or no provocation. This flogging was for sharing his meagre ration with a prisoner who'd been denied food after a minor flouting of the rules.

He sensed, rather than saw, Fraser raise his whip with its cat-o'-nine tails, and his body jerked each time the leather thongs screamed their way across his back, still scarred from his previous flogging. At first, anger at the unfairness of his punishment blocked out the agony he was undergoing, but his yells intensified with each lash and his old wounds opened up once more. Blood slid down his skin, leaving a crimson puddle on the deck. His strength deserted him and long before the fifty lashes were completed, he'd lost consciousness.

Handing the blood-stained whip to a junior rating, Fraser strode off towards his cabin.

Ginger came to as his friends were cutting him down. He continued to drift in and out of consciousness as they carried his sagging frame, his back a mass of raw flesh, to the convict accommodation below deck, where they laid him, face down, on to his filthy mattress. A tin mug was held to his lips and he gulped the water down greedily.

'I'm sorry laddie, but we canny let infection in.' Tom's voice was little more than a whisper.

Jack and Will held Ginger's arms, while Tom bathed the gaping wounds with brine. The only antiseptic available to them, it stung mercilessly, and his yells rose up to the deck. His friends were then forced to leave him, writhing in agony, to go and join their work gangs.

During the following hours, it was only Ginger's desire for revenge on Fraser that kept him alive.

He would bide his time.

CHAPTER TWO

Plunkett Point Mine, Saltwater River Penal Colony, Van Diemen's Land

April 1848

Ginger stared into the pitch blackness, darker even than the hellish conditions in the mine. He'd lost track of how many days he'd been incarcerated in this dungeon cell. Resentment still ate away at him over the unfairness of his sentence; seven years' hard labour in a penal colony for stealing some food from a street market in Glasgow when he was destitute. It had been steal or starve.

On their arrival in the colony six months ago, Fraser had seen to it that Ginger was sent straight to Plunkett Point mine. Kept in chains under constant heavy guard meant there was almost no chance of escape. Several prisoners had already died when the mine flooded.

During his time of slavery at Plunkett Point, he'd been forced to work at quarrying, splitting timber, or burning lime and charcoal. It was while harnessed together with three other prisoners to drag the coal cart along the tramline from the mine to the beach that he'd hatched his plan of escape. He'd failed this time but vowed to find a foolproof way to release himself from this nightmare.

His punishment had been solitary confinement for fourteen days. No sunlight reached into his dank underground prison and the fetid stench in his cell choked him. Apart from his two hours of exercise every day, he spent the remaining twenty two hours breathing in musty air.

He swallowed a mouthful of the tepid water remaining in his tin mug, then spat it out, the taste making him want to vomit. The daily ration of one pound of bread and an unlimited quantity of water barely sustained him.

He clung to life for one reason only, his driving wish to

get even with Fraser.

On arrival at Saltwater River, his three mates had been sent to the agricultural camp, where they could at least toil in the open air. He missed them, especially Tom. He and Tom had been chained together in the horse-drawn police van taking them to begin their sentence and, as time passed, he'd begun to look on the older man like the father he'd never had.

Early on in their friendship, Tom had confided in Ginger about his past life. How he'd been in a happy marriage but, after his wife died in childbirth along with their stillborn baby, he'd turned to alcohol for consolation. His addiction led to him losing his home and job and saw him turn to thieving to get by.

Ginger's thoughts now moved to his mother, who died when he was 12. Left to fend for himself, he'd searched for work in Glasgow but his fiery temper lost him various jobs. One day he hitched a lift in a wagon to Ayrshire, where he found work on a dairy farm. He'd enjoyed his time there but when Farmer Wallace sold the farm, he'd drifted back to Glasgow, where destitution forced him to resort once more to stealing.

When his cell door clanked open, Ginger squinted in the dim light that flooded through the doorway. 'Get up, ya filthy piece o' scum,' his jailor growled.

He pulled himself off his bunk and staggered towards the door, his chains grating across the stone floor.

'Get a move on.' The jailor gave Ginger a shove that almost knocked him off his feet.

Two guards dragged him along the passage. When the prison doors were pushed open, he was blinded by the bright sunshine outside. After a fleeting glimpse of the outside world, he was returned to hard labour in the mine.

CHAPTER THREE
Old Friends Re-united
October 1848

Pushed and prodded between two guards, Ginger arrived at the forbidding red brick building. Inside, the thick beard of moss growing in the crevices of the dank walls gave off a foul smell. Hauled roughly along the corridor, his bare, calloused feet rubbed on the gravel floor. Around him, screams of other tortured souls rang in his ears, adding to his own torment.

One of the guards threw open a cell door and tossed Ginger inside like a bag of rubbish. The door clanged shut behind him, and he remained crouched down where he'd landed, until his eyes adjusted to his poorly-lit surroundings. The cell, built to house no more than half a dozen prisoners, had a row of at least a dozen hammocks strung up on both sides, with a narrow passageway down the middle.

The airless cell seemed to be empty; he supposed his fellow convicts were in the washhouse. Then some hushed voices reached him from the far end of the cell. Gradually, he made out their shapes; there were three of them, huddled together in a circle on the ground. One of the men stood up and came towards him.

'They've sent me here from Plunkett Point,' Ginger muttered through cracked lips as the fellow, dressed in the same grey prison garb as his own, helped him to his feet. In the dim light, he looked an inch or two shorter than himself.

'The mine's been closed due to poor quality coal so they've brought you to the agricultural camp.'

'Tom, is it you?' Ginger asked.

The man looked closer. 'Ginger, oh laddie, it's so good to see you.' He called to the others. 'Will, Jack, look who's here.'

Will slapped Ginger on the back and Jack offered him some water from his bottle.

'We hoped you'd survived your time in the mine,' Tom said. 'At least here, although we're worked like mules, we're out in the fresh air.'

When the work bell rang, they went outside and joined the line of convicts. Ginger was allocated to the same team as his three mates, and ordered to dig trenches for drainage.

As they were forming into their work gangs, a group of female prisoners were marched past them. Their garb was grey serge like the men, but they wore bonnets of the same material. The women were employed in the fields, planting or reaping. Ginger saw a smile and a wink pass between a female prisoner and Jack, confirming that love could still blossom even in this hellhole.

'Is Fraser still an officer in this camp?' Ginger asked Tom, as their line was marched off towards the trenches.

Tom nodded. 'We didn't see much of him when Plunkett Point was working but he's been back in the past few days.'

Ginger didn't reply until a guard marching at their side moved further up the line. 'He's always been out to get me,' he said. 'Because of him, I had a stretch in solitary confinement.'

'Try and stay out of his sight from now on, laddie,' Tom advised, as they were directed to their work stations.

CHAPTER FOUR
Escape
September 1849

Ginger crept out of his cell just before dawn and made his way over to the latrines. The dysentery was waning, but his belly still ached and his mouth felt tinder dry. He got back to the cell as the prisoners were stirring.

Tom laid a hand on Ginger's arm. 'Heard you go out, laddie.'

'It's easing off. I'm hungry now.'

'Well, swallow some o' that muck they call porridge. If it disnae make ye vomit, it'll keep your strength up.'

After lining up for their miserly portion of the breakfast 'porridge', they went into their work gangs. The four pals were sent to build new huts to house convicts due on the next transport. Most of them would be men, but there were usually women too. They tended to be put into wooden huts, and the cells kept for male prisoners.

Jack and Will hammered the wooden frames together while Tom and Ginger cut, prepared and carried the wooden slats, dropping them into a pile. Despite his age, Tom was strong, and worked as hard as the others.

Ginger relished the whiff of newly-cut wood, a pleasant change from the coal dust he'd been exposed to previously. As he worked, he drifted off into memories of his time on the dairy farm in Scotland, where he'd watched Farmer Wallace carving wood in the evening.

His thoughts were cut short by a gruff voice. 'You there,' the overseer, Spenser, barked, pointing to where the four mates were grafting.

Hearing the instruction, Tom stepped forward but Spenser's hand dismissed him. 'Not you, him with the red beard.'

Ginger had noticed the overseer sucking up to Fraser

and he was sure Spenser, at Fraser's command, was keeping a close eye on him. He bristled at the overseer's tone of voice and Tom laid a restraining hand on his arm. 'Easy, laddie, do as he says.'

But anger flooded through Ginger and he shrugged off Tom's hand. Unable to keep the resentment from his face, he strode across to the overseer.

'Report to the tree-felling squad immediately,' Spenser yelled, giving Ginger a shove. 'The old man can continue on his own.'

Forcing back his desire to strike the overseer, Ginger headed off. When he reached the place where the tree-felling gang were slaving, an overseer approached him and pushed him roughly towards the other prisoners. 'Right, get to work, we're behind schedule. Any slacking and you'll feel this,' the man added, cracking his whip on the ground at his side.

When they were finally permitted a ten-minute break, Ginger laid down his tools and walked into the shade of the trees. Some loose branches snapped under his feet and at that moment something snapped inside him; he had to free himself.

Last month two prisoners had escaped but were later captured and died by hanging. The noose might await him if he was caught, but death was better than his present existence. Much of Van Diemen's Land was forest, easy to get lost in. Harder though to get off the island. But he'd find a way; he wasn't going to spend another four and a half years in captivity.

While the overseer was being replaced, Ginger slipped cautiously behind a line of trees. None of his fellow prisoners saw him go and, when no shout of alarm rang out, he bolted off deeper into the forest. The new overseer wouldn't miss him and he wanted to be well away by the time the evening roll call took place.

The forest grew denser the further he went; massive strong-smelling eucalyptus, myrtles and pines, all merging together to form a vast canopy above his head. So thickly crowded that they blocked out both the sky and the sun. He kept going, tripping up from time to time on the rough roots of the trees criss-crossing one another on the narrow path. His elation at having escaped ran side by side with the fear that gripped him.

The sun was setting by the time Ginger allowed himself to rest. He hugged a large eucalyptus tree, known as a ghost gum because of the white colour of its bark, and leaned against its trunk. He closed his eyes and listened to some muffled birdsong. Over to his right he heard a horse neigh. The animal, tethered to a trunk, was visible through the trees. Ginger remained silent and watched the horse shake his head around, before nosing through some leaves on the ground.

Another whisper of movement, something hitting water. He crept towards the sound, taking care not to stand on a loose branch. Ahead the forest floor took a dip and the trees thinned out into a small clearing around a lake. A figure slowly began to take shape under the darkening sky.

Ginger stood motionless. The naked man was throwing pebbles into the lake, his long hair hanging down over his shoulders. Nearby was what looked like a bundle of clothes, left there while the man had a swim. The red tunic on top of the pile told him they belonged to an officer. A muscle in Ginger's neck pulsed when the man turned his face to the side. Peering through the gloom, Ginger knew with certainty that it was Fraser, alone in the clearing.

A red haze passed over Ginger's eyes. He lifted a thick, heavy branch lying nearby, with vicious-looking knotted pieces of bark on it, and edged closer to his prey. He was very close to his quarry when something stayed his hand, and into his head came his mother's soft voice. 'Son, you be the better man.'

As he stooped to put down the branch, a twig cracked beneath his foot. Startled, Fraser looked round.

Recognising who was behind him, a look of pure evil crossed his face. Ginger turned away and began to climb the slope but he drew back in pain as a large stone rained against his shoulder, a second one striking his cheek. Before he had time to recover, Fraser grabbed him from behind and pushed him down towards the lake. Ginger scrambled to his feet, as his enemy charged at him again. He threw his weight against the bully, whose torso was still damp. Fraser's wet soles slipped on a pile of leaves and he slumped down, striking his head on a large boulder.

With Fraser's unseeing eyes staring up at him, Ginger began to tremble. If he was caught now, he'd be branded a murderer, and they'd hang him without a trial. He had no tools to bury Fraser, so he dragged him to the edge of the lake and into the water. Picking up the branch he'd meant to use as a weapon he pushed the corpse further away from the bank.

He left Fraser's horse tethered to the tree trunk and also his clothes. A search party would be sent out when the officer failed to return to the camp and it would look like he'd drowned while swimming. But before he left the scene, he dug into Fraser's tunic pockets and brought out a money pouch and a penny knife.

It was pitch black by now and Ginger knew the work gangs would have been marched back to the camp long ago. He hoped that Tom and the others would have found a way to cover up his absence, for a short time anyway. He was sorry he wouldn't see his friends again but it was safer for them that they knew no details of his escape.

He had to get as far away from the camp as he could before daylight.

In silence he vanished yet deeper into his forest kingdom; the only eyes to witness his flight were those of a family of koalas resting on the branches of the gum trees.

CHAPTER FIVE
Flight to the Mainland
November 1849

As dawn was breaking, Ginger came to a sleepy hamlet, with a row of weatherboard houses. He crept along the back of the houses, and spied a line of washing outside one of them. He climbed the wooden fence and grabbed a pair of breeches and a shirt.

Disappearing into a cornfield, Ginger became almost invisible in between the rows of tall corn stalks. He removed his convict clothes and replaced them with the stolen ones. They fitted perfectly. Further on, he found an old, gnarled gum tree and stuffed his prisoner garb into a large cleft in the trunk, out of sight of passers-by.

He'd emerged from the forest after what he thought was about eight weeks, but it had been difficult to keep track of the days during his period in hiding. Since leaving the forest, he'd trekked for many days through the countryside in the direction of Port Arthur.

When the sun came up fully, he made himself a nest inside some bushes. He slept fitfully all day and walked on when darkness came.

He followed this pattern over the next few days, foraging for food on the way. Hunger drove him to eat berries that could have been poisonous, and he drank from any water holes or inland lakes he came across. Once he swallowed wild mushrooms and was violently sick. Somehow he survived.

Arriving on the deserted dock, he hid behind some piled-up fish boxes. The stink coming through the slats was overpowering but gradually he got used to it.

Crouching there, his thoughts went back to his time as a fugitive. On one occasion he'd come close to capture. Within touching distance of the soldier's red tunic, Ginger held his breath, rubbing his birthmark. He was certain he was going to be discovered, but luck was on his side when another soldier called out and the fellow vanished. Relief washed over Ginger, but it had been a close shave.

No further searches had been undertaken over the following days, and Ginger hoped they'd assumed he'd died from starvation or drowned. He didn't think Fraser's body had been discovered, otherwise the hunt would have continued.

From his present hiding place, he looked at the blue painted fishing boat tied up nearby. The boat was called Blue Wren, named after a tiny bird that Ginger had seen often around the camp and which he'd been told was a native Australian bird. The boat was empty so he guessed the crew were holed up in some rooming house for a sleep before they started their day's work.

At first he'd thought of becoming a stowaway but had decided to use Fraser's money to pay for a place on the crossing. His beard had grown bushy while he was in the forest but, using the penny knife he'd found in Fraser's pocket, he'd yanked away some of the fuzz.

The sky had lightened by now and soon he heard voices from a short distance away. When footsteps became audible in the clear morning air, he cautiously made his way to the back of the empty wharf building. Unseen, he watched three crew members arrive and climb aboard the fishing boat. They pulled the fish boxes that had hidden him, and some nets, on to the deck and the sail was hoisted, with the Union Jack flying from its mast. Ginger knew that Australia was still a colony of Great Britain, but he wondered how long it would be until the people demanded to have their own Australian flag.

Half an hour later the vessel's Master appeared, barking orders at his men.

Ginger stepped forward. 'Any chance of a passage to the mainland?'

The stern-faced man with gipsy-black hair looked

round when he heard the voice.

'I'll pay you,' Ginger said, holding up the money bag he'd taken from Fraser's pocket. 'I'll make it worth your while to take me across to Melbourne.' Tom had told him that Melbourne, the main town in Victoria, lay directly across the Bass Straight from Van Diemen's Land. 'I would wait for the passenger ferry but I've had word that my wife is ill in Melbourne and I'd like to get to her as soon as possible.' He'd seen from the timetable posted up on the wharf building that the ferry only ran two days a week, and today wasn't one of them.

The Master squeezed his chin between his thumb and his forefinger and stared at Ginger for a long time before he spoke. 'We don't land our catch in Melbourne.' Before Ginger had time to reply, he spoke again. 'Can take you to Duff's landing, along the coast from Melbourne,' he said, and quoted a price for the crossing.

Ginger was sure he was being cheated but he was desperate to reach the mainland. 'Duff's landing's fine by me. I can make my way home from there.'

'Deal.' The Master strode towards him and shook his hand, then waited while the money was counted out.

Ginger boarded the Blue Wren and, during the crossing, kept himself out of the crew's way. Once out in the Strait, he watched them haul in fish-laden nets, the whiff of freshly-caught crab wafting over to him sitting in the aft section of the boat. His ticket allowed him to use a bed below-decks, but this reminded him too much of the crossing on the Waverley and he spent the night up on deck. The sea remained calm throughout the journey and it was early next morning by the time the vessel neared the mainland.

Ginger's heart raced and his hands felt clammy. He didn't know what to expect in the settlement known as Duff's landing, but at least he had distanced himself from the camp.

'Good luck. Hope you get to your wife on time,' the

Master said, when the Blue Wren pulled in close to Duff's landing. Suspicion was written all over the man's sun-burned face.

'Thanks,' Ginger muttered. He climbed down the rope ladder and jumped into the shallow water of the bay. Then he waded quickly on to the shingly beach, and dried his boots on some reeds growing at the shoreline. When he looked back, the crew were unloading their catch on to the landing. Two men pushing a cart arrived from the township and began to pile the boxes of fish on to the back of it.

Coming off the beach, Ginger had to cross bushland for a considerable distance to get to the settlement. Once there, he got himself a bed at the first inn he found. It was no more than a shack but after Ginger's time in the forest, the thought of a proper bed seemed like luxury. The landlord raked his fingers through his hair as he studied the stranger facing him. 'One night only?' he asked, telling Ginger the cost per night.

'Yep,' Ginger replied, and handed over the money. Having no other prices to compare it with, he had to pay what was demanded.

The landlord held up his key. 'Room 4 upstairs, supper served in the bar at 8. We have freshly-caught barracuda on the menu.'

Ginger assumed barracuda was fish and wondered if it was from the Blue Wren's catch. He nodded towards the sign advertising shaving equipment for hire. 'I'll have a razor.'

Now as he stood in his room, staring into the mirror, he hardly recognised himself with his beard removed and his head shaved. The sunshine filtering in through the window cast a pattern of light and dark stripes over his bald pate.

He left the inn next morning after an early breakfast, served by the landlord's wife. She seemed sour and uncommunicative, which suited Ginger perfectly.

He followed the coast towards Melbourne, crossing fields and walking through forest areas where possible to avoid being observed on the coastal path. He'd kept a few apples and a chunk of bread and cheese from breakfast to sustain him during his long trek and quenched his thirst from streams he came across.

At last, as darkness descended, he finally saw the lights of Melbourne in the distance. Deciding he would make his way into the town at dawn, he lay down under the starry sky and fell asleep almost immediately.

*

In Melbourne town next morning, Ginger was on the alert, merging in with the maelstrom of humanity flocking around the markets and bazaars. He drew himself up sharply when a whistle blew, his hands going to his birthmark. Next minute he was almost bowled over by a man being chased by a Police Officer, shouting, 'stop thief'.

After the incident, Ginger allowed himself to breathe once more, but still kept his eyes and ears open. At one of the stalls he bought a rough sack, with a drawstring top and shoulder straps and at another got a shirt and a wide-brimmed hat. He dropped the shirt into the sack, which he slung on to his back.

Feeling hungry, he searched out a hostelry, where he sat at an outside table under the shade of a flowering bush to enjoy a glass of ale and a pork pie. He wolfed down the pie and asked for another. A light breeze whipped up for a moment and some purple blossoms fell on to the table. He picked one up and sniffed the flower's musky smell, almost woody. He'd seen these bushes at Saltwater River but didn't know what they were called.

'I'm trying to remember the name of this bush,' Ginger said to the waiter, when the man returned with another pie for him.

'Jacaranda, flowering early this year, they don't usually bloom until nearer Christmas. More ale?' he asked, as he laid the pie on the table.

'No thanks.' Fraser's money pouch was getting lighter. A short time later, he turned into a dingy side street and entered a grubby-looking rooming house.

'G'day. Trotter Crane at your service,' the stout, red-faced landlord greeted him.

Ginger was hit by the reek of beer wafting over from the man, added to the putrid smell of overcooked cabbage coming through the open kitchen door. He removed his hat and sat it on the counter. 'Any spare rooms?'

'Only one left. It's upstairs at the back of the house. Privy out in the yard. Room only or meals included?'

'Room only.'

'One night or one week?'

'Tonight only.' As he replied, Ginger looked up at the price of rooms listed on the wall behind Crane. It was cheaper than the room in Duff's landing, although still too much for this stinking hole. 'I'll take it,' he added.

'Payment in advance.'

He counted out the money and laid it in the landlord's outstretched palm.

'Could you sign your name, please?' Crane pushed the register towards him, laying a quill pen and inkwell beside it.

The thought of a dump like this owning a register brought a smile to Ginger's face. He dipped the pen nib into the inkwell and wrote Henry Black, thinking it prudent to use a false name. He was grateful that his mother had taught him to read and write.

Crane took back the register and gave Ginger his room key.

The room was as poky and dirty as he'd expected. He used the jug and ewer to wash, then changed into his new shirt. Giving the privy a miss, he made his way back to the main thoroughfare and went into a pub with a notice outside advertising cheap grub.

*

After a fitful sleep, Ginger rose early to wash and dress. He could hear his mother's voice telling him, 'remember Son, cleanliness is next to Godliness', and he felt once again the tenderness of her hands stroking his face. She'd always smelt lovely too, as she wore a lavender scented sachet inside the bodice of her dress.

He pulled on his breeches and stuffed his spare shirt into his sack. It was as he was ready to leave the rooming house that he heard voices. He moved closer to the top of the stairway, and crouched down. Two policemen were at the reception desk and he heard Trotter Crane say Henry Black as he showed them the register. The boat owner must have alerted the police about the passenger he'd brought over to the mainland.

On hands and knees he crept back to the room. There was only a short drop to the ground so he climbed out on to the windowsill and leapt down, landing softly on the grass verging the property. He got to his feet, limbs intact, and ran off. He kept walking and around midday found himself a hiding place in the bushes until darkness came. He trudged on through the night, wincing at the pain in his toes where his boots pinched him. By the time daylight arrived, his feet ached. He lay down on the ground and removed his boots to ease his bleeding and sore toes. He'd no idea where he was or how far he'd walked, but would only relax once he'd got himself well away from Melbourne town.

CHAPTER SIX
A Change of Luck
November 1849

Daylight was breaking through when Ginger rested against a fence. He'd been walking for weeks and thought he must be close to the New South Wales border. He'd worn a massive hole in his left boot and the right one wasn't much better. Since fleeing from the Melbourne rooming house, he'd slept by day and trekked through the night, drinking from any water holes he came across. He'd existed on wild berries and fruit, and even resorted to eating raw vegetables when he came across any.

One night he'd caught a hen in a farmyard, and wrung its neck to stop it squawking. Within minutes an upstairs window in the farmhouse was thrown open, and a man leaned out, holding a candle. Clutching his next meal against his chest, Ginger hid behind the henhouse, relieved when the house was plunged into darkness once more.

Back in the dense bushland, he'd rubbed two stones together and lit a fire, taking great care not to set the foliage alight. The smell of the bird cooking made him drool and before it was properly done he'd pulled the skin off the flesh and stuffed the meat into his mouth. With the leftovers in his sack, he'd doused the fire by scattering soil over it.

Sitting here now, he leaned his head back against the fence, glad to have a rest. Using his hat to shield him from the sun, his eyes closed and he drifted off. When he wakened, he felt refreshed.

He stood up and stretched his legs and back. Over to his left, some branches hung low over the fence, heavy with peaches. The ones he'd seen in the Melbourne market had looked and felt hard, but these ones were more inviting. He pocketed two peaches, put a few more into his sack, and ate one there and then. When he bit into its delicious tasting flesh, the juice ran down his chin.

He'd finished his snack and was about to move on when he heard the wail of an animal coming from somewhere nearby. His eyes followed the call of distress, and he saw a cat stuck on the high branches of a gum tree inside the fence.

Forgetting his throbbing feet, Ginger vaulted the fence and ran over to the tree. He shinned up and got himself on the sturdy branch beside the cat. It had a longer, bushier tail than the cats back home. He stretched out to lift it, but the animal bared its teeth and struck out at Ginger's hands with its claws, drawing blood.

'Ouch,' he yelled, and licked the blood away.

Meanwhile, the cat climbed up, with ease, to a higher branch. Winding its tail around the branch, the animal hung from it, giving him the evil eye. As Ginger began to shin down the trunk again, his foot slipped and with a yell he landed on the grass below. Still a bit dazed from his fall, he heard the sound of hooves, and when he opened his eyes, a man was standing over him, while a black stallion grazed nearby.

The man helped Ginger to his feet, and propped him up against the tree trunk.

'Thanks,' Ginger mumbled, running his hands down his legs and arms.

'Don't think you're any the worse of your tumble,' his rescuer said. 'You do know your trespassing on private property?'

'Sorry Mister, I heard the cat wail, and I climbed the fence to get him down. All I got for my trouble were these,' he said, holding out his cut and blood-spattered hands. Then he picked his hat up off the grass and stuck it on his head again. The man was sturdier built than himself, and a few inches taller, but he reckoned they were about the same age.

'What cat?'

'Up there.' Ginger pointed to the higher branches of the gum tree, where the cat was still hanging. 'With the bushy tail.'

The man threw back his head and roared with laughter. 'Struth, that ain't no cat. It's a possum, they roam freely around the property, and don't usually come out until night. It spends most of its time in the trees, foraging for food.' His bright blue eyes sparkled with mirth. 'But just as well I came across you, my pa is harder on folk who trespass on his land. How'd you get here anyway?' he asked, looking over the fence at the desolate bush country surrounding them.

'I've walked from Melbourne. It's taken me weeks. Hoping to get work in the first town I come to.'

'Not many of them around here. Nearest would be Dubbo. This is an agricultural area, mainly farms and bush country.'

Ginger took off his hat and scratched his forehead. 'Is this Victoria or New South Wales, Mister?'

'New South Wales. Could you not get work in Melbourne?'

'Nothing doing.' Noticing that the man was taking in his dishevelled state, Ginger's eyes dropped to his bloodied and swollen toes sticking out of his ripped boots.

'I'm Olly Jenkins,' the chap introduced himself.

Ginger said the first name that came to him. 'Ben Harker.' He rubbed his sweaty forehead with his arm, then put on his hat again.

'This is a sheep station. Ever worked with sheep?'

'No, but I was a labourer on a dairy farm in Scotland. I'm not scared of hard work.'

Olly studied him a bit longer, then said. 'I'll talk to my pa about you as we could do with an extra farmhand. I think you need a clean-up. Hungry?'

'Starving.' Ginger hardly dared believe his luck was changing.

'Right, come with me and we'll get you some tucker.'

'I was sure it was a cat,' Ginger said, as he and his new friend walked towards the homestead, Olly leading his horse by the reins.

Olly grinned. 'You certainly won't have seen any possums in Scotland.'

'He's a fine animal,' Ginger said, patting the stallion's flank. 'What's his name?'

'Major.'

When they reached the homestead, a black and white collie lay outside, resting his head on his front paws. The dog opened one eye and stared at Ginger, who stooped down to stroke the top of his head. 'What's your name, boy?'

'It's she, and her name's Jess,' Olly told him. Opening the door, he spoke to someone inside. 'Maud, this is Ben Harker, he had a tumble from one of the gums, when he was trespassing on our land,' he said, the laughter clear in his voice.

The room was dark after the bright sunlight outdoors and it took Ginger's eyes time to adjust. Maud was a buxom woman, her rosy cheeks glowed from working at a steamy stove, and some damp strands of mousey-brown hair fell out of the mop cap she wore. Ginger reckoned she'd be in her forties.

She wiped her forehead with the back of her hand as she looked at the stranger standing in the doorway. Then her eyes crinkled at the sides and she gave him a cheery smile.

Olly threw his arm casually around Maud's shoulders. 'Maud's our wonderful housekeeper cum cook and we'd be lost without her.'

'General dogs-body around here, so I am,' she said, but gave Olly such an adoring look that it was obvious she didn't mean a word of it.

Olly winked at her. 'Admit it, you love ordering us around. Now, be a pet and get Ben something to eat and drink. He's been travelling so he's in need of nourishment.'

She dried her hands on the apron covering her dress and moved over to the stove. 'I've got some broth and have just taken a loaf out of the oven. That do you?' she asked Ginger.

'Sounds wonderful, thanks.'

'I'll go and cut some more logs, Maud,' Olly said. He turned to Ginger. 'I'll leave you in Maud's hands,' and, whistling cheerily, he sauntered outside.

'You can wash your hands and face in the sink over there,' Maud directed Ginger, while she was slicing the bread. Once he was seated at the table, she plonked a big bowl of broth in front of him. 'Get that down you, lad,' she said, and brought over some thick chunks of bread on a platter and a glass of milk.

Ginger tucked in, the food tasting like nectar.

Maud hauled some sheets and towels out of the copper boiler. Using a contraption with two rollers, she turned a handle to put the wet linen through the rollers, to drop into a basket sitting on the floor. Then she went outside to peg the washing up in the yard. When she returned, Ginger had cleared his bowl and finished the bread. 'More?' she asked and he nodded.

'Have you worked here long, Missus?' he asked, while she was re-filling his bowl.

'More years than I can remember,' she told him, and brought the soup and some more bread over to the table. 'I came here when Mistress Evelyn was a young bride. After her death four years ago,' she went on, her eyes welling up at the memory, 'I stayed on to look after the Master and Olly.'

'So you'll have known Olly all his life,' he said, as he pulled off a chunk of bread and dipped it into the broth.

'I have that. I was with the Mistress when she gave birth to him.' The kitchen chair scraped across the stone floor when Maud pulled it out and sat down facing Ginger. Tears streamed down her face, and she wiped her eyes with her apron. 'A loveable little rogue he was, and just as dear to me today, so he is. Don't tell him I said that, of course. We can't be making him too fond of himself.'

'What's the name of this property?'

'Wattle Trees, with 14,000 sheep. Master Lawrence's Da owned the station afore him. It's one o' the biggest in the area.'

'How come Wattle Trees?'

'Because of the number of wattles that grow around the property.'

'The trees with the bright yellow flowers?' he asked, and she nodded.

'Olly and his father are lucky to have you, Missus.'

'This is my home and they're good to me, so they are. And less o' the Missus, lad, Maud's fine.'

'Are you Irish, Maud?' he asked.

'I am, and proud to be so. I was born and reared in Enniskillen in County Fermanagh. I came to Melbourne over twenty-five years ago; with my folks in the ould country long since passed on, Australia's home to me now.' As she was speaking, she cleared away Ginger's dishes. 'I hear from your talk that you're a Scot.'

'Yes, from the east coast of Scotland,' he told her, looking up as Olly came back into the kitchen, carrying an armful of chopped logs, which he dropped into a box beside the range.

'You two seem to be getting on well,' he said, smiling from one to the other. 'Have you made sure our man here has staved off his hunger, Maud?'

Ginger got in first. 'She's done me proud. I've had double helpings of soup and bread.' He almost added 'so I have' but stopped himself in time, worried that he might offend Maud and she'd think he was making fun of her.

Olly disappeared for a few moments and returned with a pair of sturdy boots, which he laid on the floor beside Ginger. Although a bit scuffed at the front, there were no breaks in them. 'Try these on for size.'

Ginger took off the remnants of his boots and pushed

his feet into the others. He stood up and walked around the table. 'They fit great, Mister. Are you sure I can have them?'

'They're yours, we can't have you walking around in these things.' Olly lifted the old boots as he was speaking and tossed them into the fire. Green and blue flames hissed over the leather uppers, licking around what was left of the soles. Ginger stared in fascination and very soon the boots were no more.

'Seen your pa around?' Maud asked.

Olly shook his head. 'No, he's working in the top paddock. Maud, does Mrs Walters at The Pines still take boarders?'

'Think so.'

'Right,' Olly said, laying some coins on the table in front of Ginger, 'that'll pay for an overnight stay at The Pines.' He brushed away Ginger's attempt to decline the offer.

'Thanks a lot, Mister … Olly,' he added, unsure how to address his benefactor. He lifted the money and dropped it into his shirt pocket.

Olly grinned again. 'Drop the Mister, Olly's fine.'

'Have you loaded the ewes?' Maud asked Olly.

'Yep. I'm taking the wagon to the market Ben so I can let you off at The Pines. Tomorrow morning, if you can find your way back here, I'll have spoken to my pa about the possibility of taking you on. Can't promise anything, mind. Pa does the hiring.'

At The Pines, Olly spoke to Mrs Walters about hiring a room. 'G'day, till tomorrow,' he called over his shoulder to Ginger, as the horses set off at a trot.

*

Next morning Ginger was glad to have a proper wash at The Pines and while he was having breakfast Mrs Walters brought him good news.

'Farmer Lawson, my neighbour, is taking some hay over to Mr Jenkins at Wattle Trees this morning, and he has agreed to take you with him.'

Ginger beamed at her. 'Thanks.' His luck seemed to be changing, and if he got the job with Olly and his pa, it would solve his money problems good and proper. But he didn't want to get too far ahead of himself.

Aboard the wagon, Ginger perched on top of a hay bale. When they got to Wattle Trees, he thanked the farmer for the ride and jumped down.

Olly and an older man were standing outside the homestead. 'Ben, come and meet my pa, Larry Jenkins,' Olly called. Mr Jenkins nodded to Ben, and then went off to speak to Mr Lawson.

'Did Mrs Walters treat you okay?' Olly asked, folding his arms.

'Like a king. It was great to sleep in a proper bed again.'

'Told my old man about you last night, and how you tried to rescue the possum, which you thought was a cat.' He grinned. 'Pa seems fine about taking you on as a hired help, on a trial basis at first. Says he'll trust my judgement. Let's go inside.'

Maud welcomed Ginger back. 'Sleep well, lad?'

'Like a top.'

Mr Jenkins joined them soon after. 'Olly tells me you worked with animals in Scotland,' he said, in a gravelly voice.

Looking at Larry Jenkins, it was obvious where Olly got his honest face and bright blue eyes. Larry's dark hair was peppered with white but, although he had to be middle-aged, his face and physique were that of a much younger man. 'That's right, Sir,' he said, 'I was a hired hand on a dairy farm but I lost the job when the farmer retired.'

'So is that what brought you over here?'

Ginger clenched his fists at his sides, but knew he couldn't tell the whole truth. 'Yes, there's so much unemployment in Scotland that I thought I'd get work easier here. I'm used to hard graft.'

'You'll get plenty of that here. Right, we'll give you a

trial and see how it goes. Why don't you show Ben round the property, Olly? And get Maud to organise a bed for him in the outhouse. I'm going to move the sheep from the top paddocks,' he said, when the three of them went outside, whistling to Jess who got up and followed him. He untethered his horse from the wooden rail, then mounted and was off, the horse's hooves kicking up dust as they went, with Jess racing along at the horse's side.

'Beautiful beast,' Ginger said, once the dust had descended and he could see again.

'That's Montgomery. Pa reared him from a colt.'

Maud came out of the kitchen, carrying a couple of floor rugs, which she slung over the washing line in the yard. She began using a carpet beater on them but stopped when Olly called to her. 'When you finish that, Maud, will you make up the bed in the outhouse for Ben?'

'I surely will,' she replied, then returned to her carpet beating.

Olly led the way to the stables. 'I take it you can ride,' he said, as he opened the door of the first stall and led Major out of it.

'Farmer Wallace let me work with the horses during ploughing. Clydesdales they were and suited for the work. He let me ride some of the other farm horses too.'

'Good. You can ride Pharaoh in the next stall to Major.'

When the horses were saddled, the two men set off. Ginger was amazed at the vastness of the property, and the way the sheep wandered for miles to seek good areas of grassland. He drew his fingers through Pharaoh's thick mane as they trotted back from the middle paddocks. The horse's flanks were warm against his legs and he felt really at home in the saddle. 'Do you need to round up the sheep at night?' he asked Olly, riding at his side.

'No, they're outside all year round. They're a hardy breed and are happy in the paddocks, even in winter. Right, I've shown you enough for today. You'll see the rest of the property tomorrow.' With the horses back in their stalls munching on some of Farmer Lawson's fresh hay, the two men made their way to the outhouse.

'This was an old, broken-down storeroom,' Olly told him, and pushed open the door, which creaked in resistance. 'We had new storerooms built a couple of years ago, and this was furnished as sleeping quarters.' He led the way inside. 'Sometimes one of our casual workers uses it during the shearing season or, if there're a few of them, we bed them down on mattresses on the floor. But right now it's yours.'

The smell of wood filled Ginger's nostrils when he entered. It took him back to the last time he'd been with his mates at the colony, when they were building the wooden huts. The sadness he felt when thinking of his lost friends was overtaken by his delight in seeing his new bedroom. The room was spotlessly clean; the furniture, though sparse, was in good condition and the brass headboard on the bed was gleaming.

'Maud's used some of her usual magic,' Olly stated, as he looked around. He pointed towards a metal container in the corner. A good size, almost a bath tub. 'The creek runs behind here and you can use water from there or you can fetch some from the tank outside the homestead.'

'Good your pa seems alright with me being here.'

Olly nodded. 'Pa's getting on in years and knows he'll want to retire one of these days so he leaves more decisions to me.' He grinned. 'Trusts my judgement, so you better not let me down.' He turned to leave and said when he got to the door, 'I'll see you at dinner. Maud likes us at the table at 6 o'clock sharp.'

'You mean you want me to eat with you and your pa?'

'Yep. Since Ma passed on, we don't stand on ceremony.'

After Olly left, Ginger lay on the top of the bed for a shut eye. When he wakened, he used the bucket sitting beside the metal bath to collect some creek water. He gave himself a good wash down and put his clothes back on.

When he went into the kitchen, Olly and his pa were already at the table, facing one another. Ginger sat down beside Olly, leaving the other seat for Maud.

'What's for tucker tonight, Maud?' Larry asked.

She smiled broadly as she carried over a large dish. 'Tis your favourite pumpkin pie, Master Lawrence,' she told him, putting the dish down in the middle of the table. She served it up before sitting at the table, next to Larry.

He threw an arm round her shoulders. 'And here I was, telling Montgomery when we were on our way back to the stables that I could just do with some of Maud's pumpkin pie.'

His words had the desired effect and Maud's rosy cheeks became even redder with the compliment to her cooking.

After eating, they moved into the parlour, where Maud served them their coffee. Larry puffed contentedly on his pipe, while Olly lit a cigar. He held the pack out to Ginger, who shook his head. Very soon the room was full of smoke rings.

Around 9 o'clock, Ginger got to his feet. 'Think I'll turn in now.'

Olly yawned. 'Yeah, same here. We usually bed down around now as we've an early start in the morning. Maud has breakfast ready at 6 am.'

'See you tomorrow, lad, bright and early.' Larry raised his hand in farewell, as Ginger made his way to the door.

'G'nite, lad, sleep well,' Maud called to him as he went through the kitchen.

Ginger enjoyed his walk back to the outhouse. Darkness came early here in Australia and he stood at the open door, looking up at the starry sky. Tom had once pointed out to him a cluster of stars, saying that it was called the Southern Cross. That shape could be seen clearly tonight.

When sleep beckoned him, he closed the door and went inside.

CHAPTER SEVEN
A Scary Moment
April 1850

Jess rounded up the sheep and Ginger separated them into two groups; one lot directly to the shearing shed and the others herded into an enclosure to wait. Looking down at the dry, yellowed grass, he understood Olly's concerns about serious drought conditions ahead. 'One bad season can wipe us out,' he'd said. 'We need a hefty rainfall to save that happening.'

Pulling his fingers through a ewe's thick coat, Ginger guided her along the fencing towards the shearing shed. As he gave the animal's rump a slap, another one took off. Jess barked loudly and chased after the runaway, returning her to the queue waiting for a haircut.

Once his other chores were finished, Ginger stopped at the shearing shed on his way back to the homestead. He was hit by the warm smell of lanolin from the fleeces piling up on the wooden floor. Ten or more men were in the shed and their banter, together with the bleating of sheep, caused the sound to reverberate off the tin roof. Ginger stood for a few moments in the open doorway, holding his fingers in his ears against the din. Rivers of sweat coursed down the shearers' backs, despite wearing only sandals and shorts.

Back at the homestead, Olly was in the kitchen drinking tea. Ginger made some for himself, and it wasn't until he sat down at the table, that Olly spoke. 'A couple of hours ago, I had a visit from two policemen.'

Ginger froze, and his fingers played across his birthmark. He shivered, tasting bile in his mouth, as he tried to remain calm. He was sure Olly could hear the thumping of his heart. 'What did they want?'

Olly drew circles on the table with his fingertips. 'They

were searching for a convict, one who'd escaped from a penal colony in Van Diemen's Land. They've found a man's body. He disappeared around the same time as the con. Asked if I'd seen or heard of him. They're checking all the sheep stations and farms around the area.'

'What did you tell them?' Ginger tried unsuccessfully to control the tremor in his voice.

'Said I hadn't seen an escaped con, nor had there been any strangers around here recently. I asked when the man had escaped and they said it was in September of last year.' This time Olly looked straight into Ginger's eyes.

Ginger let his gaze drop to the table top, sure the hangman's noose was beckoning him. He felt breathless and found it hard to swallow.

'It was lucky I was alone when the police called. Did I tell them the truth?'

Still no response.

'Ben, I think it's time you came clean. You owe me that, at least.'

Ginger began slowly, then the words tumbled out. 'I changed my name to Henry Black when I arrived in Melbourne, after my escape from the Saltwater River camp. I changed it again to Ben Harker when you found me trespassing on your property.'

Olly sat back in his chair, with his arms folded. 'Who are you really?'

Ginger told him his real name. 'I was known in the camp as Ginger because of my red hair. Are you going to give me away?' he asked, raking his fingers through his thick mop.

'Probably not, especially if you're honest with me.'

'My father died before I was born. My mother loved and took care of me, but we were so poor, we often couldn't eat for days at a time, and I ran around in bare feet.' He stopped speaking for a moment and stared through the kitchen window, lost in his memories of that time. 'I was 12 when she died, and I was left to fend for myself … I spent most of my time on the streets, begging.'

'Did you not go to school?'

'Schooling costs money. But my mother had some education, and she taught me to read, write and count.'

'And what about work?'

'I did factory and farm work, but mostly was unemployed and living on the streets.'

'Were there no hostels where you could stay?'

'There was the workhouse.' Ginger squirmed in his seat at the thought. 'But with everything I heard from folk who'd been there, I think I was safer on the street.'

'You said you'd been a hired help on a dairy farm,' Olly reminded him.

'That's true. Mr Wallace took a liking to me and was kind, a bit like your pa has been. But when he retired, the new farmer brought his own workers so that was me out of work and homeless again.'

'What did you do to be sent over here as a convict?'

'I was caught stealing food from a market stall in Glasgow. They took me up before the Magistrate, who sentenced me to seven years' hard labour in a penal colony in Van Diemen's Land.'

'Seven years for stealing when you're starving?'

'It's what happens over there.' Ginger clasped his hands together, the knuckles tight. If Olly gave him away, he'd be sent back to Saltwater River to face the hangman.

A short silence fell between them, broken by Olly, his facial expression giving nothing away. 'And the body that's been found?'

'It'll likely be Fraser, an officer who took a dislike to me and made my life hell. When I escaped into the forest, I found him there on his own and … and we fought. He'd just come out of the lake and was still wet … he tried to charge at me and his feet slipped on some leaves …'

'And?' Olly tapped his fingers on the table as he asked the question.

'He fell backwards and hit his head off a boulder.'

'Dead?'

Ginger nodded and stood up. He let his shirt drop to his waist, revealing the scars. He'd never bared his back before, even when sweating profusely out in the fields, always making the excuse he was protecting his fair skin.

Olly stared at the scars in silence.

Ginger pulled on his shirt again. 'Fraser flogged me twice, the second time I nearly died. I really hated him, Olly, but I swear I didn't kill him. I fought him in self-defence, but that won't keep me from hanging if I'm caught.'

'From what you've told me, and what I see on your back, it seems the brute had it coming. Thanks for your honesty, Ben. You're a good worker and cause no trouble, so I won't break your secret to the police, or to anyone.'

'Thanks.' Ginger's voice was hoarse with emotion.

Olly got up and carried their two mugs over to the sink. 'I know you said you were known previously as Ginger but to me you're Ben Harker. I met you as Ben and that's who you are.'

'I do really think of myself as Ben.'

Their conversation stopped abruptly, when Maud came into the kitchen, followed by Larry, carrying the provisions they'd brought from the market.

CHAPTER EIGHT
Dubbo Market
October 1850

'Going to the sheep sales at Dubbo tomorrow, Ben, and thought you could come along,' Larry said, as they were enjoying Maud's Irish stew and dumplings at dinner.

Ginger wiped his mouth on his napkin. 'I'd find that interesting, Sir.' He was keen to learn more about the running of a sheep station and attending a market would add to his knowledge. He'd never left the property since he'd arrived at Wattle Trees, fear still niggling about being arrested. But the thought of visiting Dubbo was inviting. 'You going Olly?'

'Sure thing. We can see to the stock before we leave. Pa'll drive us in the wagon so Major and Pharaoh can have a rest day.'

'How far away is Dubbo, Sir?' Ginger asked Larry.

'Not far at all, it's the nearest town to us, a small country town. And Ben, how many more times do I have to tell you, drop the Sir. Larry or Mr Jenkins will do.'

'Thanks, Sir, I mean, Mr Jenkins.' Ginger felt calling his boss Larry was a step too far, although he was pleased to have been offered the chance.

Olly stood up and pushed back his chair. 'I'm off for a smoke. The stew was delicious, Maud,' he said, and blew her a kiss. Soon afterwards, Larry and Ginger followed him into the parlour.

*

When the wagon arrived in Dubbo next day, Ginger looked around from his seat behind Olly. The township nestled amongst gently rolling hills. So different from the industry-dirty, humanity-pulsing Glasgow of his past.

Larry jumped down from the wagon and secured the horses. The sheep trailer, hitched to the back of the wagon, had slowed them down on the rough country tracks. Ginger stood still, trying to take in the vast acres of emptiness around him.

'Welcome to Dubbo, Mate,' Olly said. 'It was opened up back in the '30s with vast runs of sheep, and it's thrived ever since. Pa once considered buying a station here.'

They made their way to the sales area, edging into the group of people surrounding the show ring.

'G'day,' a voice said behind them.

'Hi, old cobber.' Olly slapped the man on the back. 'Pete, meet Ben Harker, who's been with us for a year now.' He turned to Ginger. 'Pete owns Fairfields farm, next to ours, and his son Barry is a mate of mine.'

'Yeah Olly and my Barry were at school together,' Pete said, nodding at Ginger.

'How's tricks, Pete?' Larry asked, when he returned from speaking to another group of local farmers.

'Good, thanks.'

The auction started up then, and all conversation ceased. Larry bought three rams from a breeder he trusted, plus a dozen ewes. Pete got himself a ram at a knock-down price and he bid successfully for twenty black faced ewes. Ginger became engrossed in the bidding war that took place and he was amazed at the large amounts of cash that changed hands during the sale. Money like he could only dream of.

'Fancy joining us in the pub?' Olly asked Pete, once the sale was over and folk were beginning to disperse. 'Think Pa needs some lubrication after all that bidding,' he said, grinning at Larry.

Larry shrugged. 'Suits me to wet my whistle before the drive home. The beer's good in The Kerosene Lamp.'

Leaving the bright sunshine outside, they entered the dull exterior of the pub. True to its name, the place was lit by kerosene lamps, some sitting on the counter and others placed in crevices in the solid stone walls.

Olly went over to the bar for their drinks while the

other three found a table in a corner near the window. 'Get this down you,' he said, returning with four beers, two pewter mugs held in one hand and two in the other.

Some liquid slid down one of the mugs, leaving a puddle of froth on the wooden table top. Larry mopped up the liquid with his handkerchief and raised the mug to his lips. He took a long drink, then let out a contented sigh.

'Howdy, old man.' A young farmer, a cigar hanging out of the side of his mouth, thumped Larry on the back as he passed by their table.

Larry grinned. 'Less of the old, Phil. Don't forget, I can still hammer you at cards.'

The younger man took his place beside his mates, and chuckled. 'You ain't never goin' to let me forget that.'

Olly downed his pint in one go. 'Been to any games recently, Phil?' he asked.

'Nah, too busy. I've lost a couple of hands in the past two months.'

'I'll let you know if I hear of anyone looking for work.'

'Thanks,' Phil said, and started up a conversation with his mates.

'How'd you find the auction, Ben?' Pete asked.

'Couldn't believe there was so much cash floating about.' Ginger slurped down the remainder of his beer. 'Anyone want another?'

Larry whipped a note out of his pocket and held it up. 'You get them, lad, but it's my shout.'

Half an hour later Larry took his timepiece out of his waistcoat pocket. 'We best get off home before Maud nags us about a burnt dinner.'

When the four men emerged from the pub, the sky had clouded over. 'Looks like rain,' Ginger said.

Olly raised his head and followed Ginger's gaze. 'Yessir, the ground could sure do with some heavy falls though none expected for a few weeks yet. Hope we don't lose as many sheep from drought as we did two years ago.

Some days we picked up over forty dead ones from the paddocks. Almost wiped us out, didn't it, Pa?'

'Yeah, but we've survived to see another season.'

When they approached the wagon, they could hear the sheep bleating inside the trailer. Once Larry had checked that it was firmly attached to the wagon, he said, 'Ben, you jump aboard and we'll be off.'

They called farewell to Pete and sang all the way back to Wattle Trees.

'And how did you enjoy the auction?' Maud asked Ginger during dinner that night.

He swallowed his last forkful of Maud's homemade steak and kidney pudding, and washed it down with some milk, before he replied. 'I loved it, the bidding and all.'

'You've to keep your wits about you, so you have. My first auction in Australia, I got so carried away that I almost bought a house, with no money to pay for it.'

Olly roared with laughter. 'How did you manage that?'

'I was jumping up and down in excitement, so I was, and threw my hand up in the air at the wrong time. I near fainted when the auctioneer took is as a bid. Then somebody else called out with a higher bid, thanks be to God.'

The three men were still laughing about Maud's experience at the auction when they went into the parlour for their after-dinner coffee.

CHAPTER NINE
A New Hobby
November 1850

Ginger sat under his favourite wattle tree, its branches heavy with blossoms. He enjoyed this time of day, when he could practice his new skill. Holding a chunk of wood in one hand, he used his bowl-shaped knife to scrape away at the wood, until something resembling a leaf was gouged out. His only other tool was Fraser's penny knife.

During their midday break, he'd scoff the tucker Maud prepared each morning, and then spend time on his hobby. He'd often watched Farmer Wallace back in Scotland carving pieces, but hadn't had the chance to do any himself until he'd come here.

Things had gone well for him in the year he'd been at the farm. The police search had remained on his mind a lot of the time, but it was six months now since they'd spoken to Olly, and no more lawmen had come looking for him. He was Ben Harker now. Sometimes he even forgot he'd been a prisoner, so carefree his life had become. By now, he'd moved into a room in the homestead, leaving the outhouse free for any casual labour.

'Hey, that looks pretty good.' Olly, who'd been sitting at the other side of the tree, was now standing over him. 'Have you done any carving before?'

Ginger squinted up, unable to see his friend's face for the sun. 'No, but I used to watch Farmer Wallace, when I worked on the dairy farm. He made furniture too.'

'Where d'you get the tool?' Olly nodded at the knife he was using.

'Found it on a shelf in the old outhouse when I was sleeping in there. Hope you don't mind, I didn't mean to steal it like.'

'No worries. It's probably been there for years, maybe

one of the shearers was also a wood carver. So, if you can use it, you're welcome.'

Olly leaned down and took the wood from Ginger's grasp. ''Struth, that's bonza. Looks like you got a natural gift for wood carving.'

Ginger shrugged and got to his feet. 'Just passing some time,' he said, and dropped the wood and the knife into the deep pockets of his work overalls. 'D'ye want me to tend the sheep in the middle paddock?'

'Yep, and there's a couple of ewes ready to lamb.'

'Okay, I'll watch out for them.' Unlike in Scotland, where farmers helped the sheep to deliver their lambs, here in Australia the animals were left to get on with it themselves.

Major and Pharaoh had been grazing nearby during the lunch break. Ginger fed some pieces of turnip and apple to Pharaoh, who nuzzled his hand as he took them. Ginger had formed a close relationship with the horse over the past year. He rode off, leaving Olly to return to the homestead to attend to paperwork.

CHAPTER TEN
An Interesting Suggestion
November 1852

'You've got a real talent you know, Ben,' Larry said, when he walked into the shed where Ginger was carving an owl. The lad spent every hour of his leisure time on his craft. Ginger's hands moved swiftly and surely over the wood, gouging out a circle for the bird's eyes. He'd discovered he was good at drawing too and always made a sketch of his subject before he began to carve it.

Ginger stopped what he was doing. 'Do you think so, Larry?' Having worked here for three years, he was now on first name terms with his boss.

'Fair dinkum.' Larry sat down at the table and picked up the acorn sitting there. He ran his fingers over the precise shapes of the piece of art. 'You're a natural, lad. Ever thought of taking up a career as a wood carver?'

'Wouldn't know how to start. Anyway, I enjoy working with the sheep.'

Larry clasped his hands under his chin and looked thoughtful. 'You could start up a carving business and help us in the busy season. Steve and Brady are a good help, but we value your expertise with shearing.' Having watched the professionals for years, Ginger had become adept with the shears.

Larry leaned forward and patted his arm. 'I think you have a future in carving, with the new settlers demanding high class locally made goods. Think about it lad,' he said, getting to his feet. 'You can stay here with us for as long as you see fit.' As Larry strolled outside again, it occurred to him how fond he'd grown of Ben, and looked on him as kin.

From the kitchen window, Maud saw Master Lawrence coming out of Ben's carving shed. It was the master's shed of course but they all looked on it as Ben's space. While she pegged out the washing, Maud pondered over how well Ben had settled in during the past three years. He'd become more like family to the master and Olly, instead of hired help. The lad was easy to chat to but he'd always seemed unwilling to discuss his life back in Scotland, preferring to speak of Australia.

Back in the kitchen, she sang The Foggy Dew as she busied herself with her chores. She often hummed ditties from the ould country, usually shedding a few tears as she did so. But Australia was now home and she'd no desire to return to Ireland. Nothing would be the same as she remembered it so best to leave it in the past. She fetched the apple pie from the oven and laid it on the range to keep warm until dinner time. While preparing the rabbit casserole, she sang Will you Come to the Bower? Her eyes filled with the memory of her mother, God rest her soul, singing it as she worked in their cottage back home. 'Mam's gone to her maker long since, so she has,' she said aloud, 'so there's no point in crying over it. She's in a better place, after all.' Master Lawrence and Olly often teased her about speaking to herself and her response would be, 'I don't get anyone arguing with me that way.'

*

'Have you thought any more about a new career?' Larry asked Ben next evening, when they were drinking coffee in the parlour, with Jess lying beside them in front of the fire.

Ginger fondled the sheepdog's ear. 'I've thought of little else, but don't know if I've enough ability.'

'You're a darned sight more able than you give yourself credit for, lad. That work you produce would be snapped up by the new settlers.' Stretching down to lay his empty coffee cup on the hearth beside him, Larry sat back in his armchair and began to fill his pipe. 'Grandpa Jenkins started up Wattle Trees when he first arrived in the colony. My pa inherited from him, then the station was passed on to me and Olly will take it over next. I'm sure the same will happen to you and your descendants, once you marry and have nippers.'

Before Ginger could reply, Olly joined in. 'Pa's right, Ben. I hope you'd still live here, as we've gotten to think of you as kin, but your talent's too good to be wasted.'

'You could sell your carvings on the market stalls in Dubbo. And life would be more exciting there than here in the backwoods.' Larry winked at him. 'Think of all these Sheilas, just waiting for you to snap them up.'

'I'd like a wife but want to be able to offer her something, and not have to count the pennies. Still, maybe I should give it go.' Ginger felt spurred on by their encouragement.

When Maud came in to clear away the used coffee cups, Olly caught hold of her hand. 'We're trying to convince Ben that he should start a carving business. What do you say?'

'I've told Ben his skills are too good to waste,' she said, as she lifted the tray and returned to the kitchen.

Larry turned to Ben. 'There you are, lad. I rest my case.'

CHAPTER ELEVEN
The Plan Finalises
December 1852

Olly and Ginger had spent the day repairing fences in the top and middle paddocks and hadn't seen Larry since breakfast time. But that evening as they tucked in to Maud's roast lamb, Larry brought up Ginger's proposed new venture.

'I took my black-faced ram over to Fairfields today, to service the Robinsons' ewes, and Pete and I got talking about your carving, Ben. He owns stalls in Dubbo market, and one of his stallholders is retiring next week so you could rent the stall at a fair rent.'

Ginger almost choked with excitement. 'I'd like that just fine.'

'You could open your stall in time for Christmas. You'll sell masses of stuff,' Olly assured him. 'And you could also sell some of Maud's embroidery.'

'I could too.' Ginger smiled over at Maud. 'Would you be happy with that?'

'I would that, Ben. I've got a pile of stuff I've worked on over the years, so I have. And you could maybe sell some Christmas flowers from around the property, if Master Lawrence is agreeable of course.'

Larry smiled. 'No worries on that score, there're masses of bushes coming into flower right now. You and I could drive over to Fairfields on Sunday to discuss things with Pete?'

'Great,' Ginger replied, and the discussion continued over their coffee.

*

'Right lad, climb aboard and we'll get off,' Larry said to Ginger on Sunday after breakfast. 'Will you stay and keep an eye on the boys, Olly?' Although Steve and Brady tried hard, they weren't as quick learners as Ben had been.

'Sure, no worries,' Olly said. 'Good luck, Ben,' he called, as Ginger got into the wagon beside Larry.

'Good to see you both,' Pete said, waving as they climbed down from the wagon at Fairfields. 'Hannah's brewing some tea.'

Despite her work-worn hands, Hannah's face shone with health. She invited them to sit at the kitchen table and placed a pot of tea and freshly-baked fruit bread in front of them.

'How are your two extra hands doing, Larry?' Pete asked.

'Coming along just dandy. Mind you, they're slower than Ben in picking up instructions, but they're willing to graft.'

Pete stood up once they'd finished eating. 'If we go into my office, I've had my lawyer draw up a contract for you, Ben.'

In the office he slid the contract across the desk to Ginger. 'All I need is your signature at the bottom, lad, once you've read it through and are happy with the conditions.'

Larry and Pete discussed their new stock while Ginger read through the document. 'This all seems fair to me,' he said, when he'd finished reading and took up the pen Pete pushed towards him to sign on the dotted line. Ben Harker, he signed, and wrote the date beside it. The name no longer felt like an assumed one. 'I'll pay the first rent now,' he said, taking the money out of his shirt pocket, and counting it out on the desk.

'Thank you, lad, it's a pleasure doing business with you.' Pete beamed at him and they shook hands on the deal.

'That you away then,' Hannah said, as they were leaving, 'remember and give my best to Maud and Olly.'

CHAPTER TWELVE
A Friendship Renewed
September 1855

Ginger held his head high as he strolled along Dubbo High Street towards his business premises, rubbing his fingers down the front of his blue silk waistcoat. His navy suit had been delivered the previous day by Mr Pomfrey from Orange, a tailor recommended by Pete Robinson.

He halted outside his shop. Even though he'd opened it over two years ago, he still found himself staring in awe at the frontage, painted green with AUSSIE CRAFTS scrolled in fancy gold lettering on it. A shiver of satisfaction ran through him each time he looked at the words Proprietor: B. Harker in smaller lettering above the shop doorway. Ben Harker, a well-respected shopkeeper. Yes, Australia had provided him with a good life. He hoped his mother would have been proud of him.

Ginger found time to help out at Wattle Trees when asked, aware of how much he owed to Larry and Olly, and he still had his room at the farm.

Since he'd first opened his market stall three years ago, he'd built up a good relationship with his customers and he was now receiving commissioned work from the owners of town houses and mansions. He turned the door sign to Open and, as he laid the cash book on the counter top, he was humming to himself.

A few minutes later, Joe came into the shop. 'Morning, Mr Harker,' he said, smiling cheerily at his boss.

'Morning, Joe,' Ginger replied. Once the business had taken off, he'd put a notice on the shop window, advertising for an assistant. At 14½, skinny wee Joe, just finished with school, had jumped at the chance of a job in the craft shop. That was two years ago and, with his beaming smile and fair spiky hair, he'd become a favourite with the customers.

Joe blew into his palms and rubbed his hands together. 'Nippy this morning, Mr Harker. Will I make us a brew?'

'Good idea.'

Ginger was moving some of his smaller carvings to a table nearer the door, when the bell jangled. He looked up at the two policemen standing inside the doorway. Ginger's fingers went to his birthmark, and he held his breath, his frame rigid. The older and stouter of the two men stood where he was, the buttons on his grey New South Wales police shirt strained across his rotund figure. The younger officer walked towards Ginger.

Trying to relax his jaw, Ginger smiled at the policeman. 'G'day Officer, what can I do for you?' His eyes remained firmly on the officer's hat badge with NEW SOUTH WALES POLICE DEPARTMENT engraved on it.

The man took his hat off and held it under his armpit. 'Looking for a gift for the wife's birthday. She already has some of your carved animals, so thought I might add to her collection.'

Relief flooded through Ginger, but he managed to keep his expression relaxed. 'Why don't you have a look at the display?' he suggested, pointing out the carved pieces on the table beside them.

The policeman studied them and lifted a squirrel, sitting on a tree trunk. 'She's sure to like this,' he said, 'the bushy tail is a work of art. Do you carve them yourself?'

Ginger nodded, almost beginning to recover from his scare. 'Thanks, Joe,' he said, when his assistant placed a mug of tea on the counter.

'You'll be needing that this morning,' the customer said.

'Sure do.' Leaving the lawman to inspect the other carvings, Ginger cradled the mug in his hands, and sauntered over to the window and watched the sun breaking through the heavy clouds. The policeman decided to buy the squirrel and, while Joe was wrapping up the purchase, the doorbell jangled again and a well-dressed gent, carrying a cane, came in. The older police officer stood aside to let the man pass.

'Hope your wife likes your choice,' Ginger said to the lawman, before turning to the new arrival. 'G'day, Mr Stanley. What can I do for you, Sir?'

Mr Stanley removed his top hat and sat it, along with his leather gloves, on the counter. 'Mrs Stanley has been saying for some time that she needs a cabinet in which to store her china goods. You know what women are like with their precious treasures, always wanting to put them on show.'

Ginger nodded, even though he didn't really know much about women.

'So I would like you to carve me a cabinet, with glass doors, for her to display the items.' Mr Stanley tapped his cane on the shop floor as he was speaking, something Ginger had noticed him doing previously, whether from impatience or simply habit he wasn't sure.

'I can certainly do that, Sir. I work with a glassmaker on such items and I can negotiate a price with him.'

'That would be excellent.' Mr Stanley's cane continued a rhythmic tap tap tap on the wooden floor as he was speaking.

'If Mrs Stanley could come into the shop to see the designs I've carved previously on furniture, then she could choose her favourite.'

'Capital idea. I'll arrange for her to come tomorrow.'

'Fine, Sir, and I'll have my estimate for the cost of the work ready by then.'

'Perfect.' Mr Stanley gave a few more taps, then nodded his goodbye and donned his hat once more.

Once the gentleman had gone, Ginger turned to his assistant, who'd been dusting down the furniture on display. 'Joe, can you look after the shop, while I go and finish a couple of jobs I started on last week?' Olly had helped Ginger to convert the outhouse at the rear of the premises into a workshop. Two massive benches and a large selection of carving tools allowed him to undertake any jobs asked of him.

'Of course, Mr Harker,' Joe replied, laying aside the duster as another customer came into the shop.

*

At midday Ginger turned the door sign to Closed, and went outside to pull the green and white striped sunshade down over the front of the shop. He was getting ready to carry the long pole back inside, when he heard a familiar voice.

'By God, I don't believe it. Ginger, is it really you?'

Turning round, Ginger leaned the pole against the window and stared at the man facing him. Then his face crumpled, and with recognition came tears. They rolled down his face as he gathered the man into a bear hug. 'Tom, my old friend, you've survived,' he said, in a choked voice.

Despite his delight at seeing Tom again, Ginger checked that there wasn't anyone standing nearby. If the police saw him talking in a friendly manner to an ex-convict, they might start to investigate his background. Guilt surged through him at allowing such a disloyal thought into his mind.

Tom held him at arms' length and studied his attire. 'By Jove lad, you're a sight to behold. A swanky gent.'

He laughed. 'That's as may be, Tom, but I'm still Ginger.'

His heart went out to the older man when he saw the gauntness of his frame and his unkempt appearance. It crossed his mind that he must have looked the same to Olly at their first meeting. Oh, how much he owed to Olly and Larry.

'Come away in, Tom, and tell me how you got here. Did you escape?' he asked, as the door closed behind them, and he stood the pole back in its place.

'No, I was released last year. Got my Ticket of Leave.'

Every convict who completed his seven years in the penal colony was given this to show he was now a free man.

'Of course, I'm forgetting how long I've been in New South Wales.'

Ginger led the way into the staff room, where Joe was having his lunch. 'This is Tom,' Ginger told his young assistant, 'my friend and fellow Scot. We haven't met for a few years.'

Joe looked up with his half-eaten sandwich in his hand and smiled at the older man. Busy leafing through Ginger's copy of The Sydney Herald while he ate, Joe didn't appear to notice Tom's untidy state.

'Would you be able to look after things here, Joe, if Tom and I go to the pub for something to eat? I've put the Closed sign on the door.'

'Of course, Mr Harker, no worries.'

Tom gave Ginger a grateful look, and then looked down at his filthy hands. Ginger signalled to the washroom, and when Tom came out, his hands and face were spotless and he'd tidied up his hair.

'An outside table, Tom, or indoors?' Ginger asked, when they got to the The Wallaby, a ten minute stroll from the shop.

'Outside's fine for me,' Tom assured him, savouring the delicious smell of cooking drifting out of the pub.

They'd scarcely sat down when the waiter came over to their table. 'G'day, Mr Harker,' he said, nodding at Ginger, 'are you two gents ready to order?'

'A pork pie and a pint?' Ginger asked his friend, who nodded, and the waiter went away again.

'What's this Mr Harker?' Tom asked, once the waiter was out of hearing.

'It's the name I gave when I arrived here, and it's what I'm known as now.'

'We often wondered if you'd managed to stay alive in that forest. We heard you'd escaped from the tree-felling gang. Then, when Fraser disappeared, we wondered if you'd had anything to do with that?'

Ginger trusted Tom and wanted to be honest with him. 'I discovered him alone in the forest. He was dripping wet after a swim in the lake. By God, how I wanted to kill him, but I didn't. Then he saw me and chased after me. As we were wrestling, his feet slipped on some leaves and he fell and cracked his head off a boulder.' He stopped for a moment, and looked down at the table. 'I put his body into the lake, because I knew if they found it, they'd accuse me of murder.'

'I'm glad he died, laddie. Nobody would shed any tears for him, that's for sure.'

Ginger rubbed his fingers over the table top, before resuming his story. 'I spent almost eight weeks in the forest, then walked to Port Arthur, where I crossed the Strait on a fishing boat. I was lucky to be taken on as a hired hand on a sheep station and then, three years ago, I opened a market stall selling carved goods. When that became too small, I rented my shop. But, what about Jack and Will, how're they?'

A shadow crossed Tom's wizened face. 'They didn't make it. Jack escaped but was soon caught and hanged. We were all lined up and forced to watch the hanging. Will died a few months later. They've both been buried somewhere in Saltwater River.'

The grim news hit Ginger hard, and he blinked away the tears. 'I'm so sorry to hear that. But it's wonderful you've survived, Tom.' He stopped speaking when the waiter brought their order to the table. While they were eating, Ginger asked the question that had been going through his mind since he'd first set eyes on his old friend. 'Where have you …'

Tom started to speak at the same time as Ginger, then signalled for his friend to go on, while he sank his teeth into the pork pie.

'Where have you been since you were released, Tom?'

'I stayed on in Van Diemen's Land after my release.

Without money, I couldn't do anything else. I got to Hobart, the largest town, by walking most of the way and hitching a lift on a hay cart for part of it.' He returned to his pie and, watching him, Ginger wondered when he'd last eaten.

'I've never been in Hobart. What's it like?'

'Quite big. Most folk were unwilling to employ an ex-con.' He rubbed his forehead, lost in the memory of that time. Ginger was about to speak, when Tom took up his story once more. 'I did get some casual work and stayed in rooming houses when I had money. Then later I stowed away on a ferry to Melbourne …' Tom's face was lined with concentration as he thought back to those difficult days. Ginger could see the pain in his friend's eyes, reminding him of his own dark days getting here from Melbourne.

'In Melbourne I'd the same trouble finding someone to take me on their payroll and most of the time I slept on the streets or on the grassy banks of the Yarra river.'

'And what then?'

'I heard about the gold that's been found in Bendigo and I tried my luck with that, but had no success.'

'Don't think many of the speculators have been lucky so far. Mind you, there're plenty of folk still searching.'

Tom shrugged. 'I gave up the goldmining lark and arrived here two days ago. I was looking in the shops to see if they needed hired help when I saw you outside yours. Couldn't believe my eyes at first.' He took a slug of beer from the mug that had been placed in front of him, and ate the final piece of pie. Some of the jelly inside dripped down on to his chin, and he used his fingers to scoop it up and put it into his mouth.

'I'm glad you recognised me.'

Refreshed once more, Tom returned to Ginger's story. 'What about you, laddie? You've obviously done well for yourself.'

Over a second beer, and another pie for Tom, Ginger

told his old friend about Wattle Trees station, and the kindness of Olly, Larry and Maud. He explained how he'd discovered his art for carving and that Pete Robinson had offered to rent him the market stall, before he moved into his shop.

Tom's eyebrows raised at the mention of the carving. 'That sure was good of the folks at the farm helping you. They must've taken a shine to you, laddie.'

'Yes, I owe them a great deal.'

Ginger took some pound notes out of his pocket and laid them on the table beside Tom. 'Use this money, Tom, to get yourself a rooming house for a few nights. No, take it,' he said, brushing aside his friend's objections.

An idea was forming in Ginger's mind but he needed to speak to Larry and Olly first.

*

That night over dinner Ginger told the others about Tom.

'He's a friend of mine from Scotland, and I couldn't believe it when he turned up at the shop today.'

'How did he know where you worked?' Larry asked.

'He didn't. I was pulling down the sunshade at the shop when he walked by.'

'Is it long since you've met?' Olly asked, and his face told Ginger that he suspected Tom was from the camp. Ginger decided to tell Olly the truth, but not until they were alone.

'A few years now. Tom went up to Bendigo from Melbourne because he heard about the goldfields. With so few getting lucky, he moved on from there and arrived in Dubbo the other day. I was thinking I could take him on as my delivery driver.' Ginger had recently bought his own wagon, so that he wasn't constantly borrowing Larry's.

Larry nodded. 'Good idea, Ben. You've got so much work to do that you really need someone to deliver the goods for you. When will he start?'

'If he takes the job, straight away. I also hoped you could advise me about the rates of pay for delivery drivers.

I don't want to use our friendship to pay him under the going rate.'

'I don't think you'd ever do that, lad, but sure we can discuss it.'

'Tom has booked into a rooming house for a couple of nights but I wondered if he could rent the outhouse from you temporarily, Larry, until he gets something permanent? He would pay his way.'

Larry looked at Olly, who nodded. 'The outhouse is empty at the moment,' Larry said, 'I'll ask Maud to sort it out for him. He can go with you to the shop each day.'

'Thanks, Larry. I really appreciate you doing that for him.'

'You know any friend of yours, is ours too. Think I'll turn in. Early start in the morning,' Olly said, and left Ginger and Larry talking about Tom's rate of pay.

*

The next day dawned as grey and depressing as its predecessor and temperatures remained stubbornly low, even for this early in the spring. Unlike yesterday the sun refused to come out. It had taken Ginger years to get used to the seasons here being the reverse of Britain. He still found it strange to have Christmas in sunshine, and any snow in New South Wales fell between June and August. A topsy-turvy world indeed.

All morning the shop was busy with customers. Nearer lunchtime, Tom came in, looking rested after his overnight stay in the rooming house.

'Good to see you again, Tom?' Ginger greeted him.

'Same for me, Ben,' Tom replied, hoping he'd remember to call his friend that name when anyone else was around.

'Would you like to see my workshop out at the back?'

'Sure.' Tom followed Ginger out to the rear of the premises. He whistled when he saw the carvings sitting on the benches, with pieces of furniture stacked against the walls. 'Did you make these yourself? Without any lessons?'

'Yep. Took it up while I was working on the sheep farm. Used to carve pieces of tree bark during my lunch break.'

Tom ran his fingers over the beautiful shapes his friend had created. 'These are so good. You have a gift, laddie.'

'Let's go to The Wallaby again and we can talk more.'

'See you later,' Tom said to Joe, as they left.

They took a table inside the pub. While they were tucking in, Ginger brought up his suggestion. 'Tom, would you be interested in becoming my delivery driver?'

Tom pushed his empty plate away from him. 'Don't feel obliged to take me on, Ginger. I'm just happy to have met you again …'

But Ginger brushed his friend's objection aside. 'No, Tom, for some time now I've found it hard to work on all the commissions I get, and deliver the goods as well. Joe's a great help in the shop, but he's too young to handle the horses that pull the wagon.'

'Then thanks, pal. I'd be happy to be your delivery man.'

'That's settled then. And I've arranged with Olly and his pa that you can sleep in the outhouse at the farm. I used it when I was first there and you'll be comfortable.'

Tom's eyes filled and he wiped his hand over them. 'It's good of you to help me laddie. Is it just Olly and his pa working …'

Anticipating the question, Ginger interrupted. 'No, there're two other workers. Young ones, Steve and Brady, they're good lads.'

'I'll pay rent from my wages.'

'And if you're sleeping at Wattle Trees, you can come into the shop with me each day. I've got my own wagon and horses now.'

'I'm so lucky to have found you again, Ginger.'

'Lucky for me too. The horses are stabled out at the back of the shop during working hours, so you could look after them too?'

'That would be no bother to me, laddie. I spent my time with the horses when I was a farm hand. Oh, Ginger, you sure are a blessing to me,' he added.

'We're pals Tom? It's what pals do for one another. One thing though, I've only told Olly my true story. Do you think you could keep my secret from Larry and Maud?'

'Of course I can. From now on you're Ben. Ginger has gone.'

Ginger took his timepiece out of his waistcoat pocket. 'I better get back Tom, as I don't want to leave Joe too long on his own. You go and let the rooming house know that you won't need to stay after tonight and I'll ask Maud to get the outhouse ready for you tomorrow.'

'Thanks, Ben,' Tom said, and the two pals waved goodbye and went their separate ways. On his walk back to the shop, Ginger felt happy he'd been able to help Tom, but sadness surged through him when he thought of the fate of Jack and Will.

Later in the afternoon Ginger looked up from the bench where he was working, when Joe came into the workshop. 'Mr Harkins, that's Mrs Stanley from Ripponlea House in the shop, asking to see your designs for her cabinet.'

'Thanks, Joe, I'll be there in a minute.'

Ginger took off his grey button-through overall, and washed his hands. Taking his jacket off the hook behind the staff room door, he went into the shop where Mrs Stanley, wearing a large, wide-brimmed bonnet and satin gloves, stood at the counter. 'Good afternoon, Madam. It's good of you to come to the shop.'

She indicated to the young girl at her side. 'This is my daughter, Meg, who will help me make a decision on the design we'd like.' Meg was the most beautiful girl Ginger had ever seen, her blonde hair dressed in ringlets, and her blue gown matching her eyes.

Forcing himself to pull his eyes away from the girl, he

addressed her mother once more. 'If you'll come with me to the workshop, Madam, I can show you some of the designs I've done on furniture.'

'Sorry for the wood shavings, ladies. Joe is constantly sweeping them up, but it's a never-ending task.' Mrs Stanley lifted her skirt and walked through them to the bench, with pieces of wood, each with a different design, sitting on it. Meg followed her mother's example and trod through the shavings.

'Mr Stanley told me you were an artist, Mr Harker, and he was right. These are truly magnificent. Don't you agree, Meg?'

Meg stepped forward and slipped off her lacy glove to touch the flower design on one of the carvings. 'A work of art,' she breathed, then smiled shyly at Ginger and stood back at her mother's side.

'And so many to choose from, I can't make up my mind,' Mrs Stanley told him. She turned to Meg. 'What is your favourite, darling?'

'I like the rose, the leaf and also the acorn, Mama. But I do believe I like the rose best of all for the cabinet. It will match the roses on some of your china.'

'Good idea, darling,' Mrs Stanley said, deciding there and then. 'We will have the rose design, please, Mr Harker. Can you carve roses around the outside frame of the cabinet?'

'I can indeed,' he said, and escorted the two ladies back into the shop. 'It's quite a bit of work, so might take a number of months to complete. Is that alright with you?'

'Perfectly alright, Mr Harker. I've been asking Mr Stanley to buy me a cabinet for years. My daughter will help me to arrange my pieces of china into the cabinet, won't you darling?'

'Yes, Mama,' Meg said sweetly, once again looking down at her feet.

'Could you pass this estimate for the work to your husband, please, Madam? And I will deliver the cabinet to you at Ripponlea upon completion.'

'Excellent. When you arrive, Elliot, our butler, will show you round to the back entrance and direct you where it should be placed.'

'Very good,' he said, and escorted the two ladies from the shop. He'd go with Tom to deliver the cabinet, as it would take two of them to handle such a large piece of furniture. He also hoped to get another sighting of the beautiful Meg. Even thinking her name caused his heart to flutter.

CHAPTER THIRTEEN
Delivery to Ripponlea
December 1855

Tom lay on his bed in the outhouse. The rain's pitter-patter kept up a steady rhythm on the tin roof above his head. He'd fitted in well at the farm, and Maud had taken a shine to him, often slipping him an extra-large helping of food. She was a fine looking woman, and here in the privacy of his room he admitted that being in her company made his heart beat faster.

It was almost three months since he'd started working at Aussie Crafts. He and Joe got on well, and the lad was always keen to hear stories about Scotland. Beginning to yawn, Tom's head sank deeper into the pillow, the lullaby of the rain soon drawing him into sleep.

He wakened just before daylight and threw off the bed covers. The overnight rain had ceased and from the open door he watched dawn break over the tops of the tallest gums. He breathed in the fresh morning air; this was his favourite time of day and he hated to waste a minute of it being indoors.

'Morning folks,' he said, when he entered the kitchen a short time later.

'Morning Tom.' Maud turned from stirring the porridge to give him a beaming smile. He joined Larry and Olly, already seated at the table, where they were discussing the chores to be undertaken today. Ginger, Brady and Steve all came downstairs as Maud was handing round the bowls of porridge.

When Ginger had eaten his porridge, he pushed his empty bowl aside, and stretched out for a slice of toast. 'Think we're ready to deliver the cabinet to Ripponlea today, Tom. It'll take both of us to carry it.'

'Sure, Ben,' Tom replied, through a mouthful of food.

He was getting used to thinking of his friend as Ben. If he ever slipped up, he could say that Ben was known as Ginger back in Scotland because of his red hair.

'Is that the Stanley place?' Olly asked, sliding the butter dish towards Ginger.

'Yep, he's been a good customer.'

'Obviously values your work, lad, and so he should.' Larry got to his feet and looked across at Steve and Brady. 'I need you boys with me today. There's a load of fencing to be repaired.' The two lads got up from the table and followed him out, Brady cramming his last slice of toast into his mouth.

*

'Right, Joe, you're in charge until we get back,' Ginger said, when Tom halted the wagon outside the shop.

'That's fine, Mr Harker. You can depend on me.' Enthusiasm was written all over Joe's face at this new responsibility. Ginger was happy with Joe's work, and had even considered offering to give him carving lessons. But he hadn't mentioned it to Joe yet, not until he'd made a definite decision.

With the cabinet strapped to the trailer, Tom took care on the rough tracks they were driving over. He had to tighten the reins and steer the horses around any holes in the road.

Ginger sat beside Tom, admiring his friend's handling of the animals.

'What's Ripponlea like?'

'It's magnificent. Stone built, with turrets up above and pillars on either side of the entrance. Never been inside but I'm sure it's worth seeing.'

Tom flicked the reins and urged the horses on now that the track was better. 'So our Mr Stanley must be worth a pretty penny.'

'His family came over in the latter part of the last century, long before he was born. They lived in a large town in the English Midlands. He's a developer and has built up a thriving business.'

'Not so bad that he's worked for it,' Tom said. 'Not like these folk who get it handed to them on a plate.'

By the time they entered Orange, the sky had darkened and the air felt thundery. A flash of lightening cut across the sky and the loud thunderclap that followed startled Matt, the name Tom had given the chestnut stallion. Nostrils flaring, the animal reared in fright, swinging the wagon to one side in the process, and Norm, the white horse, twisted round to join his partner. One of the wagon's wheels left the road and plunged them into a ditch. Ginger was thrown off and landed under the wheels.

Meantime, Matt broke free of his harness and shot along the main road ahead, before Tom got himself out of the upturned wagon. 'Ginger, are you alright?'

'I'm fine Tom, but I need your help to get out of here? Did Matt bolt?'

'Aye, he shot off before I could catch him,' Tom said, as he struggled to release Ginger's arm that was pinioned by a wheel. Once he was on his feet again, Ginger found he could move his limbs easily, and rubbed the mud off his jacket and trousers.

Tom pointed ahead. 'There's Matt. He's been stopped outside the police station.' Two burly law officers were in the process of calming the horse down.

'Relax Ginger, and take it easy,' Tom advised, seeing his friend tense up at the sight of the law officers. 'Thanks, Officer,' Tom called to the policeman who was walking towards them, leading Matt at his side. 'The thunder frightened him and he bolted.'

'You two guys okay?' Seeing them nod, the man called to his sidekick. 'Fred, come and give us a hand here.' The two policemen, along with Tom and Ginger, managed to lift the wagon out of the ditch and Tom attached Matt again in his place beside Norm.

'Where you going with that?' one of the officers asked, pointing to the cabinet, which Ginger was now checking over for any damage. It had been thrown around a bit but was somehow still in one piece. It had fallen on to its back, so the glass doors were unbroken.

'We're delivering it to Mr Stanley at Ripponlea,' Tom informed him.

The man nodded and waved as he and his fellow officer crossed the road again.

The town pavements had grass nature strips along them, pretty poppies and other early summer flowers in the tubs festooned at intervals along the streets. On the slopes behind the road stood the mansion houses of the privileged.

At the entrance to Ripponlea, Ginger jumped down from the wagon and chugged on the circular bell-pull at the side of the massive iron gates. The gatekeeper came out of his cottage and opened the gates to allow them entry. They trotted up the winding path, the horses' heads nodding in time to the clip-clopping of their hooves. After a good ten minutes of following the lines of tall trees on either side of them, the path widened and the trees gave way to some flowering bushes. At the moment the buds were still tightly closed, but they'd soon open out in a profusion of colour.

'My God, I was beginning to wonder if we'd ever see it,' Tom said, as he got his first sight of Ripponlea, sitting in its extensive grounds. Two stone lions stood in front of the door pillars, guarding the entrance. From the front windows, the residents had a view over a wide expanse of parkland, with flower beds laid out at intervals. The sound of water tinkling down from the fountains in between the flower beds added to the peace.

The butler was standing at the bottom of the front steps when the wagon slowed. 'Good day, Mr Harker,' he said.

Ginger stepped down from the wagon. 'Good day, we've brought the cabinet for Mr Stanley.'

'So I see. If you follow me, I'll direct you to the back

entrance.'

'I'll leave this with you,' Ginger said, and handed his folded account to the butler.

The man nodded. 'I'll give it directly to the Master.'

Tom unstrapped the cabinet and between them they lifted it and followed the butler, his pin striped trousers pressed with military precision, around the side of the house.

'Collins,' the butler instructed the footman who opened the back door, 'show Mr Harker and his driver where Madam wants the cabinet to sit.'

'Very good, Mr Elliot,' Collins replied, and he stood back while Ginger and Tom manoeuvred the large piece of furniture in through the door. Then he led the way upstairs, watching all the while that no paintwork or door frame was damaged. The room he guided them into was spacious and afforded a magnificent view over the lush grounds. Through the open window, Ginger could hear the water playing in the fountains.

They sat the cabinet down in the middle of the room, where Ginger again checked for any chips or damage following the accident. 'Perfect condition,' he said to Tom, once he'd finished his inspection. Then he turned to Mr Collins. 'Where would you like us to put it?'

'Madam's instructions are over there, in the corner against the wall, away from direct sunlight.'

They moved the cabinet to the spot indicated, ready to be filled with Mrs Stanley's ornaments. The roses the glassmaker had put on the doors matched perfectly the carved ones on the wood.

'I'll show you out,' Collins said.

On the way downstairs, Ginger glanced up at the intricate cornicing. This floor seemed to have the main rooms and he guessed the bedrooms were on the floor above. The staff would likely be in garret rooms up at turret level.

Outside again, they made their way back to the wagon.

As they passed some formal gardens, the gate clicked open and Meg Stanley came through it. She was wearing a purple dress, the material rustling as she walked. Tom moved on but Ginger stopped in his tracks.

'G'day, Miss Stanley,' he murmured, hoping she couldn't hear his heart pounding.

'Hello, Mr Harker, have you delivered Mama's cabinet?' She was hatless but had an enormous bow in her hair that matched exactly the shade of her dress. She blushed when he looked at her, appearing almost as tongue-tied as he was.

'I hope it will be to Mrs Stanley's satisfaction.'

'I'm sure it will. Papa has said what a fine craftsman you are, Mr Harker.'

He gave her a sort of bow. 'Goodbye, Miss Stanley.'

'Goodbye, Mr Harker,' she replied.

As he turned to leave, a face peered out of a downstairs window. Perhaps the butler, but he couldn't be sure. He joined Tom in the wagon and, as the horses trotted off down the drive, he looked back and saw Miss Stanley standing outside the front door.

'A pretty lass,' Tom said, as they were driving down the path towards the entrance gates.

'She is that.'

Tom said no more but, out of the corner of his eye, Ginger thought he saw his friend smile, and was sure that Tom had seen his infatuation with Meg Stanley. Not that I have any chance there, he thought, as they cleared the gates and headed out on to the road again.

*

The next morning, Tom and Joe were out on deliveries, and Ginger was alone in the shop.

He'd been so busy with customers that he hadn't been able to get any carving work done. He was attending to a lady, interested in the carved animals on display, when the shop door opened. Ginger turned round as Olly walked in. He signalled that he'd wait at the counter until Ginger was free.

'I really like this rabbit,' the woman said, holding up one of the carvings. 'I can't decide between this and the sheep.'

'If you buy both, I'll give you them at a lower price,' Ginger offered.

Without any hesitation, the lady accepted his offer and he sat the carvings on the counter top while she went over to view the stand with Maud's lavender bags and embroidered handkerchiefs. Maud had been delighted to expand her range of pomanders and lavender bags when he'd opened the shop, and her embroidered initialled handkerchiefs were great sellers.

'Busy day?' Olly asked.

'Yes, sales have been brisk. Surprised to see you here,' Ginger countered, smiling at his friend.

'I was in town to order some new equipment and thought we could go together for a bite to eat.'

'Excuse me,' Ginger murmured, when the customer called him over.

'Mr Harker, I'll have three lavender bags and two of the initialled handkerchiefs.'

'What initials do you want?'

'I'll have one with the letter J and one with a B. I want to give them as gifts. Could you get me one with a K on it?'

'I can ask my supplier to make one especially for you. I should have it by the end of this week,' he told her, aware of how quickly Maud could embroider one. With Maud's kindness to him over the years, he'd been happy to give her the chance to earn something from her handiwork.

The woman accompanied Ginger to the counter to pay for her goods and, once she'd left, Olly returned to their previous conversation. 'I thought when you close for lunch, we could go to that pub along the road.'

'The Wallaby, I go there most days.' Ginger looked up at the clock on the wall behind the counter when it chimed midday. 'Joe has a key for when he and Tom get back.'

Last week he'd promoted Joe to assistant manager, and he and Ginger took turns of who came in early and opened the shop.

The Wallaby wasn't busy. 'G'day, Mr Harker,' the landlord said, nodding at Ginger, who was a regular by this time. 'We've got rabbit pie on the menu today.'

They decided to have that and the landlord pulled each of them a pint. They carried their drinks to a table near the window, to wait for their food order to be brought to them.

'I'm a bit worried about Pa,' Olly confided, once they were seated. 'He tires easily these days and I'm trying to take the heaviest of the work to spare him, but he's so determined to do as much as previously.'

'He's aged a lot since I first came to Wattle Trees, but he knows you'll take over at the helm as soon as he feels the need. He's a great man, your pa.'

'He sure is and you should've seen how energetic he was when Ma was alive.' Olly clasped his hands and looked down at the table top. For a moment, Ginger thought he was praying, and when he looked up, his eyes were moist, and he brushed the back of his hand over them. 'After Ma died, he was never quite the same. Understandable, I suppose, as they'd been so happy together.'

'Losing your ma must have been hard on you too, Olly,' Ginger suggested, remembering how life had been for him when his own mother passed away.

'Sure was, but Pa and Maud helped me a lot to get my grieving done and carry on. I feel guilty that Pa didn't get time to deal with his own sadness for helping me. Wish I could help him now, but getting him to admit to feeling tired is almost impossible. He's worked all his life and I think he'd give up altogether if he became an invalid.' He stopped speaking when their tucker was put down in front of them.

'I'm sure he'll be fine,' Ginger said, lifting his cutlery. But he too was concerned about the change in Larry.

'Tom's settled in well at the homestead,' Olly commented, while they were eating. 'I'm guessing he was with you at Saltwater River.'

Ginger nodded. 'He's a good man, Olly, or I wouldn't have asked you and your pa to rent him the outhouse.'

'He's the tops, and the secret's safe with me. I respect loyalty.'

Ginger laid his knife and fork down on his plate once he'd swallowed the last mouthful. 'Tom was like a father to me in the colony and kept me out of trouble many times. We formed a group of four with Jack and Will. All of us were transported from Scotland for petty thieving when we were starving.'

An angry look passed across Olly's face, and he thumped the table top. 'It's an injustice that you had to suffer such treatment for minor offences. What about the other two?' he asked, and was visibly moved when Ginger told him of Jack and Will's fate.

'It's a miracle that Tom got out alive,' Ginger added, his voice shaking with emotion, 'after the punishments and hard graft he had to endure over so many years.'

'He's a good guy,' Olly said, sliding his empty plate away from him. Then he laughed. 'Between you and me, I think Maud's got quite a crush on him.'

Ginger smiled. 'I think Tom feels the same way about her.'

'Hope they get together.' Olly glanced up at the clock above the bar and pushed back his chair. 'Righteo, guess I better get on my way. It's my shout,' he called over his shoulder, as he went over to the bar to pay.

CHAPTER FOURTEEN
The Soiree
April 1857

'Will we go to the soiree on Saturday?' Olly asked, as he poured milk into his tea.

Ginger's face wrinkled. 'I can't dance.'

'There'll be lots of Sheilas.'

'If I was younger, I'd be going,' Larry chipped in, chuckling as he waltzed around the kitchen. 'Drink up Olly, we should be heading to the sheep dip.'

Ginger remained silent when he and Tom were driving to the shop. 'Thinking of the gorgeous Sheilas?' Tom asked, guiding the horses around the potholes in the rough track.

'Not sure I'll go.'

'What's to stop you? And don't say because you can't dance. Most of the other critters there'll be the same.'

'Don't know if I'm ready for romance.'

Tom shook his head. 'Laddie, I know you better than you know yourself. Put the past behind you and get on with the future. You're Ben Harker now, a successful businessman.' When he drew up outside Aussie Crafts, all conversation about the soiree ceased.

*

Ginger wrestled with the cravat Olly had lent him. He tossed the cursed thing aside and mopped his brow with his handkerchief. The rain that had been forecast hadn't come and the heat was intense. He ran his fingers along the back of his neck, where the stiff collar of his shirt was rubbing. He was dreading the soiree but felt obliged to accompany Olly. There was a knock on his bedroom door and Olly poked his head around it. In no time at all, he'd fixed Ginger's cravat into place. 'See you downstairs,' he said, as he left.

Ginger stared into the mirror at his oiled hair, and pulled down the edges of his silver-grey, cut-away, waistcoat, before putting on his white scarf and gloves. As he joined Olly downstairs, lightening flashed against the night sky. 'It's come at last,' he said, raising his voice against the rain battering on the window panes.

During their journey to the Assembly Rooms, the only light came from the lantern beside the driver. They heard music as soon as they stepped out of the carriage. The rain had eased slightly and a doorman ushered them inside, where the entrance hall was bathed in golden lamplight. A member of staff came forward to collect their coats and Ginger followed Olly's lead in placing his scarf and gloves inside his hat.

When they entered the ballroom, they were offered champagne from a silver tray. They carried their drinks to the far corner of the room, where they could view the dancers. Olly nudged Ginger's arm. 'There's a fine looking Sheila on the dance floor, the tall one wearing the red dress.'

Ginger glanced at the girl, her dark hair in ringlets. 'Yes,' he murmured, 'pretty right enough.'

The music stopped and the girl returned to her group of friends. 'I'm going to ask her for this dance,' Olly murmured, and drifted into the melée.

At the opposite side of the ballroom, Ginger saw three people huddled together at the edge of the dance floor. He held his breath, sure his eyes were deceiving him. But no, it was indeed the Stanley family. Meg stood beside her mother, looking even more beautiful than he remembered from their meeting at Ripponlea eighteen months ago.

Supper was in the adjoining room, and Ginger was standing in the doorway when the Stanleys made their way to the table. Mr Stanley gave him a nod and Ginger bowed his head to each of the ladies in turn. Mrs Stanley opened her brightly-coloured fan, while Meg dropped her eyes to the floor. Her gown was heavy with embroidery and the string of pearls around her neck shone in the lamplight. Ginger's heart pounded with desire.

Olly appeared beside him with the girl in the red dress. 'This is Vicky Chambers,' he introduced her, and 'my friend, Ben Harker,' he said to Vicky. One of her hair ribbons had come loose and her dark brown eyes sparkled with life. She chatted easily to Ginger as they joined the queue at the buffet table, unlike the Stanleys who were being served by waiters.

'Them and us,' Olly said, following Ginger's gaze. 'Even though here we don't stand on ceremony, there's still some of the class system hanging on.'

'Never mind,' Vicky giggled, 'I'm sure the food's better on our table.'

They carried their plates over to the window, and laid them on its ledge. Ginger found it difficult to concentrate on what the others were saying, with his veiled gaze constantly moving to Meg. Supper over, Meg and her parents left.

At the end of the evening they left the Assembly Rooms with Vicky.

'Can I call on you one day next week?' Olly asked.

'Yes, I'd like that. I live at No 5 Lilac Grove, it isn't far from here.' She walked towards her father, waiting beside a carriage to escort her home.

'Nice lass.' Ginger winked at Olly.

'I think she's the one for me, Ben.' He hailed a carriage, which stopped beside them.

On the journey back to Wattle Trees, Ginger tried to keep up a conversation but it was obvious that Olly was so smitten by Vicky that he couldn't think of anything else, so eventually Ginger lapsed into silence.

CHAPTER FIFTEEN
A Christmas Wedding
December 1857

Maud pointed to the corner above the kitchen window. 'Pin this up over there,' she said, handing Ginger a multi-coloured paper garland.

He trailed it behind him, to where the stepladders were placed against the wall. The parlour was already festooned with garlands, and a magnificent ten foot high Christmas tree stood in front of the window. 'I've forgotten the name of these bush cuttings decorating the pictures in the parlour, the one with the red flowers,' he said, as he climbed the rungs to fix the pin into the wall.

'The Waratah, it grows mainly in Botany Bay, but there are bushes around here too. It's popular at Christmas time, because it reminds folk of the red berries on the holly we used in the ould country. Prop the ladders against the table, there's a good fella, and I'll hold them fast till you pin this end to the centre of the ceiling.' Maud twisted the garland a bit more before giving it to Ginger.

'Where are the others?' he asked, balancing himself on the ladders, his hair brushing against the ceiling.

'You get yourself steadied on the ladder and I'll bring them to you.'

He waited, with one foot on the ladder and the other on the sturdy farmhouse table until she returned with the remaining garlands, and a sprig of mistletoe. He whistled as he pinned it up above the table. 'I'll need to catch you at the table, Maud, to collect my Christmas kiss.'

'Och, away with you, lad, and behave yourself. There're plenty more lasses to kiss in Dubbo than ould me.'

'Better not let Tom hear you saying you're old. He's the same age as you and likes to think of himself as a spring chicken.' When he bent down to take another garland from Maud she was blushing. Knowing Tom's feelings for Maud, he thought there'd soon be a second wedding at Wattle Trees.

'That's great, Ben,' Maud said, once he'd pinned up all four garlands. 'Good to have the kitchen brightened up, especially with the guests arriving here after the service tomorrow.' After a whirlwind romance, following their meeting at the Soiree in April, in August Olly asked Vicky's father for her hand. His blessing received, they'd wasted no time in arranging their Christmas Eve wedding. Maud had spent months in preparing the feast that awaited the guests tomorrow. Nothing but the best for my Olly, she'd told Ginger.

Since Olly's engagement, Ginger had fantasised about asking Meg's papa for her hand. But he knew Mr Stanley wouldn't consent to his daughter marrying so far beneath her. He probably had a suitor from some well-to-do family lined up for her. And anyway, Ginger constantly reminded himself, he didn't know if Meg returned his love.

'G'night, Maud,' Ginger said, once he was sure that everything had been done to her satisfaction. As he undressed for bed, he was anxious about his best man's speech and hoped he didn't let Olly down. He'd read it again in the morning, to make sure he hadn't missed anything out. After the wedding, when Olly and Vicky had left for their honeymoon in Sydney, he could relax and enjoy the remainder of the Christmas period with the others at Wattle Trees. He smiled as he recalled what Olly told him the first time he'd celebrated Christmas at the farm. 'Three days in a row when the grog will be flowing, so prepare yourself for a massive headache after the celebrations.' How true Olly's words had proven.

As he settled down between the crisp sheets, Ginger thought how different his Christmases were nowadays from the ones during his childhood. Maw had tried her best, but with their lack of money they'd had little to celebrate. And after her death, he'd roamed around the streets on the outskirts of Glasgow on Christmas day, often raiding discarded food dumps outside the homes of the wealthy. He'd been caught many a time too, even having a piece of cloth ripped from his breeches and a bite on his backside from a guard dog he'd disturbed.

When he finally drifted off to sleep, Meg's face was in front of him, and his last wakeful thought was a futile desire to celebrate Christmas day with her at Ripponlea.

*

Next morning Ginger took time over his toileting and dressing, keen to do Olly proud as his best man today.

The door creaked open and Olly popped his head round it. 'Are you ready for our buttonholes?' he asked. 'Maud has wired them for us.'

Ginger smiled at his friend and took the small sprays of wattle from him. They'd been cut freshly this morning from one of the trees on the property. 'Let me pin yours on first, and then we can deal with mine.'

Olly stood still while Ginger fixed one of the sprays to his lapel. Once Ginger was satisfied with his handiwork, Olly said, 'now it's my turn,' but his fingers were shaking so much, that Ginger ended up doing his own buttonhole.

'I'm surprised you're so nervous.'

Olly grinned. 'Wait till it's your turn. But your main job as best man is to keep me calm. And not to use your speech to give away any of my secrets,' he added, tapping his nose.

'No, your secrets are safe with me. But thanks for reminding me about my speech.' Ginger took some sheets of paper out of the top drawer of the bedside cabinet and placed them safely into his inside pocket. He'd put the finishing touches to his speech when he'd had a wakeful period during the night.

'Pa's going to come in the carriage with us,' Olly told him, as they made their way down to the front door. Maud and Tom were there already, dressed in their Sunday best, while Steve and Brady were staying behind to look after things at Wattle Trees.

'You look magnificent, Maud,' Ginger told her. 'That pink shade suits you.'

She shook her head. 'Not pink, lad, mauve.'

'Is it not more of a wine colour?' Tom suggested.

'No, I'm telling you, mauve.'

'Anything you say, Maud.' Tom raised his eyebrows at Ginger over Maud's head.

When the carriages arrived, Larry sat in the front seat beside the driver, with Olly and Ginger behind, and Maud and Tom sat together in the second carriage. Larry and Ginger kept up a steady conversation to help keep Olly relaxed. They got out of the carriages at the High Church in Orange, and made their way inside, where Vicky's mother was already seated, with other guests in the pews behind her.

When Vicky and her father arrived, the organist struck up the wedding march and the assembled guests rose from their seats as one. From their position in front of the altar, Olly and Ginger glanced round as Vicky, looking wonderful in her cream-coloured gown embroidered with pink rosebuds, walked down the aisle on her father's arm. There were some matching flowers on her bonnet and on the parasol she carried.

*

'So how do you think it's gone?' Olly asked, when he and Ginger were standing together in the kitchen, while Vicky had gone upstairs to change into her travelling clothes.

'Really smoothly, and Maud did her usual excellent job with the catering.'

'Yes, she's a wonder is our Maud. And she's promised to keep an eye on Pa while I'm in Sydney.'

Ginger had noticed a decline in Larry's activity level over recent months but he still pulled his weight around the farm. 'He stood up well to today's excitement, and now he can relax over Christmas.'

'Just watch he doesn't over-indulge in booze. He can't

hold the drink like he could years ago.'

'Don't worry, Maud and I will keep him on the straight and narrow. Here's your beautiful Missus,' Ginger said, as Vicky came into the kitchen to join them.

Olly threw his arm around her waist. 'Ready for the road, Darling?'

'Sure am. I've always wanted to go to Sydney.'

Remembering his best man duties, Ginger ushered them into the parlour again. 'Ladies and Gentlemen, our bride and groom are about to take their leave.' Immediately the guests milled around the happy couple, wishing them well, and made their way outside to wave them off. Before she climbed into the carriage with her new husband, Vicky gave her parents a big hug.

When the guests returned to the parlour, Ginger went into the kitchen for a drink of water. He forgot about the water when he was stopped in the doorway. Maud and Tom clung together, kissing under the mistletoe. Smiling, he turned away, quietly closing the door behind him. Yes, he thought, there will soon be another wedding at Wattle Trees.

CHAPTER SIXTEEN
Expansion
February 1859

'Thank you for your custom, Mrs Froggat,' Ginger said, handing over the gift pouch containing the carved wombat, before he wrote her purchase into the sales ledger.

Having had his store in Dubbo for four years, he'd recently thought it time to expand. When he opened this shop in Orange, he'd retained the name Aussie Crafts. Keeping to the same colour and design on the shop frontage had been intentional, as he had dreams of building a chain of stores across New South Wales. He'd begun to think the Magistrate had done him a favour in sending him to this wonderful country, although memories of his time in captivity haunted him at times.

He looked up when Tom entered the shop. 'How did the deliveries go?'

'Joe's a treasure. When I got to the shop this morning, he had the furniture sitting near the door ready to be loaded on to the wagon.'

'Yes, I made the right decision.' When he opened this shop in Orange, he'd had no hesitation in putting Joe in charge of the Dubbo store, with an increase in salary, and his hunch had proved to be a good one. He wasn't so sure about Ted Jackson, the new employee he'd taken on to assist him in this shop. Ted had not been pulling his weight; he was lazy and took days off without good reason. Ginger had received many complaints from customers that he'd been rude to them. In addition to these problems, Ginger suspected him of stealing from the business, and he'd decided he must get rid of Ted.

'I'll go and feed Norm and Matt,' Tom said, breaking into his thoughts, 'and then I'll make us a brew when the boys have eaten.'

'Great.' Ginger smiled at how fond Tom had become of the horses. As he'd suspected, Tom and Maud wed six months after Olly and Vicky. To show his appreciation for all that Maud had done for him and Olly, Larry decided to build the newlyweds a little weatherboard house on the property, a few minutes' walk from the homestead, which would offer them some privacy. The blissful couple moved in immediately the house was completed, with Maud still housekeeper and cook at the homestead.

The homestead was rather full anyway, with Olly and Vicky having moved in after their honeymoon and now Frances, born nine months after their wedding, was part of their family. Despite Vicky's difficult pregnancy, Frances was blooming with health and the apple of Olly's eye. At 5 months old, with her pale blue eyes and fair curly hair, the little girl was adored by her grandfather, and was thoroughly spoiled by everyone at Wattle Trees.

*

It was later that day, when Ginger was on his way to The Emu Inn for lunch, that he saw her. Although it was two years since their paths had crossed, he still dreamt about her.

Water splashed on to his trousers when the wheels of the dark wine carriage ran through a puddle left from overnight rain. But his eyes were on the occupants. Mrs Stanley used her frilly umbrella to shield her face from the sun, with Meg wearing a large bonnet but no umbrella. Looking after the carriage, he could have sworn that Meg smiled at him.

'How's business these days, Mr Harker?' the landlord of The Emu asked, as he laid the menu down on the table.

'Pretty good, thanks, George.'

'What can I get you to drink?'

'My usual pint, and a jug of water, please, George.'

Having paid for his lunch, Ginger was picking up his hat and gloves to return to Aussie Crafts when he saw Meg looking through the window. Pleasantly surprised, he joined her on the pavement outside. 'G'day, Miss Stanley,' he said, giving a quick bow of his head.

'Please call me Meg,' she murmured, lowering her eyes as she spoke. She indicated with her hand that they should walk together in the direction of Aussie Crafts and Ginger moved towards the edge of the pavement, allowing her to walk inside nearer the buildings.

'I saw you with your mother in the carriage earlier,' he said, moving aside to let a young woman with a perambulator walk between them.

'Yes, Mama wanted new curtains and brought me along to help her choose the material. She's still in the shop but I felt a headache coming on and said I'd have a stroll in the fresh air.' Ginger dared to hope she'd made the excuse to see him.

When they reached the door of Aussie Crafts, a sudden gust of wind blew her bonnet back and it was all Ginger could do to stop himself stroking her hair and drawing his fingers down her beautiful face. Blushing, she quickly pulled the hat on again.

'Why don't you step inside and have a look?' He turned the key in the lock and held out his hand in invitation.

She hesitated for a moment, and then placed her soft, gloved hand into his larger one. He helped her over the threshold, and felt bereft when she removed her hand again.

'I can't stay long, as Mama will be looking for me directly she comes out of the fabric shop.' Staring around the large, uncluttered area, Meg's eyes fell on the display of carved animals. She pulled off her glove and picked up a koala. 'You're so talented, Mr Harker.'

He would have given it to her as a gift but didn't think her parents would approve of her accepting it.

'Thank you, Miss … er, Meg. And I'd like if you'd call me Ben instead of Mr Harker. At least when we're alone, like we are now.' He wondered if he'd gone too far with familiarity, but was glad to see pleasure on her face.

'Yes, I'd like that, as long as Papa and Mama don't know.'

'It's our secret,' he whispered, and kissed the back of her hand. His heart was singing so loudly he was sure she'd hear it. 'Maybe we could stroll together another day, providing your parents have no objection.'

She giggled, her eyes shining. 'Our secret. And now, Mr Harker, I mean Ben, I must go before Mama becomes anxious about me.' And with that, she quietly left the premises and disappeared out into the street.

CHAPTER SEVENTEEN
Illness Strikes
January 1860

The shop was quiet after the pre-Christmas rush, and Ginger had considered lowering some of the prices to entice shoppers in. But with Sydneysiders on their summer holiday from work, their custom helped offset the post-Christmas slump. He'd dismissed Ted Jackson last year, and that ended the pilfering. Dave who'd replaced him was worth his weight in gold.

The shop door jangled and he looked up, thinking it was Tom returning from his morning deliveries. But excitement coursed through him when Mrs Stanley and Meg entered. Since the day, almost a year ago, when Meg had come into the store with him, he'd only seen her once, and on that occasion they hadn't been able to steal any time alone.

'G'day, ladies,' he greeted them, his smile encompassing both of them.

'Good day, Mr Harker.' Mrs Stanley cooled her cheeks with her fan. 'I want to purchase a carved piece as a birthday gift for my mother-in-law.'

'Perhaps you'd like to look over my display,' he suggested, aware that Meg was following behind her mother. As he was pointing out various pieces to Mrs Stanley, his gaze wandered over to Meg, as beautiful as ever in a pale green dress. How he longed to be with her alone.

Tom arrived while Mrs Stanley was choosing her gift, and he slipped quietly into the staff room. Choice made, Ginger packed it carefully and took the payment from Mrs Stanley. 'Thank you for your custom,' he said, handing her the change, and she placed the purchase into her wicker basket. Although Meg didn't speak, her eyes smiled at him, and he felt a flutter at his heart.

As mother and daughter took their leave, a group of holidaymakers came into the shop and he turned his attention to them.

*

As soon as Ginger and Tom arrived back at Wattle Trees that evening, Maud's white, drawn face told them that something dreadful had happened. 'It's Master Larry,' she told them, and began to sob.

'What's happened?' Tom asked, taking her into his arms.

Ginger pushed past them and went into the parlour, where Olly stood, his head resting on the window pane, shoulders shaking.

Ginger put an arm on his back. 'What's wrong with your pa, Olly?'

There was a catch in Olly's voice when he spoke. 'He collapsed in the upper fields an hour ago. I sent Brady to fetch the doctor from Dubbo, then managed to get Pa on to Montgomery's back and walked them home.'

Ginger was lost for words. 'What a shock for you Olly,' was the best he could come up with.

'I couldn't be sure he was still breathing by the time we got here, but Maud took over and put him into bed. That'll be Dr Duffy now,' he said, when they heard footsteps on the gravel outside.

'Where's your pa, Olly?' Dr Duffy asked, when Maud showed him into the parlour.

'In his bedroom,' Olly said, and led the way.

After what seemed like an eternity, the doctor took his leave, and a few minutes later they heard him drive off in his carriage.

When Olly returned to the parlour, his eyes were heavy with grief. He sat in his pa's armchair, while Ginger poured a large measure of brandy. Olly drank the contents in one go.

Maud brought in some tea and, when she'd laid the

cups down, turned to Olly. 'What did Dr Duffy say?'

Olly's voice shook with emotion. 'The doc's amazed that Pa is still alive, he says a lesser man wouldn't have survived the apoplexy. But he thinks Pa will recover, providing he stops working. And I'll make sure he does,' he vowed.

Maud wiped her eyes on her apron. 'Does Master Larry need anything?'

'No thanks, Maud. Vicky is sitting with him, in case he wakens.'

'Okay. I'll go and attend to our meal. Then I'll go up and relieve Vicky so she can have some rest.'

'Yes that would be good, Maud.' Vicky was now five months pregnant with their second child and with 16-month-old Frances to look after she didn't get much rest.

It was a very subdued household at the table later, with their thoughts on Larry.

CHAPTER EIGHTEEN
The Fire
February 1860

Maud sat at the side of Larry's bed, feeding him some chicken broth she'd made that afternoon. The rest of the family had enjoyed a bowl at dinner but Larry wasn't recovered enough to join them at the table.

'Well, Master Larry, you've cleared the plate, shows your appetite's coming back.' When he looked up at her, the twinkle had returned to his eyes, and she felt a surge of relief that his deathly pallor had cleared.

'Will I ask Master Olly to help you into your chair by the fire?' Beads of perspiration glittered on her forehead, but Dr Duffy had said to keep the room warm for Larry.

Larry's head nodded slightly and he lifted his hand a fraction. His speech was still poor but they were finding ways of communicating with him, mainly using sign language. 'Needs must,' as Maud had remarked to Tom the other day.

Maud was washing the dishes when she heard footsteps on the gravel path outside. She opened the kitchen door to a man dressed in a New South Wales police uniform.

'Evening, Ma'am,' he said, raising his hat to Maud, and showing her his identification card. 'I'm looking for Ben Harker.'

'I'll get Mr Harker for you, Officer,' she replied. 'Do you want to wait here in the kitchen until I do?'

The policeman nodded and closed the door behind him. Leaving him there, Maud bustled into the parlour where the family were sitting. They all looked up when she walked in, but her gaze fell on Ben. 'There's a policeman here asking for you, Ben.'

Ginger caught his breath, and got to his feet at once, sure the others could hear his pounding heart. He brushed past Maud into the kitchen.

Once again the policeman held out his badge. 'Mr Ben Harker?'

Ginger clenched his fingers behind his back. The last time police officers had called at Wattle Trees, they were looking for an escaped convict, but Olly had kept his secret. By now he was a respected business man, so surely they weren't still searching for him.

'That's me,' he said slowly.

'I'm Officer Matson. Sorry to bring you bad news, Sir, but there's been a fire at your shop, Aussie Crafts.'

Ginger gasped, but forced himself to remain calm. 'Dubbo or Orange? I have two shops.'

'Orange. If you want to accompany me, I'll take you there now?' As the policeman was saying this, the others filed into the kitchen, having heard the man speak of a fire.

Ginger turned to Tom. 'Could you get the wagon and follow us to Orange?'

'Will do, Ben.' Without waiting for further explanation, Tom headed out to the stables to hitch Matt and Norm to the wagon.

Sitting next to Officer Matson in the police wagon, Ginger smelt burning as they drove into Orange, the road ahead blocked by plumes of dense black smoke. They got out of the wagon and walked to the shop, where Ginger made to run to the front door, but Officer Matson pulled him back. 'No Sir, don't try to enter, there're sparks of burning embers all around us. Once the Fire Brigade has done its work, they'll let us know when it's safe.'

The firemen were on ladders up near the roof level, from where they trained their hosepipes on the blaze coming from the direction of the back shop. The men in charge of the water wagon were turning the wheel in a furious attempt to keep up a steady supply and douse the flames. Vivid reds and yellows lit up the night sky.

They waited helplessly as the men fought the blaze, with Ginger in dread of what damage had been done. He kept asking himself if Ted Jackson had started the blaze. Surely not, but the notion refused to leave him. It would have been easy to set the premises alight in this tinder-dry weather, but the only thing to back up his suspicion was Jackson's promise to get even with him. The man was drunk at the time, and Ginger hadn't taken his threat seriously. Now, he wasn't so sure. He was still trying to dismiss the idea, when Tom arrived.

The firemen worked through the night, climbing the ladders in turn, with others taking over from them when they needed to rest. One of the firemen who'd come down to rest, crossed in front of them. He was wearing green overalls and a helmet, his eyes blackened with soot, and there were dark smudges on his forehead. He wore a mask over his mouth and nose but, despite this protection, he was choking and coughing.

Finally, as dawn was breaking over the rooftops, the chief fireman came over to them. 'You can go inside now, gents, but please don't attempt to go upstairs, as the stairway has been left in a dangerous state.' The chief removed his helmet, leaving a blackened band across his forehead. He spoke directly to Ginger. 'A lot of the wooden carvings have gone, but hopefully some will be saved. It was burning for some time before it was reported, which is why it's taken so long to put it out.'

'Do you know how it started?' Ginger asked.

'Not sure yet, it could be arson or perhaps the embers in the fireplace hadn't been doused properly and a spark has caught on to something nearby.' When one of his men called to him, the fire chief excused himself and moved away.

Ginger said to Tom, 'I'm the one who doused the fire tonight, so if that's been the cause, then it's due to my carelessness.' He made no mention of Ted Jackson.

'But you're always careful, Ben.'

'Well, I guess now I'll need to be doubly careful.'

The three men entered the premises, handkerchiefs

covering their mouths and noses. A tide of foul-smelling air hit them and their eyes smarted in the strong, smoky atmosphere. Particles of glass from the shattered windows littered the floor. The charred remains of carvings were scattered around the floor and on the remnants of tables, but the fire appeared to have been contained mainly in the rear area of the building. The front part of the shop had been spared from the worst of the flames, although had suffered from water damage.

Ginger looked in dismay at all the debris lying around. 'The whole place will need repainting when the roof and walls have been repaired.'

'Your insurance company will cover these costs, Sir,' Officer Matson assured him.

'I hope so,' Ginger replied. 'I must try and find the person who called in the Fire Brigade tonight. Otherwise, the damage could have been much worse. I want to reward him for his swift actions.'

'That's very generous of you, Sir,' Matson said. 'I'll get the man's name and address for you.'

Just then, the workmen who'd been summoned to board up the shop door and windows arrived at the scene. With no more to be done until the insurance assessors had visited, Ginger and Tom heaved their weary limbs up into the wagon. 'We better call at Dave's house to let him know not to go to the shop today,' Ginger said to Tom.

When they got back to Dubbo, the family at Wattle Trees was seated around the breakfast table. Relieved to see them in one piece, but aghast at their bedraggled state, Maud jumped up and ran over to them.

'Don't come too close, love,' Tom said to her, 'we're reeking of smoke.'

Olly sprang to his feet. 'How bad was it?'

Ginger massaged his forehead as he replied. 'Not as bad as we expected. Most of the building and some of the stock has been saved. It's a mercy I had the place insured.'

'At least no-one was hurt in the fire, belongings can be

replaced.' Then, as was normal for Maud, her thoughts turned to sustenance. 'Now, can I get you both something to eat or do you need sleep more?'

'Sleep please,' they said in unison. Tom headed out to the cottage he shared with Maud, while Ginger trudged past the family room on his way upstairs. A weak voice called from inside, 'so … good …'

Ginger poked his head round the open door, but Olly squeezed past him. 'Pa, you've spoken,' he said, dropping on to the arm of the chair and cradling his father's head. When he looked up at Ginger, his eyes were moist. 'Pa felt well enough to join us this morning and it looks like your safe return has brought back his speech.'

Larry stretched out his hand, as far as he could, towards Ginger, who moved nearer to the armchair. 'Hey, old fella,' he said, a smile replacing his weariness, 'good to hear you again.'

Noticing that Ginger was near to collapse, Maud shooed him off to bed for a few hours' rest, before she went to the cottage to check Tom was alright.

*

'You're looking better,' Olly said, when he came in from the fields at midday to find Ginger sitting with Tom at the kitchen table, both supping Maud's homemade broth. Even on hot days like this, Maud made her soup, which was relished by the others in the household. Ginger gave Olly a strained smile. 'I'm to visit my insurance company this afternoon. I'll also need to make out a list of the losses I've sustained.'

'It's a blessing that passer-by reported the blaze. Did you get his name?'

'He's called William Wallace, and was on his way to the pub when he saw the flames. When I heard the name, I thought immediately of the famous Scot of the same name, who was executed by the English.' Despite his lack of education, Ginger had read as many history books as he could lay his hands on.

Olly raised an eyebrow. 'Never heard of him, what was his crime?'

'He was accused of treason.'

'Who was?' Maud asked, having caught the tail end of the conversation when she came indoors after hanging out the washing.

'William Wallace.'

'Does he live near here?' she asked.

Olly and Ginger both laughed but let the subject drop, as by now Maud was concentrating on getting the dishes washed and put away.

Before Olly went back out to the fields, he went into the parlour, where Ginger was writing out his list of losses. 'Hope it goes well with the insurance company,' he said, 'how easily a fire can start.'

Ginger laid his pen down on the table and looked up at his friend. 'I'm still not sure if it was arson.'

'What do you mean?' Olly propped himself on the edge of the table.

'Do you remember last year I had to get rid of Ted Jackson?'

'Is he the one who was lazy, and rude to the customers?'

'That's right, and I also had my suspicions that he was pilfering money from the shop. But as I couldn't prove anything, I simply told him that he wasn't suitable for the job and gave him a couple of weeks' pay to keep him until he got other work.'

'And do you think this Jackson fella had anything to do with the fire?'

'I'm not certain, but it's possible. He threatened me in the street a few months afterwards, but I put it down to him being drunk at the time. I haven't seen or heard from him since.'

Olly had been chewing his fingernail while Ginger was speaking. 'What did he threaten you with?'

'He said he'd get his own back on me. I didn't pay

much attention to his promise at the time, but now I'm not so sure.'

'If you think this Jackson fella had anything to do with the fire, you should tell Matson.'

'I did mention it to him, and he is going to investigate Jackson for any previous acts of arson but, without evidence, it's difficult to prove.'

Olly nodded slowly. 'Difficult, I agree. I'll leave you to it then,' he said, and left Ginger to pick up his pen once more.

CHAPTER NINETEEN
A New Arrival
April, 1860

It was on a Friday morning, with the autumn tints vibrant on the trees, that Ginger caught sight of the Stanleys' carriage passing the front door, and his heart began to pound.

He'd so nearly lost everything in February's fire. The insurance company, the one Larry used to cover the farm buildings and stock, had paid up promptly. The owner, a man of high integrity, had guided Ginger through the whole process.

In the office he warmed his hands at the log stove. He sat down at the desk, leaving the door ajar, to hear if a customer came in. While writing up the order book, his thoughts kept shifting to Larry and how well he was doing following his illness three months ago. His speech and mobility were poor, and Larry had accepted he couldn't work on the farm any longer but was happy to help Maud with small tasks around the homestead.

A short time later, Ginger had a run of customers coming in, and soon he was serving a queue of people. After he'd attended to the second last in line, he turned to the only remaining customer, and gasped in surprise.

Meg Stanley gave him her usual enchanting smile. 'I'm not in to buy anything, Mr Harker … I mean Ben … but as it's a long time since we spoke, I thought I'd come in and say hello.' She looked towards the door as she was speaking.

'Yes, Meg, it is, but I've thought of you constantly since then.' He stopped speaking, wondering if he'd been too outspoken, but her answering smile put his fears at rest.

She looked up at him through lowered eyelashes, high

colour on her cheeks. 'You've been in my thoughts too, Ben.'

'Do you think your papa would allow us to walk out together? I could come to Ripponlea and ask for his consent.'

'I don't think so. My parents are anxious for me to marry well and are very strict about the men I associate with. I'm sorry, Ben, I must sound rude … I mean, I know you have done very well in your business but …' she stumbled to an end, blushing furiously.

'Don't worry, Meg, I understand what you are trying to say. I'm not in your class and I'm sure your papa will have a more suitable gentleman lined up for you.'

She nodded her head slowly then sighed deeply. 'But not one I would want to marry.' Before she could say any more, Meg looked out of the window and, following her gaze, Ginger saw Mrs Stanley strolling along the pavement on the opposite side of the road. 'I'll have to go, Mama will be looking for me.'

As she crossed the shop towards the door, Ginger called after her. 'I would really like to see you again.'

She stopped in the doorway for a moment and looked back at him. 'Can you come to Ripponlea on Sunday afternoon? I'll sweet talk James, our gateman, to let you in and we could meet in the woods nearby?'

'But what about your parents?'

'The woods are dense and you can't see the house from there.'

She hesitated for a moment longer, her hand on the door handle. 'Come at 3 o'clock. I'll make an excuse to come outside. My parents know I'm safe in our private woods so they won't object.'

'I'll be there at 3 o'clock sharp,' he called after her retreating form. He usually helped Olly on the farm on Sundays, but was sure his friend would be understanding.

'I must go,' she repeated, and once outside she moved swiftly, walking in the same direction as her mother had gone.

Ginger's heart turned somersaults, as he watched her graceful figure vanish from sight.

*

But after all Ginger did not discuss his plans for Sunday with Olly when he and Tom got back to Wattle Trees, as something much more urgent was taking place.

'Vicky's labour has started,' Maud told them, before she disappeared upstairs with a basin of hot water and a bundle of towels under her arm.

Ashen-faced, Olly sat in his armchair, cradling 19-month-old Frances. Sound asleep on his lap, the little girl's chubby hands rested on his chest. Larry sat in his chair opposite, and stared into the flames that flickered and danced in the fireplace. 'Maud and Dr Duffy are with Vicky,' Olly told them, his dark-circled eyes trained on their faces. 'It's too early, the baby isn't due for over a month yet.'

Ginger laid a hand on his friend's shoulder. 'Don't worry she's in good hands,' he said. Vicky wasn't very robust, and they'd all been concerned about how tired she'd looked during this pregnancy, much more so than before Frances was born. They sat down and tried to block out the cries of pain coming from the bedroom upstairs, with Maud appearing from time to time to collect something needed to help the mother-to-be.

Eventually, after many hours, they heard the first cries of a baby, and the sound of footsteps coming downstairs. 'You have a son, a healthy boy, thanks be to God,' Maud told Olly, ruffling his hair as she passed his chair on the way to heat some milk for the baby, until Vicky was able to suckle him herself.

Olly got up immediately and placed Frances in Ginger's arms. 'And Vicky?' he called to Maud, his eyes wide with fear, as he headed for the stairs.

'Overjoyed with her son, and asking for you.'

Half an hour later, with Frances by now awake, Olly appeared back in the parlour, his face shining with joy.

'They're both fine,' he told them. 'Vicky's fallen asleep now and my son is bawling lustily for more milk. Maud's gone to get some for him.' When Frances held up her arms to him, Olly took her and cuddled her. 'You're a big sister now, Darling, and soon I'll take you upstairs to see your brother, Herbert.'

'You've named the bairn already then,' Tom said.

'Vicky and I picked his name before she fell asleep.'

Larry stood up and threw his arm around Olly's shoulders. 'I just wish your ma could have lived to see this day,' he said, his face wet with tears.

'Me too, Pa.' Before Olly could say any more, Frances wriggled in his arms. 'Mama,' she whimpered, and her thumb went into her mouth. Olly held her closer. 'You'll be able to kiss Mama, my darling, as soon as she wakens again.' Comforted by his words, the little girl clutched her favourite dolly and snuggled into her father's neck.

Maud carried Herbert into the parlour, and sat in the armchair near the fire to feed him. Frances, her blonde curls cascading over her brow, climbed down from Olly's knee. Dropping her dolly on to the floor, she came over to stare down at her baby brother.

'Here's your big sister come to say hello, Herbert,' Maud crooned to the baby, who was by now sucking contentedly on the teat.

Frances moved closer. 'Erbert,' she said, and patted his tiny face.

'Gently, Darling,' Maud said softly, as the little girl's pats became harder. 'Remember he's a baby and we have to be very gentle with him.' Herbert had finished the little milk Maud had prepared and seemed quite satisfied.

'Small,' Frances said, and kissed his forehead.

Maud smiled at her. 'You were small like Herbert, when you were born. And look at what a big girl you are now.'

Frances stood up tall at her words. 'Play?' she asked.

Maud chuckled, as she lifted the baby against her

shoulder to wind him. 'Herbert will play with you when he's bigger, but right now I'm going to take him back to his crib.'

When Maud and Herbert left, Frances toddled back to Olly. 'Mama,' she said, touching his knee to interrupt his conversation with Larry and Ginger.

'Mama might still be sleeping, Darling, but let's go and see her anyway,' he said, taking Frances' hand.

'Mama,' she repeated, and tottered along with him towards the stairway.

CHAPTER TWENTY
A Clandestine Meeting
April 1860

Ginger was saddling Pharaoh on Sunday afternoon when Olly strolled up to him. He'd been happy to give Ginger the day off to meet Meg. 'Good luck,' he said, and winked.

Ginger hummed quietly to himself on the way through Orange and he felt at one with his steed. Astride Pharaoh's back, he sensed a ripple of excitement coursing through the animal, as though he was happy to share in the adventure too. Ginger's wide-brimmed hat kept him shaded from the glaring sun, his cotton shirt cool against his back.

At Ripponlea James, the gatekeeper, gave Ginger a brief nod, before pointing to a path on the right of his cottage. Ginger dismounted and led Pharaoh into the private woods. He tethered the horse to the trunk of an ancient gum, and sat down on the ground to wait for Meg. Cocooned by thick foliage, with the trees above forming a canopy, they would not be seen by anyone from the house. He saw a flash of blue through the trees and jumped to his feet as Meg appeared beside him. Her blue bonnet had slipped off and sat at the back of her neck. The dappled sunlight coming through the trees painted patterns on her hair and face.

He couldn't think of anything to say and made do with, 'Meg, how wonderful to see you.' She, on the other hand, looked much less tense than on their previous meetings, perhaps due to being in familiar surroundings.

'Let's walk,' she said, slipping her arm through his. He heard running water and, through a gap in the trees, saw a humped bridge ahead of them. They stood close together on the bridge, listening to the brook gurgling its way over the stony bed below, with the chorus of parakeets sitting in the nearby branches adding to the tranquillity. Running his hand over the rough stonework, with the occasional patch of moss growing on it, Ginger wished they could stay like this forever.

'Was it difficult to get out of the house?' he asked, sensing her closeness.

'I told Mama I had a headache and wanted some air, as the house is always stuffy in this weather. She was busy with her embroidery and Papa was in his library reading.'

They drifted over to an aged gum tree, and sat down with their backs against its massive trunk. 'Do you live here in Orange, Ben?'

'No, in Dubbo, at Wattle Trees farm. A large property with over 14,000 sheep. Larry, the owner, and his son Olly, employed me and I've become a part of their family. Olly is married to Vicky and they have two children, Frances and baby Herbert.'

Her sigh when it came sounded wistful. 'No doubt a place with laughter and noise, the very opposite of Ripponlea. How is it you live on a farm but work as a shopkeeper?'

'Larry and Olly taught me all I needed to know about sheep farming, but when I found I had a talent for wood carving, Larry encouraged me to start up my own business. I started with a stall in Dubbo market and, when business increased, I opened the shop in Dubbo and then later the one here in Orange.'

He couldn't stop himself from kissing her and the look of pleasure on her face when he did so gave him cause to hope. 'Meg, I love you so much. Let me come to the house with you, and ask for your papa's blessing on our courtship.'

'I love you too, but Papa has a husband in mind for me,' she told him, misery etched on her face.

'But surely, he wouldn't force you to marry without love?'

'In my world, Ben, daughters are forced to marry for

money and title, no matter their feelings for the husband-to-be. And Lord Lamont is old enough to be my father, if not my grandfather.' She lay in his arms and wept.

He soothed her until the crying eased. 'That's cruel. How old are you, Meg?'

'I'll be twenty-one in August.'

'Almost a year older than I was when I arrived in Australia, back in '47.'

'So you're aged …'

'Thirty-three. You probably think that's ancient,' he said, smiling.

'No, Lord Lamont is at least twenty years older than you,' she told him, and her sobbing recommenced.

'Dearest Meg.' He took out his handkerchief and dried her tears. 'Couldn't you speak to your parents about us, and let them know you can't marry a man you don't love?'

'Papa will never see it my way.' She was unable to keep bitterness out of her voice.

'But can't your mother speak to him?'

'Mama agrees with him in everything.'

'Now we've found one another, Meg, we must be together.' He pulled her up on to her feet and tightened his arms around her. 'We can't let them separate us,' he whispered.

From a distance away, a voice rang out. 'Meg, darling, where are you? Is your head any better?'

'It's Mama.' Meg pushed him away, and brushed the moss off her dress.

'Coming Mama,' she returned her mother's call, patting her curls back into position. Then she dropped her voice again. 'Wait until we've gone, Ben, and James will let you out.'

'But when will I see you again?' he murmured, his voice urgent with frustration. 'I love you, Meg.'

Meg raised her face to his and kissed him. 'And I love you, but we mustn't be caught, or I'd never see you again. Come again next Sunday, and I'll try to get away,' she whispered, as her mother's voice called to her once more.

'Nearly there, Mama.' She put her bonnet on and was tying the ribbons under her chin when she turned away from him. She quickly disappeared from Ben's sight, as she made her way out of the woods. He heard her speak to her mother once she was on the open grassland and soon their voices dimmed as they walked towards the house.

He stayed in his hiding place for some time after Meg had gone. Pharaoh whinnied as Ginger approached. He untied the animal, and led him back to the gatehouse. Silently, James opened the gates and let horse and rider out.

*

When Ginger rode into Wattle Trees, Olly was cutting down some native bushes outside the homestead and he saw the despondency on his friend's face. He walked alongside Ginger and Pharaoh to the stables. Ginger led the horse into his stall, where he removed his saddle and rubbed him down.

Olly plucked a piece of rye grass and began to chew it. 'What's wrong, Ben? Didn't she come?'

'Oh she came, and she loves me, but there's no way we can be together.'

'Why on earth not, if you love one another?'

Ginger sighed and rested his head on Pharaoh's back for a moment. Then he looked at Olly with a defeated air. 'Because her father has arranged for her to marry a man called Lord Lamont, who is old enough to be her grandfather.'

Olly grimaced. 'He'll be one of the Lamonts from Orange, a very powerful family in the county. But surely if you both speak to her pa …' he came to a halt, only too aware that Lamont would be considered by Mr Stanley as a good match for his daughter.

'It's no use, we both know it,' Ginger said, as they headed back to the homestead.

When they got nearer, Maud opened the kitchen door.

'You're back then, Ben. Dinner will be on the table in ten minutes.'

'Thanks, Maud,' he replied, bending to fondle Jess' ears. 'I can't talk about Meg right now,' he whispered to Olly as he straightened up.

'No worries, I won't say anything.' Olly threw his arm casually around Ginger's shoulder and they went indoors, where Frances was waiting to show them her new dolly.

CHAPTER TWENTY-ONE
Maud Voices Her Concern
August 1860

Olly and Brady had eaten breakfast early and were already at work, repairing the shearing shed roof. Ginger and Tom were still at the table, finishing theirs. 'How do you feel Master Larry is doing?' Maud asked Ginger. She kept her voice low, aware that Larry's bedroom door was open.

'Not sure. He tires easily these days, but he eats well,' Ginger said.

'Oh yes, his appetite is good, but he sleeps a lot, so he does. I'm worried about how little interest he has in everything around him.'

Ginger threw her a puzzled look. 'In what way?'

'Sometimes I catch him staring ahead, without really looking at anything, if you know what I mean?' As she was speaking, Maud began to collect up the used dishes from the table. 'At other times it's as though he's smiling at someone who isn't there.'

'You know what a worrier you are Maud, love, he's just getting older,' Tom chipped in, brushing his hand across hers.

But she was having none of it. 'No, he definitely isn't himself these days, so he's not, doesn't even pay much attention to Frances when she chats to him.'

The two men left shortly afterwards. 'Maud seems really concerned about Larry,' Ginger said, on the way to Orange.

'You know Maud, wouldn't be happy if she didn't have something to worry about.'

'Wonder if Olly has noticed anything?'

Tom shrugged. 'Well if he has, he certainly hasn't mentioned it to me, and I'm sure he'd have spoken to you, his best mate.' When they arrived at the shop, the conversation about Larry's health was put on hold.

By lunchtime the sun had come out. Ginger had given up inviting Tom to join him for lunch as the older man preferred to relax in the back shop and read The Sydney Herald. 'I'm off to The Emu, Tom,' he said, as he was putting on his overcoat.

'Fine, Ben,' Tom replied, then raised his eyes from the newspaper. 'There's an article in here about Tasmania, and it mentions Saltwater River.'

Ben felt himself tense at the mention of that awful place. Van Diemen's land, as they'd known it, had changed its name to Tasmania four years ago but that didn't remove the nightmares he still suffered about the treatment he'd received in Saltwater River.

He was still thinking of that place as he walked to The Emu. George was clearing the outside tables when Ginger arrived. 'G'day, Ben,' he said, having dropped the Mr Harker a while since, at Ginger's request. George wiped his hands on his long apron and looked up at the sky, the clouds starting to break up. 'Want to sit outside?'

'Yes, I will. I'll have one of your home-made mutton pies, and a glass of cold ale.'

'Coming right up,' George told him, and disappeared inside with the used dishes.

While he was eating, Ben's thoughts moved to Meg's forthcoming wedding in December. Over the past few months, he'd met her in the Ripponlea woods when he could get away from the farm. The time they spent together was precious to them both, especially as it was unlikely they'd meet once she became Lady Lamont.

*

Sadly, Maud's concerns weren't unfounded, as Ginger and Tom found out when they arrived back at Wattle Trees after work.

'Dr Duffy isn't long away,' Maud told them, 'Master Larry didn't get out of bed today and this afternoon he took a turn for the worse. Olly sent for the doctor, and he sat with his pa until Dr Duffy got here.'

'But he'll be alright,' Tom said, in an attempt to reassure her.

Maud's hands were clenched and a shadow passed across her normally cheery face. 'Don't know,' she said, her voice muffled by a sob. 'It doesn't look good. Olly's sitting at his bedside.'

'I'm going to Larry's room,' Ginger called over his shoulder, 'don't keep dinner for me Maud, I ate at lunchtime.'

Ginger was shocked at the difference in Larry from a little over twenty four hours ago. His eyes were closed and it looked like he was already wearing a death mask. Olly sat in a hunched position beside the bed, and Ginger took a seat at the opposite side.

Vicky came into the room once the children were asleep. 'You go down and have a bowl of broth, Ben,' she said, 'and I'll sit with Olly and his pa for a while.'

'Will I ask Maud to bring some soup up to you, Olly?' Ginger asked as he was leaving, but his friend simply shook his head.

Nearer bedtime Ginger suggested that he sit with Larry and let Olly and Vicky lie down for some rest. 'No, I'm not leaving Pa,' Olly said, laying his hand over his father's deathly cold one. 'But you should go to bed, Vicky,' he urged his wife, 'you need to get your sleep, darling, so you can look after Frances and Herbert tomorrow.'

After a slight hesitation, she nodded and left the room.

Olly looked across at Ginger. 'She hasn't fully recovered her strength after Herbert's birth.' Ginger nodded, he too felt that Vicky's normal zest for life hadn't returned since the baby was born four months ago.

Few words passed between the two men during the hours that followed and it was shortly after one o'clock in the morning that Larry finally lost his fight for life and slipped away peacefully, with Olly and Ginger at his bedside.

*

A week later, on a cold and grey afternoon, the mourners crowded around the open family grave in Dubbo cemetery. The cemetery lay on the outskirts of Dubbo town, only a stones-throw from Wattle Trees.

'Ashes to ashes, dust to dust,' Reverend Morgan's voice intoned, as Larry's coffin was lowered into the grave, to rest beside his beloved wife. The coffin bearers were the men who'd meant the most to Larry; Olly and Ginger had the front cords, with Tom and Pete Robinson in the middle, while Brady and Steve held the cords at the back. Reverend Morgan, his cassock blowing around in the gusty wind, spoke movingly about the worthwhile life Larry had led and he assured the mourners that their loved one was now in God's safe keeping. His soothing voice comforted the family members and friends gathered at the graveside to say farewell to a beloved Pa, Grandpa, father-in-law, friend and employer.

After a further prayer, Vicky handed a sleeping Herbert to Maud, while she and Frances moved forward. Together, mother and daughter dropped flowers on top of Larry's coffin. Then a broken-hearted Olly stepped forward and threw in a handful of soil.

From his place beside Olly, Ginger looked up at the leaden sky and shivered. Winter seemed to have set in properly since the night Larry passed on, and the days leading up to the funeral had turned very cold. The dark day reminded him of a winter's day in Scotland, dreich his mother used to call it, but the Scottish winter was much harsher, with snow and ice covering the ground often for weeks at a time.

Before leaving the graveside, Reverend Morgan shook hands with Olly and the other close family members.

'Will you come back with us for something to eat?' Olly invited.

'It's very kind of you, Olly, but I have another funeral to conduct. I'll visit you all soon,' he promised, as he took his leave.

The rest of the mourners accompanied the family back to the homestead, where Maud had prepared some food in advance of the service, and drinks had been laid out for a toast to Larry's memory. Wattle Trees' residents were grateful for the support of their friends and neighbouring farmers, but they all visibly relaxed when the last of the mourners had left.

'Why don't you have a lie down for a few hours?' Maud's tone was gentle when she spoke to Olly.

He started to protest but Vicky opened her arms and hugged him. 'Maud's right, Darling, we're all grieving but you're suffering most.'

'But there's a lot to do…' he began to say.

Maud cut him short. 'There's nothing that Brady and Steve can't handle. You've been on the go since your pa was taken, and you badly need some sleep.'

'Come on, Olly,' Vicky insisted, 'Maud and I will give the children something to eat before their bedtime and the rest of us can have dinner later tonight.'

Olly finally gave in and let her lead him upstairs.

'You alright, Ben?' Maud asked, when she saw Ginger at the window, staring out at the tall trees surrounding the property.

He took some time to reply and when he did, he turned to her with a wan smile. 'I guess so, Maud. I feel as if I've always lived here at Wattle Trees, and it's hard to come to terms with Larry's loss.'

'Aye, lad,' she agreed, 'we're all going to miss him around the place but Master Larry would want, nay demand, that we all get on with things and keep his beloved farm running smoothly, so he would. So that's just what we must do.'

Ginger took her hand. 'You're right, of course, Maud. Sensible as ever,' he said, and immediately some of the strain fell from his face.

Tom threw his arm around Maud's shoulders. 'Yes, we can always depend on my Maud to keep us all going,' he said, giving her a hearty kiss.

Maud blushed with embarrassment. 'Och, away with all that nonsense,' she told him, but not before she had planted a big smacker of a kiss on his cheek.

CHAPTER TWENTY-TWO
Hatching a Plan
September, 1860

It was the second Sunday of September before Ginger was able to get to Ripponlea again. He hadn't seen Meg since Larry's death. The spring sun was warm on his back at he rode to Ripponlea and James came out and opened the gates for him. Ginger tethered Pharaoh to his usual gum tree and settled down on the moss beside the humped bridge to wait for Meg.

When she hadn't arrived by quarter to four, disappointment flooded through him. He was deciding to return to Wattle Trees, when she appeared on the path leading to the bridge. She looked beautiful in her emerald green gown, the material rustling as she walked. She stopped beside him, bare-headed and smiling. 'I'm sorry to be so late,' she said breathlessly, raising her face to his, 'but Mama had some visitors call round today and I thought they were never going to leave. I slipped out of the house while she and Papa were waving our guests off, but I won't be able to stay for long in case they miss me.'

'Was Lord Lamont in the party?' He was unable to keep jealousy out of his voice as he asked the question.

She shook her head briskly. 'No, he was engaged somewhere else this afternoon but some of his family members were here.'

They walked on to the bridge. Meg laid her head on his chest; passion surged through him and he stooped to kiss her lips. In unison, without the need of words, they moved off the bridge and sat down under the trees on the soft moss-covered ground. He cradled her face between his hands and, with their eyes locked together, his lips met hers once more. They lingered over their embrace, joy stirring in them both. Ginger was breathless when they finally drew apart, and the happy glow in Meg's blue eyes was, he felt sure, mirrored in his own.

He ran his fingers through her blonde curls, and stared at her in awe. 'Oh, Meg, dearest Meg, I love you so much,' he whispered hoarsely, afraid to speak any louder in case he broke the spell.

She clung to him tightly, her eyes closed and her lips parted in a smile. 'If only we could stay like this forever,' she murmured.

'How long have we got? I mean before you and Lord Lamont marry?' he asked, almost choking on the last words.

'The ceremony is arranged for the week before Christmas,' she told him, then changed from the unpleasant subject abruptly. 'I heard about Larry's death. I'm so sorry, Ben, I know how fond you were of him.'

'Yes, it was sad, and even worse for Olly to lose his pa. That's the reason I haven't been able to get here on the past couple of Sundays as I had to help Olly organise the funeral. But how did you know about Larry's death?'

'My maid, Anna, knows someone who works on a farm near Dubbo and he mentioned a local farmer's funeral. I asked her who the farmer was, and when she said Mr Jenkins from Wattle Trees, I knew it was Larry.' She gave a wry smile. 'While Anna is dressing me or brushing my hair, she gives me news of things outside Ripponlea that I wouldn't otherwise know about.'

'I've never met anyone before who has a maid.'

'Anna's been with us since I was a baby and, although she's old enough to be my mother, I think of her more as a friend than a servant. I miss her when she's on her day off.'

It occurred to him once again what different worlds they came from. 'What are we going to do about your wedding?' he asked, returning to the event that neither of them wanted to think about.

'I don't know, Ben. I love you so much, and can't think

of a future without you; I can't sleep or eat, and Mama is becoming concerned about my health.'

He placed his hands on her shoulders. 'I've been thinking of a way, Meg, but it would need to be kept secret. We could marry soon, before your wedding to Lord Lamont. But it would need to be done without your parents' consent.'

For answer, she clung even closer to him, her eyes ablaze with love. 'Oh, to marry you, Ben, instead of that fat old man would be bliss.'

'Are you sure you love me enough to risk losing the support of your parents?'

She nodded and lifted his hand to her lips.

'But, Meg, before we take such a drastic step, please let me come to the house with you, so that we can speak to your father together and convince him of our love for one another. It would be better for you to marry with his blessing.'

'I don't think he will agree, Ben, but …'

'No more buts,' he murmured, pulling her to her feet, 'we can't let him force you to marry a man you don't love.' He took her hand and they walked through the gardens up to the house.

Mr Elliot opened the front door as they climbed the steps. He raised his eyebrows when he saw Ginger standing on the threshold beside Meg.

'Where is Papa?' Meg asked him, leading Ginger into the house.

'He's in the library, Miss Meg.' The butler looked down his nose at her companion. 'But …'

Meg glowered at Elliot. 'We're going up to speak to him,' she said, brushing aside what he'd been about to say.

Leaving Elliot looking after them, aghast, Ginger followed Meg across the thickly-carpeted hall towards the stairway. They climbed up to the next floor and Meg knocked on the library door, opening it when her father's voice boomed out 'come in'.

Paul Stanley was sitting in a chair in the corner reading a book. He removed his spectacles and laid them with the book on the table at his side. 'Have you come to deliver something, Mr Harker?'

'No, Sir.' Ginger cleared his throat, and squeezed Meg's hand tightly. He spoke again, before he lost his nerve. 'Meg and I are in love, Sir, and we would ask for your blessing on our marriage.'

For an instant Mr Stanley looked shocked, then anger overtook it. 'How dare you come into my house with such a preposterous suggestion? And as for you Meg, have you taken leave of your senses?'

Meg rushed towards him. 'But Papa, I love Ben and he loves me. I could never marry Lord Lamont, he's much too old and I don't love him.'

Ginger gasped when Stanley gave Meg a stinging slap across her face. He moved forward to protect her, but Stanley put out a hand to stop him.

'Get out of my house, this instant, before I have you forcibly removed, and do not darken my door again.' The coldness of his tone left Ginger in no doubt that their discussion was over and he had no option but to go.

Meg made to follow him but her father grabbed her and pushed her down into an armchair. 'Stay where you are girl,' he growled, 'I'm not done with you yet.'

Meg's sobs followed Ginger as he crossed the hallway towards the front door, his anger at Stanley almost as strong as what he'd felt for Fraser all those years ago.

When he got to the front door, Elliot was still there, an inscrutable look on his face. Without a word, the butler opened the door and closed it firmly behind Ginger.

*

Ginger and Olly were left together in the parlour that evening, when Maud and Tom had gone home to their cottage and Vicky was upstairs reading a bedtime story to Frances.

'How did this afternoon go?' Olly asked.

Ginger massaged his forehead with his fingers, then threw Olly a despairing look. 'Meg's so beautiful and we want to wed but it's never going to happen.'

Olly poured two glasses of brandy. Giving one to Ginger, he sat down on Larry's armchair facing his friend. 'Go on.'

Ginger explained everything that had happened between himself and Stanley. 'Before we went to speak to her father, Meg and I worked out a plan to marry if he refused, but I'd need your help, Olly.'

'You know I'll do anything I can to help you and Meg.'

'The only way is to marry before her wedding to Lamont. It would have to be in secret of course, and with the hope that her parents don't find out.'

Olly sat quietly for a few minutes, holding his brandy glass in front of him, with the lamplight reflecting off the golden liquid inside. When he did look over at Ginger, he said, 'I doubt very much if the Stanleys will forgive Meg or you, especially as they will have to cancel the wedding arrangements already in place. But as you're not going to get their blessing, I don't think there is any other option but to marry in secret. Is Meg prepared to give up her luxurious lifestyle?'

Ginger drained his brandy glass and laid it down on the table beside his armchair. 'Yes, she's adamant that as long as we can be together, servants and all the other benefits she enjoys will be of no loss to her. I hate to feel her parents will disown her because of me but neither can I stand the thought of her marrying Lamont.'

Olly squeezed his chin between his thumb and forefinger. 'When were you planning to wed?'

'As soon as possible. I hoped you might speak to Reverend Morgan on our behalf, to ask if he will marry us.'

'How will Meg get away to marry you?'

'I don't know that yet, it's something I'll need to consider.'

'How old is Meg?' Olly asked suddenly.

'She was twenty-one last month?'

'She's old enough to marry without her father's permission and there's no obstacle to your union as you're both single. You'd need to give notice to Reverend Morgan three weeks before the wedding. Where to you intend to live?'

'Last week I consulted Mitch Flynn, the lawyer Pete Robinson introduced me to when I bought my first shop. Mitch said there's a mansion, Deepdene, for sale in Dubbo. I've already viewed the property. It's to be auctioned next week and Mitch thinks the top price I can offer should secure me the mansion. So I might own it by the time Meg and I are wed.'

'And if not, then you could stay here with us at Wattle Trees for a time.'

'Thanks, Olly, although I'd hope not to impose on you for too long, as it's unfair to crowd you here. But it would be …' Ginger stopped speaking when Vicky came in.

'You two seem very serious. What's going on?'

Olly caught her by the hand and pulled her down on to his knee, where he cradled her against his chest. 'Well, my darling, I think our Ben here has some news for you …'

*

On the Wednesday following his confrontation with Meg's father, Ginger was working on accounts in the back shop when Daniel, a young lad he'd recently engaged, interrupted him. 'Mr Harker, a woman's come in, asking to speak to you.'

The woman, wearing a brown cotton dress and a straw bonnet perched on her greying hair, carried a wicker shopping basket. 'Are you Ben Harker?' she asked.

Ginger was struck by her open, honest face. 'I am. Can I help you?'

'My name's Anna Forsyth. Miss Meg from Ripponlea sent me.'

'Anna. Yes, Meg has told me about you. How is she?'

'She's very upset.'

'Has her father struck her again?' Ginger's hands clenched tightly. 'He slapped her with great force in front of me, and ordered me out of the house.'

Anna shook her head. 'He hasn't hit her, but he keeps her locked up in her room and cook sends her meals up to her.'

'What about her mother? Can't she do anything?'

'The mistress always agrees with the master.' Her voice, which had been quiet, lowered even more. 'Between you and me, Mr Harker, I think she's afraid of him.'

Anger welled up in Ginger. 'The man's a monster.'

'Miss Meg asked me to give you this,' Anna said, taking a letter out of her pocket.

Ginger took the envelope from her, his heart thumping as he looked at his sweetheart's copperplate writing. 'Do you still have errands to run, Anna?'

She nodded and he gave her a warm smile. 'When you've finished, could you come back to the shop as I'd like to send a reply to Meg?'

'Yes Mr Harker.'

'Please call me Ben,' he said, as she turned to leave.

Ginger went back to his desk and opened Meg's letter, the paper smelling of lavender.

My darling Ben,

I am distraught when I think of what happened on Sunday. Papa refused even to listen to how much we loved one another, and I will never forgive him for his treatment of you, my dearest heart.

Papa has locked me in my bedroom and won't allow me to go out, but I am determined I will not marry Lord Lamont. Mama has sided with him, as she always does, so I can't turn to her for help. The only person I can trust is my maid, Anna, and I am sending her into town on some errands, so she can take this letter to you.

My darling, I am desperate to be with you, and I pray you will find a way to let this happen. If I'm forced to marry Lord Lamont then I will kill myself before the wedding, and Papa can suffer guilt for making me do it.

You can contact me through Anna.

With all my love, dear heart,

Meg x

Ginger's fury at Stanley increased with every line he read. He took a sheet of parchment out of the desk drawer and dipped his nib into the inkwell.

Darling Meg,

It breaks my heart to hear of your plight and please, please, don't think of harming yourself. I have already taken Olly into my confidence and he has spoken to Reverend Morgan on our behalf. The minister needs three weeks' notice of our intention to marry but he sees no obstacles to our union taking place on the first Saturday in October. We are both single and, as you are 21, you can marry without your father's permission.

It is essential, dearest, that your parents don't hear of our intentions, so tell no-one other than Anna. When you leave Ripponlea, bring nothing with you; that way neither the butler, nor any other member of staff, will see you leaving the house with luggage. Dress as though you are going for a walk in the woods. If, however, you wish to choose a dress you want to be married in, please give it to Anna and send her on an errand again, so that she can bring it to me here. I will buy you anything else you need, dearest.

Don't escape until the day we are to be married. If you leave a letter in your bedroom, we will be man and wife by the time your parents read it. Perhaps Anna could 'forget' to lock you in after you are dressed and you could leave through a side door. Try to make it look as though you've escaped without Anna's help, to keep her from being blamed. Once you reach the woods, wait at the side of James' cottage, hidden by the hedge, and only come out once I arrive with the wagon to bring you back to Wattle Trees.

I have bought a house for us, dearest Meg, a mansion

called Deepdene in Dubbo, which I think you will like. We could move in soon after our wedding, although of course you will be able to see it before that and choose the furnishings for us. Until we move to Deepdene, Olly and Vicky are happy to have us live at Wattle Trees.

I need to bring this to a close, my darling, as Anna will be back soon to collect it from me. Send Anna to the shop with your dress, and you and I will meet for our wedding the first Saturday in October, a day that can't come too soon for me.

Sending you all my love, my dearest Meg,

Ben x

Ginger sealed the envelope and laid it on the shelf under the counter. Five minutes later Anna returned to the shop.

'It's ready, Anna,' he said, handing her the letter. 'I hope our plan to marry won't cause you any problems with your employer.'

She gave him a sad smile. 'I'm willing to risk it for Miss Meg. But I will miss her.'

CHAPTER TWENTY-THREE
A Secret Wedding
October 1860

On the day of her escape, Meg wore a plain, dark green dress. Last week Anna had delivered the dress she'd chosen to be married in to Ben's shop.

'Isn't it bad luck for the groom to see the dress before the ceremony?' Anna had said, before she left.

'This is the only way I can get the dress out of the house.'

'What about the letter for your parents?' Anna now asked in a low voice, brushing and dressing Meg's beautiful blonde tresses as fast as she could.

'It's on my dresser beside the window. By the time they read it, we'll already be married.' Last evening she'd told Bridget her room didn't need done today. Since her parents rarely came into her room now, her plan should go smoothly.

'We must keep in touch,' Meg whispered to Anna, gripping her maid's arm tightly.

Anna gently freed herself. 'I'm not sure how often I'll get into town, Miss Meg, but when I can, Mr Harker will tell me how you are.'

'You can call him Ben, and me Meg. We're friends, Anna.'

Anna smiled, but didn't make any comment. 'I won't use the key this time. I'll wait until I see you leave and then lock the door. Don't forget to leave the window open.'

'Thank you, Anna, for everything.' Meg rushed over and hugged her.

'Careful now, you don't want to disturb your hair,' Anna whispered, tears welling up in her eyes. She quickly slipped out of the room.

With shaking hands Meg opened the window, praying it

wouldn't squeak. She released her breath when it didn't, having been unaware how tightly she'd been holding it. She pushed the sheets they'd tied together over the windowsill; with the sheeting tied firmly round the leg of the solid oak dressing table, it would look as if she'd escaped via the window. She chugged hard on the sheeting and was sure it would have held her weight.

Meg had one last swift look around her bedroom. She was sad to leave her books and her collection of dolls behind, but Ben was right it was better to go empty-handed. She tiptoed along the corridor, her footsteps muffled by the carpet, and sped down the stairs to the servants' hall and kitchens. When she heard someone coming along the uncarpeted basement corridor she squeezed herself, heart racing, into a pantry, until the staff member started to mount the stairs. Leaving by the side door, she raced across the grass into the formal gardens.

She slipped through the fence and once safely into the woods, she made her way towards the gatekeeper's cottage. Creeping round the back of the building, she hid herself in against the side wall, out of sight of James and his wife. A shiver ran through her, a combination of fear and excitement, but apart from sadness at leaving Anna she had no regrets. When she heard the sound of hooves approaching, she unlocked the gates. Ginger, already in his wedding suit, helped her up on to the wagon. Relief coursed through her as he pulled on the reins and they set off, smiles lighting up their faces on the journey to Dubbo.

Olly and Vicky were waiting in the parlour at Wattle Trees, dressed for the wedding. With no time for introductions, Maud took Meg's hand. 'I'll show you where you can get dressed,' she said, smiling at the girl.

There was a collective gasp when Meg arrived downstairs again, looking magnificent in her peach satin gown, decorated with sequins. She felt herself wrapped in the warmth of their smiles. Maud would stay at the homestead and look after the children, while Tom drove the wedding party to the church.

Ginger took Meg's hand, love shining in his eyes. 'Ready?' he asked.

'Ready,' she replied, with no sign of the stressful escape she'd made.

The horses raced along, the white ribbons Tom had fixed to their manes, waving around with the motion. Reverend Morgan was waiting for them at St Luke's Church in Dubbo. He led them down the aisle to the communion table, behind which was a stained glass window depicting Jesus Raising Lazarus from the Dead. Olly and Vicky took their position one on either side of the happy couple during the short wedding service. Olly had somehow managed to organise a birth certificate for Ginger, naming him as Ben Harker, and when the vows were exchanged, the minister said a prayer of blessing on their union.

Back at Wattle Trees, Maud had prepared a wedding day feast. She'd baked a cake, with silver bells and horseshoes around the sides and a tiny bride and groom sitting on the top. There were no interruptions to the celebration and, by bedtime, with no word or angry visit from Meg's parents, the newly-weds made their way into Larry's old bedroom, freshly decorated, to start their married life.

When they climbed into bed, Meg sensed Ben shared her tension about their first sexual encounter. His reticence helped rid her of her own worries about the unknown. Ben's lovemaking was gentle, and his tenderness towards his new bride made it easy and natural for her to give herself to him.

*

Paul and Jane Stanley were having afternoon tea in the drawing room, when the door flew open and one of the maids rushed in with a loaded tray wobbling about in her hands.

'I'm sorry, Sir, Madam,' she said breathlessly, looking

from one to the other, her face red and sweaty, 'but Miss Meg has gone.'

Paul sprang to his feet, his face black as thunder. 'Gone? Gone where? I gave strict instructions she had to be kept locked in her room at all times.'

The maid cowered back a little. 'Yes, Sir, but when I unlocked her door, the room was empty and … and she wasn't there.'

Mr Elliot hurried in behind her. 'My apologies, Sir,' he said, 'I tried to stop Edna from disturbing you.' He glowered at the maid and pointed to the door. 'Get out of here immediately, and I will speak to you downstairs.' The terrified girl lowered her head and slunk out of the room.

The butler handed his employer an envelope. 'I found this in Miss Meg's room, Sir. The window was wide open and there was sheeting leading down to ground level.'

Anger had by now drained Paul's face of colour, and he stood with his back against the marble fireplace. 'Thank you, Elliot, you may go now,' he said, in a clipped tone.

'Sir,' the butler replied, bowing his head, as he backed out of the drawing room.

Only once Elliot had left, did Paul rip open the envelope.

Dear Papa and Mama,

I have never disobeyed you before, but I cannot marry Lord Lamont. He is too old for me, and I don't love him. I'd kill myself before becoming his wife.

You leave me no choice, as you refuse to accept Ben Harker as my husband. There's no need to fear for my future, as Ben is an honest and kind man.

By the time you read this, I will be Mrs Ben Harker, something that will make me the happiest woman alive. As I am 21, I don't need your permission to marry, Papa.

I still love you both and hope that one day you will find it in your hearts to accept Ben as your son-in-law.

Meg xx

Paul tossed the letter aside and strode out of the room,

the floorboards juddering under his weight.

Bending to pick it up, tears poured down Jane's face as she read of her daughter's flight. 'Oh, Meg, my darling Meg, what have you done?' she said aloud, and grabbed her smelling salts from the table at her side, as the words became faint. She'd used the salts frequently since Meg had announced her love for Ben Harker. When her fainting turn began to ease, she got out of her chair and went into the hall, where she almost collided with Elliot. Barely acknowledging his apology, she stumbled out of the house and found her husband sitting on a bench in the rose garden.

Paul looked up, his eyes narrowed. 'This is all your fault, Jane, for constantly giving in to her whims.'

She gasped at the vehemence in his tone, but shook her head vigorously. 'No Paul, Meg has a stubborn streak, and she gets that from you, not me.'

His mouth fell open, and he was struck dumb for a moment by her audacity to stand up to him. 'When we tell Lord Lamont what has happened, we'll be a laughing stock,' he growled, the vein in his neck pulsing.

'I know,' Jane murmured, sitting down beside him. She wiped her eyes with a hankie and sniffed back the tears. In an attempt to placate him, she laid her hand on his. 'Once things settle down again, we can invite Meg and her new husband to visit us here at Ripponlea.'

'Absolutely not,' he bellowed, throwing her hand away. 'They will never darken our door from this day on. Meg is no longer my daughter and her name will not be mentioned ever again.' He thundered off up the stony path, his wife following a short distance behind.

Back in the drawing room, he rang the bell and Elliot came in a few minutes later. 'You rang, Sir?'

'Send Anna in here immediately …'

*

Ginger had taken a few days off work after the wedding, to spend time with his new bride, who looked radiant this morning. The shops were in the capable hands of Joe, assisted by a young man, Martin, who had been taken into Ginger's employ four months ago.

Ginger and Meg were in the kitchen with Maud, getting ready to drive over to Deepdene to view their new home. 'I do hope you like it, darling,' Ginger said, as he helped her on with her cloak.

'I know I will, Ben,' she whispered, and kissed him. She was thrilled about the prospect of running her own home.

Maud went to answer a knock on the kitchen door. Meg gasped when she saw Anna standing on the doorstep, a small case in her hand. 'Anna, come in,' she said. Anna made a small curtsey, first to Meg, and then to Ginger.

'No need for that,' Ginger told her, noticing her ashen face. 'Take a seat,' he invited, his tone gentle, and Maud signalled she'd make some tea.

'What's happened?' Meg pulled a chair over to sit beside Anna. 'Was Papa cross?'

Anna nodded and looked down at her lap. When she looked up again, tears glittered in her eyes, but she smiled them away. 'He didn't get your letter until yesterday afternoon, when it was discovered you were missing. He sent for me later and asked if I'd helped you to get away. I told him I didn't know anything about your disappearance, but I could see he didn't believe me, and he dismissed me there and then. Told me to pack my belongings and leave first thing this morning. Cook made me some breakfast before I left.'

She turned grateful eyes on Maud, who laid a steaming cup of tea and a slice of homemade fruit bread in front of her. Maud's smile was warm and welcoming. 'Get that down you, and you'll feel better.'

While Anna was eating, Meg looked up at Ginger, pleading for help. But once Anna had cleared her plate, she spoke again.

'You mustn't worry about me, Miss Meg, I'm glad I helped you to escape and I would do it again if I had to.

There would have been little for me to do at Ripponlea with you gone, so I would most likely have left of my own accord. I have some savings that will keep me going until I find another position. But I was hoping you'd supply me with a reference on my good character, as I couldn't ask your papa for one?'

'I'll be happy to do that,' Meg started to say, but she stopped speaking when Ginger put a hand on her shoulder

'Meg, you could use Anna's services when we move into Deepdene.' Two pairs of eyes were trained on him as he continued. 'Anna would be company for you while I'm working in the shop. There are four bedrooms in the house, so plenty of room for you to live in, Anna. Seems to me the obvious resolution.'

Meg threw her arms around Ginger's neck and hugged him tightly. 'My darling, what a wonderful idea,' she said, and murmured in his ear, 'thank you.'

'We'll be moving into Deepdene within the next two weeks, so I'll pay for you to stay in a rooming house until ours is ready. No,' he said, as Anna made to protest, 'I insist, it's the least we can do for you. Maud, you won't mind squeezing another place in at the table so that Anna can eat with us here until the new house is ready?'

Maud smiled. 'Another mouth is nothing in this household, so it isn't.'

CHAPTER TWENTY-FOUR
The Move to Deepdene
November 1860

Anna came into the family room, carrying a pile of freshly washed and ironed bed linen. They'd bought both bed and table linen, when she and Meg were in town yesterday.

She stood in the doorway for a moment, listening to Meg humming quietly to herself as she polished the table and chairs Ben had made. Over the time she'd been with the newlyweds, Anna had been overjoyed to see how happy and contented Meg was as Ben's wife. She'd been transformed from an unhappy girl, being forced to marry a much older man, into a confident, self-assured woman in only a matter of weeks.

'You sound happy in your work, Miss … er Meg,' she said. Although she'd been instructed to drop the Miss, Anna was finding it difficult to leave off the habit.

Meg looked round at the sound of her voice, and smiled brightly. 'Yes, Anna, I am. Ben has made us such a beautiful dining table,' she said, drawing her fingers lovingly across the surface.

'Magnificent. I've put the table linen in the cupboard meantime, and I'll now start making up the beds.'

'Thanks, Anna, and later perhaps you could help me to hang the curtains in the parlour.'

'No worries,' Anna called back, as she started to climb the stairs.

While Anna was working upstairs, she thought back to a conversation she'd had with Meg yesterday. 'It's wonderful to have you here with me,' Meg had told her. 'It's so different from Ripponlea, here we all work as a team.'

'I do feel welcome, Miss … er Meg,' she'd replied, then laughed. 'It's going to take me time to get used to being so familiar when I speak to you.'

'Thank goodness the attitude of my parents and their friends is dying out in the new colony, and people are treated as equals.' Meg had turned away at that moment to check on some lists she'd made up, but not before Anna had seen the pain written across her face when she spoke of her parents. There had been no word or visit from them since Meg's wedding and, although Meg had written twice, she'd received no reply.

When Anna finished her chores in Meg's room, she moved on to the bedroom she'd be occupying on the opposite side of the stairway. Ben had made a dresser and a washstand for her, and a cupboard for hanging her clothes. She didn't have many clothes, so there would be ample room. The house was lit by kerosene lamps and she had her own little lamp on the dresser at the side of her single bed. Once her bed was made up, she sat on it and jumped up and down, feeling the softness of her mattress. Her room was much more comfortable than the one she'd had in Ripponlea, which she'd shared with another maid. She began to feel that Mr Stanley had done her a service by dismissing her, as life here with Meg and Ben was going to be much more pleasant.

'Do you think this would look right here?' Meg asked her, when she returned downstairs. Meg was standing, barefoot, on one of the dining chairs, holding up a picture of a pioneer's cottage, under a blazing sky, and surrounded by Australian native bushes. The figures in the foreground depicted some of the early settlers to the colony.

'It looks lovely.' Anna hurried over to help Meg lower the framed picture, a wedding gift from Pete and Hannah Robinson.

'Ben can hang it for us.' Meg looked around the room. 'I can't believe we will be moving in at the weekend, isn't it exciting?'

Anna nodded, her eyes sparkling with joy, and the two of them took hands and danced around the room.

CHAPTER TWENTY-FIVE
Happy News
April 1861

Meg went back and forward to the window frequently, watching for Ben's wagon. Since coming home from town this afternoon, she'd been unable to settle to anything; she'd pick up her embroidery for all of ten minutes, before returning to the window.

'You're like a hen on a hot girdle as my mother would have said,' Anna told her, when she wandered aimlessly into the kitchen for the umpteenth time in the past half-hour. 'It won't make him arrive any quicker, you know.'

'You're right, and I'm going to settle down with my embroidery. Unless there's anything you need a hand with,' she offered.

'No thanks, everything's under control.'

Anna, the eldest of ten children, had a lot of experience of pregnancy from the births of her younger siblings. Then there was her own personal experience and her eyes filled at the memory. She'd recognised some signs that Meg had been displaying recently; no doubt why she was so keen for Ben to come home. But she said nothing, knowing Meg would want her husband to be first to hear her news.

When the wheels of the wagon finally rolled up the driveway, Meg rushed outside and hurried towards Ben, as he was jumping down from his seat beside Tom.

'G'night, folks,' Tom called, as he turned the horses, 'see you tomorrow, Ben.'

Ginger looked round and waved his hand, as he and Meg headed indoors.

'I couldn't wait for you to get home,' she told him.

'I gathered that. What's all the excitement about?' Ginger smiled at Anna before being propelled into the family room.

Meg closed the door and they sat in front of the newly-lit fire, flames starting to lick their way over the coals. Although they weren't into winter yet, the autumn evenings were becoming cooler, and Anna always got the fire going at this time of day.

'When I was in town today, Ben, I went to see Dr Duffy.'

'You're not ill, I hope, Meg, you've seemed in such good spirits recently. Are you pining for your life at Ripponlea?'

'No, I don't miss Ripponlea one bit, I love it here at Deepdene with you and Anna.' Her eyes sparkled as she ran her hand over his face, her finger tracing its way round his lips. 'The doctor confirmed what I'd already suspected. I'm going to have a baby.'

'Darling, what a wonderful surprise.' He laid his hand across her abdomen, unable to stop the smile spreading across his face.

'Not such a surprise, we were hoping to have children,' she reminded him, her smile matching his.

'When's the baby due to arrive?'

'Dr Duffy thinks sometime in October.'

'Will we let your parents know?'

A cloud passed momentarily over Meg's face and she stared into the fire. 'There's no point, it's clear they don't want anything to do with me. It's a pity, as Mama would have loved to be a grandmother.' Then she shrugged. 'It's their fault for not accepting you as my husband.'

Ginger decided against trying to persuade her to change her mind. Despite Meg having a gentle nature, he'd discovered that she did have a determined streak. But he hoped she'd be reconciled with them eventually. Their rejection had hurt but they were still her parents.

In the kitchen, Anna smiled when she heard the father-to-be's yell of delight. So, she thought, her suspicions had been correct. She waited a bit longer before going in to tell them dinner was ready. The dining room was used when they had guests, but they were happy to eat in the kitchen with Anna at other times.

'Great news, we're going to have a baby.' Ginger's voice was joyful and Anna felt happy for them both.

'That's excellent news, you'll make wonderful parents.'

'I've suspected for some time that I might be with child,' Meg said, her face aglow, 'but Dr Duffy confirmed it this afternoon. That's why I couldn't settle to anything.'

'Yes, I knew there was something afoot. It will be lovely to have a child's laughter around the house,' Anna said, as the three of them went into the kitchen.

*

In bed that night, Meg and Ginger found themselves too excited to sleep.

'Will you carve a crib for the baby?' Meg asked, as she cuddled against him, her head resting on his chest. She liked to feel the movement as he breathed.

He bent his head and kissed her. 'Of course I will. It will be the most beautiful crib that's ever been made,' he promised. He hesitated for a moment, and played with her blonde hair, before adding, 'I think your parents would be happy to know they are to be grandparents.'

Meg tensed immediately. 'No, Ben, they don't deserve to know. Not after the way they've treated you. I can't forgive them for that. They should be proud of you, like I am, the way you have built up your business and provided us with such a beautiful home.'

Weighed down by guilt, Ginger raised himself off the pillow. He lit the lamp and, in its glow, looked at her beautiful, trusting face. Thoughts of Van Diemen's land re-surfaced and he knew he no longer wanted to keep secrets from her.

'I haven't been honest with you, my darling. About my past life, I mean.'

Fear now replaced the happiness on Meg's face. 'What do you mean, Ben? You're frightening me.'

He sat up higher on his pillow, and cradled her head

and shoulders with his arm. 'I didn't come to Wattle Trees straight from Scotland as I've always let everyone believe. I was in Tasmania, or Van Diemen's Land as it was, before I came to the mainland.'

Her arm tightened across his chest. 'I don't understand. You said you came for employment because there was little work to be found in Scotland?'

'I was in a prison camp, Meg. I was sent over to Australia as a convict.'

Meg sat up to face him. He expected her to be angry and accuse him of lying to her, but instead she said, 'Ben, you are not a convict, you couldn't be, you're kind and too much of a gentleman to have done anything wrong,' she said, a sob catching her voice.

Ginger slid down the bed, gently pulling her with him. He drew the bedcover over them, and murmured, 'I will tell you the whole story, Meg, and I promise I won't leave anything out. Even if it stops you loving me, I want to share everything with you.' He kept his voice low, afraid they might waken Anna, sleeping across the corridor from them.

Meg clung to his hand, while he told her about his life in Scotland, his transportation to Australia and meeting Tom on board. He spoke about his time in Saltwater River, and how he'd changed his name to Ben Harker when he came to the mainland. She listened intently and, when he finished, she stared into his eyes and asked, 'Fraser, he's the one who inflicted those wounds on your back, isn't he?' Soon after their marriage she'd asked how he got the scars on his back. He said he'd been thrown off a horse back in Scotland. She'd accepted that at the time but now realised they were the result of his flogging.

'Yes, I almost died from my injuries.'

'What a beast.' She cupped his face in her hands and kissed him tenderly. 'How cruel these guards must have been. I hope you were allowed time to sleep and didn't have to work day and night, no-one could survive that surely?'

'On the ship we had to sleep on mattresses on the deck but at Saltwater River we slept on hammocks. They were suspended from the walls of the cell, in two rows facing each other, sort of like sailors have on ships.'

'Was Tom in your cell?' she whispered.

'Yes, when I was transferred from the coalmine to his prison block. Once you were in the hammock, it was fairly comfortable, but there was very little space between you and the men on either side of you.'

Meg tried to imagine what he'd suffered during those years. 'It must have been hard to be so crammed together.'

'The worst part was the stench from all the unwashed bodies, mine included. We were only allowed to bathe and shave once a week on a Saturday. Also the noise of snoring made it difficult to get any sleep.'

Meg pulled a face and sighed. 'Oh my darling, what awful things you have suffered.' She lay quietly in his arms for a time, her hand in his. Her voice was a whisper when she said, 'Ben, thank you for telling me, and your past makes no difference to our love. I would have married you, even if I'd known about your time as a convict. It's a disgrace that you were ever sentenced, simply for stealing food when you were starving. Has Tom told Maud about his time as a prisoner?' she asked.

'I don't think so.'

'And who else knows about your time in the camp?'

'Only Olly, I told him in my early days at Wattle Trees, when two policemen came looking for me. Olly was alone in the homestead when the lawmen came, and he didn't even tell his pa. Loyalty is important to Olly, and I'm sure Vicky will know nothing either.'

'And you can depend on my loyalty too, Ben. Nothing that happened to you was your fault, and I'm sorry you didn't feel able to confide in me earlier. But now you have, and I don't want us to ever again have secrets from one another.' When Meg stopped speaking, she began to yawn.

'We need to get some sleep. You look exhausted and

we have to think of the baby,' he whispered, laying his hand over her stomach.

She laid her hand over his, and smiled. 'Put the lamp out, Darling, and we need never speak of this matter again. Only the future is important.'

Ginger did as she asked and when the room was plunged into darkness, he found her lips for a goodnight kiss.

Within minutes of the light going out, they both fell asleep.

*

Two days later, Vicky was cutting some late roses in the garden when she heard the wheels of Ben's wagon roll over the stony driveway. She straightened up and waved, as Ben reined in the horses. Mindful of Meg's condition, Anna climbed down first and took Meg's hand to help her out of the wagon. Ginger had been able to drive his wife and Anna over to Wattle Trees, because shops closed at midday on a Saturday in the colony.

'How lovely to see you all,' Vicky said, holding her scissors and the flowers away from her, while she kissed both Meg and Anna in turn. 'You're looking so well, Meg, in fact, you're blooming.' Meg had given Vicky the good news yesterday, when she'd called at Deepdene to remind Meg about the family's invitation to Herbert's birthday party.

Meg smiled, and lowered her head. 'They're a magnificent colour,' she said, looking at the roses. She was about to mention the flowers the gardeners at Ripponlea grew, but bit her lip, preferring not to think or speak of her parents' home nowadays.

'Yes, though I'm always amazed that such beautiful flowers have really vicious thorns. But come away in,' Vicky invited, ushering the two ladies towards the kitchen door. 'Olly's working in the middle paddock,' she called to Ben, who'd unhitched the wagon and was leading the horses away to graze in the lower fields.

'Right, I'll go up there to see if he needs a hand,' he replied. Although he no longer officially worked on the farm, Ginger was happy to give Olly a hand when it was needed.

'The birthday boy is having an afternoon nap before his party,' Vicky said, as they headed indoors, 'and Frances is helping Maud to lay all the party foods on the table.'

With a whoop of delight, Frances came racing into the kitchen from the parlour and ran straight into Meg's open arms. The 2½-year-old had taken to Meg on first sight and the pair had become great friends since Meg had joined the family circle. 'We've got jelly and ice cream,' she told Meg, 'and a big birthday cake with a teddy bear on it for Herbert.' Frances threw her hands out wide to show the size of the cake.

'And how's my beautiful girl, today?' Ben asked, as he came into the kitchen behind the others. 'Olly's just finishing up in the sheep pen,' he said to Vicky, as Frances left Meg to rush over and hug him. He swung her up in the air and she shrieked in delight.

'What are you all doing standing in here? Away into the parlour and find yourselves a seat,' Maud told them, shooing them out of her domain.

When Olly came indoors and cleaned himself up, Herbert, refreshed from his nap, was brought downstairs. Once Herbert's gifts were opened, the little boy having more fun with the wrapping paper than with the toys inside, there were games for the children. The adults joined in, and afterwards they all tucked in to the goodies prepared by Maud. When the candle on the birthday cake was lit, Herbert giggled and blew out the flame, helped by his mother, then clapped his tiny hands in glee when everyone sang Happy Birthday to you.

'It'll be great for Herbert to have a new playmate when the baby arrives,' Vicky said to Meg, once the singing had died away, and the cake cut.

Meg nodded, taking a slice of cake from the plate that

Maud held out to her.

'Me play with baby,' Frances piped up, as she licked the cake icing off her fingers.

Vicky smiled. 'Of course you can, Darling, it's just that the new baby will be closer to Herbert in age. But you can all play together I'm sure.'

Frances sat up on a dining room chair, swinging her legs back and forward. 'Me see baby?' she asked.

'Not until October.' Meg touched her little bump and beamed with happiness.

CHAPTER TWENTY-SIX
A Surprise Arrival
July, 1861

'Looks like the war in America's still raging. That's another battle been fought in Virginia, at a place called Manassas this time,' Tom said, from behind his newspaper. The American Civil War had started back in April with a battle at Fort Sumner, and the world's press had been busy reporting details of the conflict.

Maud scooped sausages, fried tomatoes, bacon and eggs on to their plates which had been warming on the range. Vicky did the cooking at Wattle Trees on a Sunday, so she and Tom could have a leisurely breakfast in their cottage. 'Now eat up and give me some peace from hearing about wars, especially ones in other countries that don't affect us here in Australia,' she scolded, putting Tom's plate down in front of him.

He grinned, aware that Maud disliked him reading at the table. 'But even though you don't like to hear of it, the war is still raging,' he persisted, lifting his knife and fork. 'The Confederates in the south are refusing to do away with slavery and the Yankees up north are determined to make them.'

Maud sat down opposite him. 'It's as my ould Mam, God rest her soul, used to say, there's nothing wrong with our world, except the folks that live in it.'

Tom stuck his knife into the egg to let the yolk run over his plate. He buttered a slice of toast, cut it in half and soaked it in egg yolk, savouring every mouthful. Maud tutted and shook her head, giving him one of her looks.

'Will we go to the market today?' He and Maud often browsed round the Dubbo stalls on a Sunday.

'Yes, we need new bed sheets, and we can also attend the church service.'

Tom made a face but nodded. 'Anything you say, Maud.' Being a devout Christian, Maud liked to attend church when she could and, although a non-believer, Tom went with her. If he drifted off during the sermon, Maud would waken him with a hard nudge.

*

'Come in,' Ginger said, and stood aside to let Maud and Tom enter. 'Meg, that's Maud and Tom come to see us,' he called upstairs, before showing his friends into the family room. 'Meg was having a lie down. As her date draws nearer she tires easily.'

Maud nodded. 'The extra sleep is good. Hope we haven't disturbed her.'

'No, she's been asleep for a couple of hours. Anna will make us some tea.'

'Is it not Anna's day off?' Maud asked.

'Anna insists on staying put, so she can be here for Meg. Even though I'm here on a Sunday, she still won't take time off. And I know Meg feels more secure with Anna nearby.'

Maud smiled. 'She's in safe hands. Anna's the oldest of ten children, so she has plenty of experience in the birthing world.'

*

Hearing Ginger call to her, Meg got out of bed and washed her face and hands. She pulled on her dress, with its front panel Anna had sewn in to accommodate her large bump. She was so grateful that Anna had come to live at Deepdene; she was worth her weight in gold, even refusing to have a day off until after the birth.

Meg stood in front of the mirror and drew her hands over her swollen belly. She loved to think of her baby growing in there, and often had a chat with him or her. She couldn't wait to hold her child. As she'd grown bigger, she'd worried that Ben would be disgusted by her size, but he often laid his hands across her belly, telling her he couldn't wait for the little one to become part of the family.

She closed the bedroom door and hurried downstairs.

Halfway down, the hem of her dress caught in the heel of her shoe and, before she could grab the handrail, she tripped and fell headlong. She landed with a thud at the bottom of the stairs and lay, stunned, staring up at the rose cornicing on the ceiling.

Ginger heard her cry out and raced into the hallway, followed by Maud and Tom.

Meg groaned. 'Darling,' he soothed, gathering her head and shoulders into his arms.

Maud knelt down on her other side. 'Leave her be for a moment, Ben,' she cautioned, 'and let her gather herself together.' She looked up at Tom. 'We'll need to get Dr Duffy to check Meg over.'

'I'll go for him,' Tom began, when Anna appeared from the kitchen. She'd heard the commotion from the back garden and straight away grabbed her coat off the peg in the hall. 'I'll go and fetch Dr Duffy, you stay here Tom and help Ben get Meg upstairs.'

By the time Anna arrived back with Dr Duffy, Meg was in bed and Maud had got her into her night clothes. She'd come round, but was still trembling from shock.

'What happened?' Dr Duffy sat his medical bag on the bedside table.

'I fell down the stairs,' she murmured weakly, moaning when the doctor took her pulse and checked her head for any cuts or bruises.

Ginger, his face ashen, wrung his hands. 'I should have gone up and helped her downstairs. If anything happens to Meg or the baby …' his words faded out and he dropped down on his knees at the side of the bed, stroking Meg's brow.

Dr Duffy laid a hand on Ginger's shoulder. 'Ben, I think Meg needs to rest, and I'd also like to examine her, so probably better if you all go downstairs.'

Meg grabbed Ginger's hand, not wanting him to leave her, but he kissed her forehead and got to his feet. 'Better to do as Dr Duffy asks,' he said, gently releasing his hand from her grip. 'I'll be downstairs, my love,' he added, as he turned towards the door.

The others made to follow, but the doctor called Anna back. 'Anna, I'd like you to help me with Meg. Could you boil some water, please, and bring up some towels?'

She hurried downstairs, where she put on a clean pinafore. Meg's cries were louder by the time she returned and the doctor was laying out things from his medical bag. Having helped bring many a younger sibling into the world Anna knew what to do, but her hands shook as she poured water into the ewer for Dr Duffy to scrub his hands and fingernails.

The doctor examined Meg internally. She grimaced and clung to Anna's hand. He rested his hand on the fundus to check the contractions. Drawing the bedcovers over Meg once more, he spoke to his terrified patient. 'You've gone into an early labour, Meg. I didn't expect you to deliver for about another five or six weeks. The fall has probably contributed to your contractions starting.'

Meg grasped his arm in a vice-like grip. 'Can you stop it, doctor?'

Dr Duffy gently prised her fingers away. 'It's gone too far and we need to let nature take its course. Try and rest, you need to reserve your strength.'

Anna sat down at the side of the bed and wiped the beads of sweat off Meg's brow. 'Try and relax, my lovely,' she said, holding Meg's clammy hand, as she was hit by another contraction.

Dr Duffy lifted Meg's nightdress and listened for the baby's heartbeat. His brow furrowed as he tried repeatedly to find sounds. Anna's mouth was dry with fear for Meg's precious baby. She remembered clearly the time this had happened to her mother and that child, her brother, was born dead. But, shaking such thoughts away, she concentrated on what Dr Duffy was saying.

Meg's eyes had been closed but now she roused herself. 'Is everything alright, doctor?' She stared up at him with fear evident in her pain-filled eyes.

'Yes, Meg, the baby has a strong heartbeat.' He nodded to Anna in confirmation of what he'd just said.

As the contractions increased, Meg's yells became louder. 'I'll give you something to ease your pain,' Dr Duffy said, then to Anna he murmured, 'I'll use chloroform, enough only to make her drowsy, as she needs to be alert enough to deliver the child.'

'Is that what Queen Victoria was given during childbirth?'

He looked slightly taken aback. 'You're right Anna. How did you know that?'

'The cook at Ripponlea house told me when I worked there, she was a strong Royalist and took an interest in such matters.'

'The sedation will ease your pain, and baby will be less distressed,' Dr Duffy said to Meg, as another strong contraction ripped through her.

Raising her head off the pillow, he placed a mask over her nose and mouth while he administered the chloroform.

Trying to ignore the fingernails digging into her palm, Anna sponged Meg's sweaty face until the medication took effect.

Many hours passed, with Meg's screams increasing each time she suffered a particularly strong contraction. Being a first baby, the labour was long and painful, and Meg cried out for it to end. At her side, Anna held her breath, praying that all would be well.

Darkness had fallen by the time the baby's head appeared. Anna moved closer, rubbing Meg's arm gently. 'The baby's coming, Meg, it's nearly over.'

'A little push and it'll be here,' Dr Duffy told his patient by way of encouragement. He tried not to think of how many of these early births resulted in a life being snuffed out before it even got going. There was a chance, God willing, that this child might survive.

In a supreme effort, Meg pushed along with the spasm

of her womb.

'Almost there, almost there. Here it is … what do we have? A little girl.' Dr Duffy cut and secured the cord, desperate to offer congratulations but knew it was far too soon for that. The baby was small, dusky and quiet. How he wished for a cry. 'Anna, keep an eye on the bleeding while I clear this little one's mouth and nose.' The blueness on the baby's lips persisted, and he held her up and patted her on the back and the bottom. Anna's eyes were anxious as she watched him working and they gasped simultaneously when the little mite gave her first mewling cry.

'Is she alright?' Meg's weak voice asked from the bed.

'Yes, Meg, she's perfect,' Anna told her. 'You have a gorgeous little girl.' She dried the baby and wrapped her in towels, making sure her head was covered. Holding the newborn in her arms and rocking her gently, Anna carried her over to Meg. Anna removed the soiled linen from the bed and pushed a clean sheet underneath Meg.

'Well done, Anna.' Dr Duffy took off his spectacles and rubbed his knuckles over his eyelids. 'The baby will need to be fed with small amounts of warm milk every hour or two, until she's able to suckle from the breast.'

'Tomorrow I'll buy a feeding bottle for her,' Anna said.

'Meantime, I suggest you use a small spoon and you can give her animal milk or condensed. You might need to feed her from a spoon or a dropper for several days until she's able to suck.'

'There's plenty of cow's milk in the kitchen. I'll go and heat some up now.'

'And, Anna, once she's fed, I suggest you light a fire in the room, as it's essential she's kept warm.' Anna always lit a fire in the evening before Meg and Ben went to bed but today's events had overtaken the normal routine. 'And I think we should let the new father come up and meet his daughter.'

*

After pacing the family room floor for hours, constantly rubbing his birthmark, Ginger heard a baby's cry. He made to leave, but Maud stopped him. 'Leave it, lad, and let the doctor finish his work. He'll tell you when to go up and see Meg and the baby.'

At last they heard footsteps coming downstairs and Ginger dashed out the door, almost colliding with Anna. 'All's well, Ben. Meg and your daughter are waiting for you.'

Ginger rushed into the bedroom. 'Thanks, so much, doctor,' he said, and shook the hand that Dr Duffy extended to him.

He brushed his hand down Meg's clammy cheek. 'Oh, my darling, I was so worried about you, thank God you're both okay. He leaned down to his daughter, still cradled in her mother's arms, and kissed the tiny forehead.

'We'll need to give her a name.' Meg's face glowed with happiness, as she cuddled her daughter. They'd discussed names previously, but hadn't come to a decision yet.

'You decide, dearest, I'll be happy with whatever you choose.'

Meg looked down at her baby and smiled. 'What about Lily? I think she's as pretty as a flower, so should have the name of one.'

'Hello, little Lily, welcome to our family,' he whispered.

Anna returned with the warm milk, which she lay on the bedside table. She lifted Lily from her mother's arms, before holding the spoon to the little one's mouth. Once the baby seemed satisfied, Anna winded her. Then she bathed the little mite in warm water and wrapped her up securely in a blanket, with a knitted hat on her tiny head. She laid Lily in her crib which now sat at the side of the bed waiting for the new arrival.

Ginger sat with Meg, while Anna lit the fire. In no time at all, it was blazing out its heat to keep their precious baby warm.

Once the afterbirth came away, Dr Duffy seemed

content that all was well. Meg fell asleep, her face free of worry by now.

Ginger and Anna went downstairs with Dr Duffy, who departed after drinking the cup of tea Maud made him. Afterwards, Maud went upstairs to peep into the bedroom where Meg and Lily were both asleep.

'What a gorgeous child,' she said, on her return to the family room. 'Now, Tom and I will get off and leave you in peace. Remember and call us if we can do anything,' she added, giving both Ben and Anna a hug on her way out.

CHAPTER TWENTY-SEVEN
Lily's Christening
October 1861

'What a pretty girl you are, my darling.' Meg tickled Lily as she lay on top of the bedspread and the baby kicked her legs up in the air. Rays of sun streamed in and threw an aura of light around Lily, making the sequins on her christening gown sparkle.

While Maud tidied away the paraphernalia that was lying around, Meg fluffed out the feathers on Lily's hat. 'I'm sorry you had a rush sewing on the sequins this morning. I can't thank you enough.'

'I'm happy to do it for little Lily,' Maud said. 'Will we go down and join the others?'

'Here comes the star of the show,' Ginger said, when Meg came in carrying the baby.

Olly and Vicky came over to admire Lily's finery. Having been witnesses at Meg and Ginger's wedding, they were now delighted to be Lily's Godparents.

'Hello, you two,' Meg said to Frances and Herbert and allowed Frances to sit in a comfy armchair for a few minutes and hold Lily in her lap.

Tom brought Ginger's carriage round to the front door and drove them the short distance to the church, with the Wattle Trees' carriage following behind. The minister waited for them outside the door.

In the usual tradition, there was a hymn, a prayer and a bible reading before the christening. Meg and Ginger stood in front of the font, with Olly and Vicky supporting them. The baby was awake when Reverend Morgan made the sign of the Cross on her forehead, and she made little crooning noises when the water from the font touched her skin.

*

'What a lovely day it's been,' Meg said to Ginger in bed that night. Lily had been given her last feed of the day and was now tucked up in her crib at the side of their bed. At almost three months old, the baby was now sleeping through the night, which allowed Meg to waken refreshed in the morning.

'And Lily behaved so well in church, didn't she?' he murmured, cradling Meg against him, her head on his chest.

'We're so lucky to have such a contented child, Ben.'

'Yes, we are truly blessed,' he whispered, and within minutes they drifted off to sleep.

CHAPTER TWENTY-EIGHT
Further Expansion
June 1865

'If you don't get a move on, you'll be late for Ben,' Maud scolded Tom, 'and you've let your toast grow cold,' she added, clearing up the breakfast dishes. Olly and the boys had long since gone to work in the fields, and Vicky had taken Frances and Herbert to school. Tom folded up The Herald, and placed it in the paper rack for later reading. The newspaper had kept him up-to-date with all the happenings during the last four years of war in America and thankfully the Civil War had ended last month. From all accounts, peace hadn't been totally restored to the country, with the freed slaves not sure what to do with their lives, after taking orders from their Masters for so many years.

He put on his new tweed cap and overcoat. 'Right, Love, I'll get off now,' he said, and gave Maud a kiss. He adored her, even when she nagged him; he knew how much she loved him and would do anything for him.

'I hope it all goes well. After the hard graft Ben's put in over the years, it's great to see his business extending.' Today was the opening of Ben's new store in Sydney. It was his biggest shop yet. He and Meg were going, leaving Anna to look after the children. They'd been blessed with the birth of their son, Gordon, two years ago and Ben was thrilled at the idea of his son one day taking over the business from him.

When Tom got to Deepdene, Ginger helped Meg into the carriage, then climbed in beside her, with a rug over their knees. He allowed himself a moment of pride, thinking how his navy blue carriage was as handsome as the one Meg's parents had owned. It was sad that they'd never contacted Meg since her marriage, and didn't know their two grandchildren.

'Penny for them,' Meg said.

'Just thinking how lucky we are.'

Tom flicked the reins and the horses set off. Matt and Norm, although getting older, were still giving great service.

When they drove into the main street of Sydney, Aussie Crafts was easily identified by the bunting around the shop. 'Looks great,' Meg said, when they stopped outside the store, and Ginger helped her down from the carriage. When they went inside, Meg looked around the vast floor space and the high ceiling, with its decorative cornicing. 'I like it, much bigger than the other shops,' she said.

The shelving around the walls was well stocked with goods made by Ben and Joe, plus the other wood carvers they'd employed over the years. Ginger pointed towards the stairway at the far end of the store. 'I'll take you upstairs, but first come and meet the staff.'

Joe and two female assistants stood nearby. Meg noticed Joe's hair wasn't so spiky nowadays, probably due to using hair oil. She smiled at the two ladies, Kathleen and Mary, who looked nervous. 'I hope you'll be happy working here, and I know you're in good hands with Joe,' Meg said, trying to put them at ease.

Ginger then took Meg through a door leading into the workshop, with sturdy benches and tools for the extra wood carvers they'd employed. A part of the room had been ringed off, with some tables and chairs and a cooker in it. 'That's where the staff can have their lunch breaks. Let me show you the upper floor before we open,' he said.

'This is great,' Meg enthused, when they got to the top of the stairs. The floor area was set around the stairway, with a rail running along the edges for safety.

Meg stood at the rail and looked down on the main shop space below. 'What are you planning to do with this?'

'I'm not sure. Any ideas?'

She stood for a moment, deep in thought. 'Why don't

you open this part as a teashop? You could set out tables around the room, inside the rail, and through here,' she said, leading him into an anteroom, 'this could be converted into a kitchen to serve the tearoom. After the customers have shopped downstairs, they could come up here for refreshments and something to eat.'

'What a wonderful suggestion,' Ginger said, throwing his arms round Meg and hugging her tightly. 'Why didn't I think of that?'

She laughed and kissed his cheek. 'Because you've been busy with the shops. I'm sure a tearoom would be well received by your customers.'

'I'll have a word with Mitch Flynn. Would you help with choosing the china and crockery for the tearoom? I mean without feeling that you were neglecting the children?'

'Of course I'll help. I'm sure Anna would enjoy spoiling Lily and Gordon while I'm here.'

'I'll go and see Mitch tomorrow. I guess we better go down as it's almost time for the grand opening.'

A large crowd had gathered outside. Joe had put some red and white ribbon across the doorway. 'Good luck, Ben,' he called, as they went out via the side door, he with his speech in his hand and Meg holding a pair of scissors.

'Good day, everyone,' Ben started, 'and welcome to the opening of our new store.' He kept his speech short, and afterwards invited his wife to cut the ribbon and make the opening official. He noticed a photographer from The Sydney Herald recording the event, pictures of which would no doubt appear in tomorrow's paper. In earlier years, the thought of his picture in the paper would have made Ginger anxious, but having been Ben Harker for so long now, his fears of arrest had vanished.

Joe opened the door and the customers flooded in. While they milled around browsing the stock, Ginger and Meg joined Tom in the carriage.

It was during the journey back to Deepdene that Meg

made her suggestion. 'Ben, you've achieved so much since you arrived in Australia. Why don't you write your memoires?'

'I hadn't thought of that, Meg, but perhaps I should. It would be something to leave for our children, and their children, when I'm gone.'

'But you're not going anywhere, my dearest, I need you here with me until we're old and grey,' she whispered, nestling her head against his shoulder.

CHAPTER TWENTY-NINE
Maud Makes a Discovery
July, 1865

Maud finished black-leading the range and tidied away everything lying on the kitchen table. She tutted; as usual, Tom had dropped yesterday's Herald on to the table, instead of putting it into the rack in the corner beside the pantry. 'When will I ever get that man trained?' she said aloud to the empty room. Then she laughed at herself, knowing how much she enjoyed looking after him.

The sheets of newsprint rustled as she lifted them and one fell on to the floor. She stooped to pick it up, and gasped. The page was headed Births, Deaths and Marriages, and from the list of deaths the name STANLEY jumped out at her. Maud sat down and read the Obituary to Meg's papa, who'd died in his sleep. The piece took up about two and a half columns, almost half of the page.

She felt Meg had a right to know about her father's death. Ben bought The Sydney Herald every day, but he often left it in the shop, so Meg might not have seen it. Although she'd been hurt by her father's behaviour, he was still her flesh and blood.

Maud recalled a favourite saying of her ould Mam, God rest her soul, family is family. Yes, she thought, I'll show it to Meg, but not today, on Lily's birthday. The newspaper gave the date and time of the funeral for next week and Meg would have time to decide whether or not she'd attend.

Maud roused herself to go and wrap up the game of snakes 'n ladders she and Tom had bought Lily for her 4th birthday.

*

'That's me off, love,' Tom said the following morning, kissing Maud as he left.

Alone in the house, she scooted around doing her chores and just after eleven o'clock walked to Deepdene in the winter sunshine.

She heard Lily and Gordon shrieking with laughter in the garden when she walked up the path. Before she had time to ring the bell, Meg had opened the door. 'Lovely to see you, Maud, come in.'

She slipped off her coat and Meg hung it on the rack near the door. Pulling out her hatpin, she laid her hat on the hall table, before following Meg through to the kitchen, where Anna was washing up the breakfast dishes. A delicious smell of baking came from the oven.

'Hello, Maud,' Anna said, 'you and Meg make yourselves comfortable in the family room and I'll make some tea.'

They took an armchair each, one on either side of the fireplace, with Maud staring into the flames, a perplexed look on her face. Meg had an idea why she'd come, but she waited for Maud to speak.

'It's very mild for mid-winter. Olly was saying the other day that we need a lot of rain before summer comes round again. The fields are parched and he thinks they might have to do some hand feeding of the sheep.'

The door opened and Anna carried in a tea tray, with some of her freshly-baked shortbread.

Meg poured their tea and while they were drinking it, Maud started to speak. 'I wanted to tell you something yesterday, Meg, but as it was Lily's birthday, I thought it better I came to see you on your own today. I saw something in the newspaper yesterday … it was …'

As she stumbled around, Meg took pity on her. 'Maud, I know what you're trying to tell me. After you'd all left yesterday, and the children were asleep, Ben showed me the Obituary for my papa in The Herald.'

Maud was relieved, although she'd thought Meg would be more upset. 'I notice that the funeral will take place next week,' she said.

'I won't be attending.' Meg spoke softly and the only sign of distress was when she began to chew her thumbnail. She watched the flames licking over the coals and when she looked up, her eyes were moist. 'I can't forgive him for the way he treated Ben and he's never tried to contact me over all these years. I am sorry that my mama has been left a widow, but she didn't stand up for me when I left Ripponlea.'

Maud swallowed her last few crumbs of shortbread. She was sad Meg couldn't find it in her heart to support her mother at the funeral and hoped she wouldn't live to regret it. 'I wasn't trying to interfere, Meg, but thought you should know about his death.'

'Ben tried to persuade me to go, and offered to come with me. But I've made up my mind.'

At that moment Gordon launched himself into the room, Lily behind him.

'And what have you two been up to this morning?' Maud asked them.

They told her about the games they'd been playing. Then Maud produced some sweets from her bag.

'Oh, thank you, Maud,' Lily said, holding up the bag of sweets to show her mother.

'Hank you,' Gordon echoed, opening his bag to peer at the goodies inside.

'Don't eat them just now,' Meg instructed the children. 'If you go into the kitchen, Anna will give you something to eat and a glass of milk. After lunch, you can each take a few sweets into the garden with you.' The two women smiled as they watched Lily head off to the kitchen, with Gordon trotting after her, his bag of sweets clutched tightly in his fist.

Maud got up then and laid her empty cup, saucer and plate on the tray, glancing at the clock above the fireplace. 'Well, I'd best get off, Meg. Thanks for the tea.'

'I appreciate you coming,' Meg told her, giving the older woman a hug.

CHAPTER THIRTY
All That Glitters
February, 1867

'Your usual?' Olly raised his voice over the wall of noise that hit them inside the pub.

Nodding, Ginger chose a table, leaving Olly to join the crowd milling around the bar, where Don was working alone, rushing between the gantry and the counter. It was a humid evening and, despite the pub door standing open, only hot air filtered through it. The kerosene lamps on the bar added to the stifling atmosphere.

Elbows propped on the table top, Ginger looked around the pub, which hadn't changed since his first visit with Larry and Olly, after attending the sheep sales in Dubbo. That seemed so long ago, and the memory brought on thoughts of Larry and his kindness.

'Poor Don, he's run ragged, the sweat was pouring down his face.' Olly laid their drinks on the table. He sat down and raised his glass to his friend. 'Finally, Ben, we get to spend some time together. Here's to us, mate.'

Ginger lifted his glass. 'To us,' he echoed, and drank some of the welcome liquid. 'Yep, nowadays there're usually children running around. So, how're things at Wattle Trees?'

Olly took a long swallow of his beer and smacked his lips in appreciation. 'I'm hoping for a wet winter ahead, after such a hot spell. Vicky's been complaining about the long hours I've put in since Brady bought his own station further up the valley.'

'Didn't he wed Pete Robinson's daughter?'

'That's right and they wanted their own place. Only natural, I suppose. Can't wait for Herbert to join me on the farm.' Olly grinned as he said this.

Ginger chuckled. 'Herbert's what? Seven, isn't he?

Think there's some way to go yet before that happens.'

Olly joined in the laughter. 'At least he's interested in becoming a farmer, so that's something. I guess you'll hope that Gordon will go into the business with you one day?'

'Who knows? Right now, Gordon's head is full of mischief, but I suppose at just 4-years-old I can hardly expect anything else.'

'He's a lucky lad, having a thriving business to take over when he's older.'

Ginger picked at his fingernails, without responding.

Olly finally broke the silence. 'What's the problem, mate?' he asked, sensing his friend's lowering of mood.

Ginger moved his beer mug around on the table top, while Olly waited. At last Ginger raised his head, concern evident in his eyes. 'You'll remember years ago I decided to plough the profits from the shops into buying shares in the Bendigo Gold Mine in Victoria.'

'Yeah, seemed like a wise decision. And didn't Mitch Flynn agree with that?'

'He did, and the dividends were used to expand the business. But the gold strikes have lessened in the past year or so and the share prices have fallen drastically, leaving the market uncertain.'

'I read that in the papers, but didn't realise it was so bad. I sold Pa's mining shares when he died, and used the money to buy some extra stock.'

'I remember you doing that. I discussed things with Larry at the time I bought my shares, and back then they were doing well. But it's changed days. At first the drop was slight, but over the past few months things have worsened, and I'm concerned now that the price might fall to zero before long. If that happens, I may even have to consider letting some of my employees go.'

'What about having a word with Mitch?'

'I've arranged to see him at his office on Friday afternoon. I haven't said anything to Meg as I didn't want to worry her, so maybe best you don't mention it to Vicky.'

'No worries, I'll keep it to myself. Mitch should give you good advice.'

'He's a good man where shares are concerned.' Ginger drained his glass and stood up. 'Enough doom and gloom. Same again?' he asked, picking up their empty beer mugs.

'Great, thanks.' Olly was concerned as he watched his friend head for the bar. He'd been so pleased for Ginger that his business was flourishing, and he hoped that this current problem would be short-lived and easily resolved.

*

'What's wrong, Ben?' Meg asked, when she came downstairs the following evening and found Ginger sitting in his armchair, staring down at his feet. 'You've hardly said a word since you arrived home from the shop.'

Ginger leaned back in his armchair, resting his head against the antimacassar. He looked up at Meg and gave her the ghost of a smile, but his eyes betrayed any attempt to hide his anxiety.

She knelt down on the carpet and laid her arms on his knees. 'Ben, I know there's something bothering you. You know what they say about a trouble shared. Are there problems in the shops?'

He twisted his fingers round the curls cascading down over her forehead. 'No, darling, the business is in a healthy state.'

'Then there's something else troubling you, isn't there?' she persisted.

His hand fell away from her hair and he clenched his fingers tightly. 'I was trying not to worry you,' he said, his hand sliding towards his birthmark.

'Well now I'm really worried because you're not sharing the problem with me. Remember we promised not to have secrets from one another.'

He bent down and kissed her forehead, then slowly began to speak. 'You'll remember a number of years ago I bought some shares in the Bendigo goldmine in Victoria. I used the profits from Aussie Crafts to pay for these.'

'Go on,' she encouraged him.

'Recently, there's been a slump, with the market making huge losses.'

She stretched up and stroked his cheek, sad to see the worry etched on his face.

He put his hand over hers for a moment, before continuing. 'The price of gold has taken a tumble, and folk are now selling their shares before it drops even further.'

'But if you hold on to the company shares, is there not a chance the price will rise again? Papa used to say they moved up and down quite rapidly.'

'That's the trouble, Meg, the market could go either way; great if it picks up but should it go the other way, then Aussie Crafts could lose a lot of money.'

'Do you think it might mean you having to lose some of your staff, or perhaps close one of the shops?'

'I hope not. I certainly don't want to be the person who leaves my hard-working staff with no employment. I haven't said anything to Tom or Joe up to now, in the hope that things would improve. But the latest fall in the price of gold makes for pessimistic reading.'

'But you mustn't blame yourself, Ben, you've enough to deal with without this added worry.' She remembered all the evil things that had happened to her husband in the past. 'The way you were treated in the camp, now that was cruelty, but this is different.'

'I've contacted Mitch Flynn for advice. Now, tell me, what mischief has Gordon caused today?' Hardly a day passed, without his son being in deep water.

'When I was buying hair ribbon for Lily at the market today, I noticed he'd disappeared from my side. You know how he tends to wander off.' Ginger nodded, and she went on. 'I dropped the ribbon and ran about calling his name. A woman at a nearby stall said she'd seen a little boy go into the public house behind the stalls. I found him sitting up on one of the high stools at the bar, watching the woman behind the counter serving the customers single-handedly. I was in time to hear Gordon say to her, 'Lady, why is your face all red, with water running down your cheeks?' The people sitting at the bar roared with laughter but the poor woman was embarrassed. I apologised for his rudeness and chastised Gordon, although I found it difficult not to laugh.'

'One thing about Gordon, he always tells the truth,' Ginger said, and their laughter lightened the worry about the gold shares.

*

The following afternoon, Ginger arrived at the Dubbo District Legal Chambers on Market Street in good time for his appointment with Mitch Flynn. The town had grown fast since Ginger first got here back in '49 and the chambers were only two years old. He strode up the stairs at the front of the grey granite building, the stonework glinting in the afternoon sunshine, and made his way to the office on the third floor. Mitch had been his lawyer since he'd started in business with Aussie Crafts, and Ginger was in no doubt of Mitch's integrity.

'Good afternoon, Mr Harker,' the secretary said when Ginger approached her desk. 'Mr Flynn is expecting you. Can I get you a tea or coffee?'

'Coffee, please.'

After a few pleasantries, Mitch invited Ginger to take a seat. 'So you've concerns about your shares.'

Ginger laid the certificates on the desktop. 'The share prices are plummeting, and I thought it was time I had a discussion with you about the best way to proceed.'

'I, too, have been keeping a close eye on the market,' Mitch told him, then stopped speaking when his secretary arrived with the coffees. He cleared a space for the tray on the highly polished desk, with its dark green leather inset.

'Thanks, Miss Penfold.' Once his secretary had left, Mitch poured the coffee, passing Ginger the sugar and milk to help himself. 'The market has been a bit volatile recently, and it's to be hoped that things settle down soon.' While Mitch was speaking, he dropped two sugar cubes into his cup and stirred it into his coffee. 'How has the business been affected up to now?'

Ginger took a few sips of his coffee, then laid the cup down on its saucer again. 'As you know, I bought a large number of shares, some from my own savings to hold for my children, but the bulk of them were bought from the profits of the business.' He stopped speaking, while he took another drink. 'I'm prepared to lose some of my own money, but I'm keen to avoid this happening to the business shares. I'd hate to have to pay off any staff, who have given me loyal service.'

Mitch nodded, then clasped his fingers together, thinking. 'Here're my thoughts, Ben. If you can hold off selling any shares at the moment, when you're unlikely to get back what you paid for them, there is a good chance that the market will become buoyant again. Since your shops are doing well, and I can see this is the case from the company accounts, what about considering a bank loan to tide you over this difficult period?'

Ginger bent his head a little, rubbing his birthmark. 'Do you think the bank manager would grant me a loan?'

Mitch nodded. 'I'm sure he would. Your business is in good health, and you have sufficient collateral for the bank to take the chance. Do you want some time to think about it, Ben, or will I go ahead and contact the bank on your behalf?'

Ginger's mouth felt parched, and he drained his coffee cup, to give him time to think. Then he smiled across the desk at his lawyer. 'I don't think there is any other way, Mitch, so yes, please request the loan.'

'I'll set the wheels in motion today and once we get a reply from the bank, hopefully a favourable one, I'll contact you again and get you to sign the necessary forms.'

When their business was concluded, Mitch stood up,

and came round the desk to shake hands with Ginger. Then he opened the door, and bade him good day.

Relief surged through Ginger as he made his way down to the entrance hall, praying that Mitch's plan worked.

CHAPTER THIRTY-ONE

Another Extension to the Harker Empire

February 1869

Under a boiling hot sun, Ginger left Aussie Crafts. He threw his jacket into the carriage and climbed aboard. 'Let's go.'

Tom flicked the reins and the horses set off. 'Everything going well in there?' he asked, glancing round at the shop they'd just left.

'Yep, Trevor's built a good relationship with the staff and sales are good. We'll see how Patrick's doing in his store.' Following an increase in Sydney's population, Ginger had acquired two more shops, one on the west side of the town, and the other on the east.

After the worry with the gold shares two years ago, and having secured a bank loan, the market had come up again, with the price of gold rising significantly. Today when he was in Sydney inspecting the shops, he and Tom would stay in a rooming house and return to Dubbo tomorrow.

Tom drew up in front of the town centre store and Ginger went inside to go over the accounts with Joe. His protégé had blossomed into a fine businessman. Meg's idea had been sound and the café was well used by local ladies.

'Are you going upstairs for some lunch, Ben?' Joe asked, once he and Ginger had finished.

'Good idea, I'll get Tom to put the boys in the field while we have a bite to eat.'

He found Tom outside, still seated behind the horses, reading his newspaper. Happy with this arrangement, Tom put down the paper and picked up the reins once more.

As he was going upstairs, Ginger smiled to himself. He'd started calling the horses the boys too; they'd been Tom's boys since the first time he used them with the delivery wagon. They were getting quite old by now, and Ginger was sure they would soon have to be replaced by younger animals. He dreaded the thought of Tom having to give up his beloved Matt and Norm, even though they would be well looked after by Olly at Wattle Trees.

Ginger ordered them both a black coffee and pushed the lunch menu across the table to Tom when he arrived. They gave their food order to the waitress, her pristine white pinafore apron worn over a smart black dress and a frilly white cap perched on top of her curly hair.

'G'day, Mr Harker,' the café manageress said, as she passed them on her way to speak to customers at a nearby table.

'G'day to you, Miss Hart.' Although Joe hadn't said anything to him, Ginger was sure that he and Deborah Hart were stepping out together, and he wouldn't be surprised to hear soon of their engagement. Deborah was a Sydneysider by birth and Joe had now bought himself a home in the town.

*

'Sounds like Trevor and Patrick are both doing well in the new stores,' Tom said, when he and Ginger were enjoying their dinner in the rooming house that evening.

'Yep,' Ginger replied, swallowing his last morsel of braised steak, before wiping his mouth with the napkin. 'And sales in the three Sydney stores have shot up in recent weeks.'

Tom laid his cutlery on the empty plate, and sat back in his seat. 'You've done so well, Ben, and richly deserved, laddie, 'cause you've worked hard.'

'But I couldn't have done it without support from Meg, Olly and you. And, of course, Larry at the beginning was the one who spurred me on. I owe a debt of gratitude to you all.'

But Tom brushed away the compliment. 'Nah,' he said, 'you've done the hard graft, and you've given us employment into the bargain.'

Mrs Neilson, the owner of the rooming house, came over to the table. 'Everything satisfactory, gentlemen?' she asked.

Ginger smiled at her. 'Highly, thanks. Will we go into the parlour for coffee?'

'Yes, please. Bessie will bring it through to you.'

'Let's have a drink to celebrate the success of Aussie Crafts,' Ginger suggested, once the two of them were ensconced in comfortable chairs in Mrs Neilson's parlour.

'Now you're talking, laddie.' Tom gave him a grin as Bessie arrived with their coffee.

CHAPTER THIRTY-TWO
Meg Discloses Good News
April 1870

When Ben walked in the front door, Lily and Gordon raced out of the family room, pushing each other aside, to reach him first.

Gordon, being taller and stronger than his sister, was the winner. 'Daddy, Daddy,' he squealed, 'guess what, I came in first in our class races.'

'Well done, Son.' Ben ruffled the excited boy's hair, still curly despite being cut shorter. Then he turned to his daughter. 'And what do you have to tell me, Lily?' he asked the pretty 9-year-old, her face the image of Meg's.

'I got nine out of ten for my spelling test, Daddy.' Still of a fragile build, she preferred the academic subjects.

Meg came into the kitchen to join them. 'Come on, you two, give Daddy a chance to change before dinner. And what about your homework, Gordon? Lily's finished hers.' Gordon made a face but returned to his school work, followed by Lily as she knew he often needed her help with his sums and reading.

'Dinner will be ready in ten minutes,' Anna told them, and Ben ran upstairs to change out of his work clothes.

*

'The End.' Ginger closed the book, Little Women, laying it on Lily's bedside table. Although very sleepy by now, she'd managed to stay awake long enough to hear what finally happened to the four March sisters.

In his bed, in the same room, Gordon had long since fallen asleep, most likely because it had been a story for girls. Ginger had it in mind to suggest he next read Thomas Hughes' novel, Tom Brown at Oxford, telling of a young boy's schooldays. He was sure it would be much more to Gordon's taste.

'Gordon gets to choose our next book,' he whispered to Lily, as he put out the lamp and tucked her up for the night. Although the children, especially Lily, were able to read for themselves, they always enjoyed being read to before they went to sleep.

'Yes, Daddy,' Lily murmured, and was asleep before he'd closed their bedroom door.

'All alone?' Ginger asked, when he joined Meg downstairs.

'Yes, Anna's gone to bed.' Anna's working day started early, especially on school days, so she tended to retire to bed around eight o'clock. 'I need to have my beauty sleep,' she would tell them, a saying which intrigued Lily.

Ginger settled himself into his armchair, facing Meg, who had been reading a book. She was also a very good writer, especially of poetry, and Ginger had, for some time now, encouraged her to send off some of her poems to a publisher. He was disappointed that she hadn't so far, but he wouldn't give up suggesting it.

'Are they asleep?' she asked, putting a bookmark in at her place.

'Yes, Gordon was sound before I finished reading,' he told her. 'It's getting more difficult to read something that suits them both. Although they'll soon feel too old for bedtime stories,' he said.

Hearing the sad note in his voice, Meg smiled. 'Soon they'll be too old to share a bedroom.'

'That'll be easily remedied, with our extra bedrooms.'

She smiled again. 'That's true, Ben, and we'll soon need them.'

He stared at her and something in her smile gave the game away. He perched himself on the arm of her chair, and drew her closer. 'Are you telling me what I think you are?'

'Yes, my darling, it was confirmed today that I'm with child.'

'Meg, that's wonderful.' He scooped her up in his arms,

then looked serious. 'It'll be alright, I mean it's seven years since Gordon was born …'

She laughed and waved her hand in front of him. 'Of course, it is. I'm only 31, after all, and women much older than that have babies.'

'You're right, and when can we look forward to our new addition?'

'Dr Duffy says probably in October.' The doctor was getting older and would retire soon but Meg was glad that he would still be able to deliver her baby. She'd had faith in him since Lily's birth.

They were still smiling over the good news when they went to bed shortly afterwards.

CHAPTER THIRTY-THREE
A Surprise Visitor at Deepdene
October, 1872

Ginger folded up his newspaper, and dropped it on to the carpet at the side of his chair. He leaned back against the antimacassar and gave a sigh of contentment. How he loved to spend his Sundays with his family, especially as nowadays Olly had employed three new farm hands, so Wattle Trees was well served.

Adam sat on the sofa beside Meg, clutching his giant teddy bear, almost as big as himself, and Sarah was sitting on the carpet at her feet, dressing her new dolly. Both toys were gifts they'd received yesterday for their second birthday. Sarah had arrived into the world first, with her twin brother following on twenty minutes later. A smile played around Ginger's lips as he thought how bossy Sarah was, with Adam doing as he was told.

Over in the far corner, Lily was painting a picture. Her eyebrows creased in concentration as she worked, her box of watercolours opened on the table in front of her. A contented girl, she spent hours on her hobby. Ginger loved all his children dearly and never showed favouritism, but there was a special place in his heart for Lily, knowing how easily they could have lost her. His gaze moved over to Gordon. He was proud of his son and hoped that one day he'd join him in the business. Gordon was an active child, and became easily bored, although right now he was happy to zoom round his railway track with his toy trains.

Not even in dreams had Ginger imagined that his life could become so happy and fulfilling. After his experiences on the ship and in the convict colony, he had expected nothing from life, sometimes even doubting for his sanity. However, fate had decreed his meeting with Olly, which had been the turning point.

There was a ring at the doorbell. 'I'll go,' he called to Anna, who was in the kitchen preparing Sunday dinner. He opened the door and was rendered speechless. Quickly recovering his composure, he stood back and ushered their visitor inside. He led the way into the family room, where Meg was helping Sarah to fasten her dolly's dress. When she raised her head, a stunned look crossed her face. She remained rooted to the sofa and it was left to Ginger to offer their guest the seat he had vacated.

At last Meg found her voice, but the look she threw at her mother was cold and unemotional. 'Mama, what are you doing here?'

'I'm sorry to arrive unannounced.' Jane Stanley's voice was quiet and she turned to Ginger to escape from her daughter's unwelcoming expression.

Sarah toddled over and stared up at the stranger. 'Who are you, lady?' she asked, her words more a demand than a question.

'This is your grandmother,' Ginger told Sarah, after a silence. Accusation and anger hung heavy on the air. Lily and Gordon stopped what they were doing while Adam, more timid than his twin, drew closer to Meg.

'She's a stranger to my children, and they know not to talk to strangers.' Meg spoke through gritted teeth and Ginger had never heard such vehemence from his wife. 'I don't know why you've come, but I want you to go.' She hurled the words as she would stones.

'Please Meg, forgive me,' Jane said, beginning to sob. She pulled a handkerchief out of her pocket and blew her nose. 'I didn't want to hurt you, but your papa …' Her words trailed off and she dropped her face into her hands.

Meg's face looked like it was set in stone, and she didn't respond to her mother's obvious distress.

'Meg, maybe it would help to talk,' Ginger suggested, adding, 'I could take the children into the garden to let you and your mama discuss things.'

'There's nothing to discuss.' Meg, rigid with anger,

averted her eyes.

'Meg, I wanted to contact you after your marriage, and have you and Ben visit us at Ripponlea, but your papa was adamant that he never wanted to see you again. He died seven years ago' … she stopped for a few moments … 'but I expect you would have read of his death in the newspaper. I … I wanted to let you know at the time but … but I was scared that you wouldn't want to see me.' Jane stumbled to a halt and, although she'd treated them so badly, Ginger couldn't help but feel sorry for her.

Meg's voice was devoid of any warmth when she finally replied. 'You were correct at the time, and nothing has changed, so now I must insist on you leaving.' She picked Adam up, and pulled Sarah towards her. Then she left the room, sweeping past Lily and Gordon, who stared at the woman that Daddy had said was their grandmother.

Jane slowly got to her feet and followed Ginger out to the hallway. 'I'm sorry,' he said, 'but Meg was terribly hurt when you both abandoned her.'

'I know,' she said brokenly, dabbing her eyes with a handkerchief, 'and believe me, I'd do anything to wipe out the past.' She looked at him, pleading for forgiveness. 'I'm so lonely at Ripponlea. I'd really like to get to know my grandchildren, if you'd only bring them to visit me. It would be wonderful to hear children's voices in the house again and, although my husband cut Meg off without a penny, I want her to have the house after me. And also your children in time.'

'Thank you, but we're doing perfectly well as we are.' He smiled, trying to soften his words, but felt he had to speak the truth.

'Sorry, I didn't mean to offend you. I'm pleased your business is doing well, and I've been following its progress in the newspapers.' Then she murmured, so quietly he could barely make her out, 'Ben, my door will always be open to both of you and your children.' She heaved a sigh and went down the front steps, leaning heavily on her stick.

'Why didn't you invite the lady to stay for dinner?' Gordon asked, when Ginger returned to the family room.

'Is she really our grandmother?' Lily asked, before he had time to reply.

'Why have we not seen her before?' was Gordon's next question.

Ginger sat down heavily in his armchair and rubbed his forehead. When he did speak, he smiled at his children. 'She is your grandmother and you haven't seen her because she and your grandfather hurt Mummy badly when we were married. Nothing for you to worry about, it happened a long time before either of you were born.'

'Mummy has never mentioned our grandparents and I thought they were dead,' Lily said, moving over to sit on the arm of his chair.

Ginger put his arm round her waist and drew her down on to his knee. 'Your grandfather died seven years ago and we haven't seen your grandmother until today. It was a shock for Mummy.'

'Will we see her again?' Gordon wanted to know.

Lily stretched up and kissed her father. 'She looked very lonely,' she said, in a sad voice, 'I feel sorry for her.'

Ginger gave Lily a hug, before she returned to her painting. He wasn't surprised at her sympathy for the old lady, since she was such a caring girl. Meg's attitude today was out of character but her papa's antagonism to their marriage still rankled.

He leaned back in his chair and closed his eyes, trying to see his mother's face. Having lost her when he was 12, to him family was everything, and he thought Meg wrong to refuse to forgive, even though he understood her reasons.

Anna, who'd heard everything from the kitchen, tactfully mentioned nothing when she popped her head round the family room door. 'Dinner will be ready in ten minutes, and we have strawberries and cream for dessert.'

CHAPTER THIRTY-FOUR

Vicky and Herbert Visit Deepdene

August 1876

Meg was engrossed in Wuthering Heights, when she heard the back door opening. A glance at the clock above the mantelpiece told her that her quiet time was over, and she pushed a marker in at her place in the book. Before she'd laid it down, Sarah and Adam raced in, jostling with one another to get through the doorway first, and both talking at the same time. They'd started attending school a year ago, just before their 5th birthdays.

Meg hugged them both. 'Go and change out of your school uniforms and put on your play clothes,' she instructed them.

'Yes Mummy,' Adam said, biddable as ever, while Sarah let out a frustrated sigh, but followed her twin out of the family room.

Gordon came in, shouting at the top of his voice.

'Shh, Gordon, don't be so noisy,' Meg cautioned, all the time aware that it was impossible for such an energetic, teenage boy to be quiet. She'd often wondered how the schoolmaster coped with her son's boisterous behaviour but, strangely enough, they'd never had any complaints from the school. Perhaps he keeps his noise for the house, she thought.

Vicky, Herbert and Lily took up the rear. At 16 and 15, the two young folk were good friends.

'Hello, Vicky, it's lovely to see you,' Meg said, giving her friend a kiss on the cheek. They'd arranged this visit today, so the three older ones could spend some time together.

Anna carried a tea tray into the family room, which she laid down on the dining table. 'The scones aren't long out of the oven, so they're still warm,' she told them. Over the years Anna had worked at Deepdene, her mousey-brown hair had gradually become splashed with streaks of grey but her round face, free of blemishes, was still that of a young girl.

Meg smiled at her. 'Thanks, Anna.'

The bright sunshine outside lured the children into the garden, leaving the two ladies a chance to enjoy their tea in peace. Meg served Vicky with sugar and milk, before holding out the plate of scones. 'Anna has spread some with butter and her homemade damson jam and the remainder with jam and cream.'

'How lovely.' Vicky put a jam and cream scone on to her plate.

'And how are things at Wattle Trees?' Meg asked, when she sat down again.

Vicky cut her scone into quarters. 'It's lambing time, so Olly and the boys have been busy. Sadly, one of the ewes lost her lambs yesterday; one had the cord caught round its neck and its twin got stuck in the birth canal, with one leg in front and the other twisted back.'

'Poor little things.'

'Olly has a few lambs left without their mothers, so he's trying to encourage the bereaved ewes to bond with the orphaned lambs.'

'And how is Frances doing in her employment? Does she like it?' Frances, now 18, had taken up a position as governess to the children of a well-to-do couple in Sydney.

Vicky wiped her fingers on the serviette. 'It's going well. It took her time to settle, with it being a live-in post. Olly and I miss her greatly, and I think Herbert finds it lonely without her.' She chuckled. 'Even if they do argue most of the time they're together.'

'Just like our children. But it's good that she comes home at weekends.'

'Do you think Lily will become a teacher?'

'She's considering that, and I think she has the correct temperament for it. Her artistic skills are also strong, so maybe she'll concentrate on that.' Noticing her friend's plate was empty, Meg got up and offered her another scone. 'And how is Maud?'

'Very well indeed,' Vicky said. 'When I left this afternoon to collect the children, she was spring cleaning, singing her heart out while she worked.'

'Maud has a beautiful singing voice.'

'Yes, she has. I've often told her she could be on the stage. But she told me she much preferred being with us at Wattle Trees.' The two women chatted on for a time, until Sarah came in sobbing.

'What's happened?' Meg asked her, lifting Sarah on to her lap.

'Gordon pushed me off the swing and I fell on to the path,' the little girl said, sniffing back the tears. She lifted her knee to let her mummy see the graze on it. Gradually her sobbing eased, by which time Anna appeared with a basin of water to bathe and bandage her knee.

*

Once the children were in bed, Ginger scoured through the paper for the items he hadn't read during the day, while Meg read her book.

Anna popped her head round the door. 'I'm thinking of going to bed now,' she said, 'is there anything else you need before I do?'

'No thanks, Anna, we're fine,' Meg replied. 'Sweet dreams.' She finished her chapter and picked up the school jersey she was knitting for Adam. With a family of four, her knitting needles were rarely idle.

Ginger folded up his newspaper and watched her nimble fingers glide across the row of knitting. 'I had an unexpected visitor in the shop today.'

'Oh,' Meg replied, taking her eyes off the pattern for a moment.

'Your mama.'

There was a long silence. Her mother's name hadn't been mentioned since the time, a few years ago, when she'd called unannounced at Deepdene. The children had stopped asking about their grandmother, sensing that it upset their mother.

Ginger spoke again, keeping his tone calm. 'She was asking for you and the children, and said how much she'd welcome a visit from us. She looked fairly well, although I can see she's ageing now, with her hair turned white.' He came to a halt and looked down at his knees, to give Meg time to digest this.

At last she laid her knitting down on her lap. 'I still can't forgive her for the way she treated you, Ben?'

Noticing a dent in her previous armour, he continued. 'I know your parents hurt you terribly, Meg, but I think the fault was mainly with your papa and your mama found it hard to go against his wishes. Don't you think she has suffered loneliness long enough, and perhaps now we could let her into our lives?' He was going to drop the subject, but gave one last push. 'She misses you, Meg, and would love to get to know her grandchildren. Will you at least think about us taking up her invitation to dine at Ripponlea with her?'

When he received no reply, he changed the subject. 'What about a game of cards before bed?' he suggested.

CHAPTER THIRTY-FIVE
A Visit to Ripponlea
September 1876

The sun was shining brightly when the family settled themselves into the carriage on Sunday morning for their journey to Ripponlea. A magnificent rainbow had appeared, following the earlier light shower, and by now there was once more an unbroken blue sky.

For the past few weeks, since Ben had dropped the bombshell about their invitation to dine at Ripponlea, Meg hadn't mentioned the matter again. Although disappointed that she hadn't taken up his challenge to forgive her mother, he hadn't pushed it further. Then on Friday evening he'd been pleasantly surprised when Meg had re-opened the subject.

'Ben, I've decided to accept Mama's invitation to lunch at Ripponlea, but it'll take me a long time to get over my hurt,' she warned him.

'I'm proud of you, Meg, and the children will be happy to see their grandmother again. I'll call at Ripponlea tomorrow and suggest that we go to lunch on Sunday?'

'Adam, eat your porridge please and stop playing with it,' Meg said at breakfast this morning. He was the faddiest eater of all their children, but she liked him to have something substantial at breakfast time. 'You know they say you should eat like a prince in the morning and a pauper at supper time.'

'Would a prince like my porridge?' Adam asked, rolling his eyes the way he'd seen Gordon do. But, hating to be in trouble, he spooned some more into his mouth.

'It's a beautiful day for a drive, isn't it?' Ginger said, when they were ready to leave Deepdene. He sat behind the horses, with Gordon perched beside him on the bench seat, while Meg, Lily and the twins settled themselves down in the carriage.

When they reached the gates of Ripponlea, Gordon jumped down and rang the bell. James, looking much older than Ginger remembered him, came out and gave them entry.

As the horses trotted up the long drive to the house, Ginger recalled the day he and Tom delivered the cabinet. So much had happened since then and he wondered what was going through Meg's head but couldn't see her face from where she was sitting.

From her seat in the carriage, Lily held her breath as the house came into view. Ripponlea, hugged tightly by bright purple wisteria, was the most beautiful place she'd ever seen. The stonework sparkled in the sunshine, and she felt a strong urge to get out her easel and paints.

The butler came down the front stairs to greet them. Ginger noticed it wasn't Elliot but a much younger man.

The man smiled a welcome. 'Good day, Madam is in the drawing room.'

'Thank you,' Ginger said, 'does Elliot no longer work here?'

'Mr Elliot retired soon after the Master's death, and I have taken over his position. I am Mr Collins.'

Of course, Ginger thought, Collins was the under-footman who'd shown them where to leave the cabinet on that earlier visit.

In the drawing room Jane Stanley was sitting by the window. The heavy brocade curtains kept out the strong rays of the sun, helping to make the room feel cool. Leaning on her stick, Jane stood up, the taffeta material of her dress rustling as she did so, and her beaming smile encompassed the whole family. 'How lovely to see you all again,' she said, opening her arms to her daughter. When she got no response, she turned to her grandchildren.

'Make yourselves comfortable, children,' she said, directing them to .a large sofa while she fanned her blushing cheeks. Meg and Ginger sat together on a smaller one at the side of the marble fireplace. 'It's wonderful to have you visit,' she said to her grandchildren, 'and, of course, your mama and papa.' Meg continued to sit with her hands tightly clenched on her lap, looking down at the floor.

'Can I get you something to drink before lunch? A sherry perhaps, and juice for the children?'

'Juice, please,' Gordon piped up, and the other children nodded.

Jane turned to the butler, who was still standing in the doorway. 'Could you get some drinks for us please, Collins?'

'Certainly, Madam,' he said, and left the room.

Still Meg remained mute, and beside her Ginger could feel her tension. He spoke to break the awkward silence. 'The grounds are looking good,' was all he could think to say.

Jane latched on immediately. 'Thank you. I've been lucky to have retained my loyal gardeners over the years. After lunch, I'll let the children see round both the house and the gardens. Would you like that?' she asked, her eyes mainly on Lily, who resembled Meg so much that it hurt.

'Yes, thank you, Grandma,' Lily said.

'Do you have swings in the garden?' Sarah wanted to know.

Jane smiled at the little girl. 'No, Sarah, no swings, but we have a rose bower with a fountain in the formal garden, and lots of fruit trees. And then of course there are the woods that you can wander through …' she stopped speaking at that point, and sorrow creased her face, as she remembered it was there that Meg had hidden on the day she'd run away to marry Ben. She looked up when one of the maids came in with the drinks tray, which she laid on the large table in front of the window. 'Anything else, Madam?' she asked.

'No thank you Edna, we'll manage fine.' Jane had grown fond of the young maid over the years since the day she'd rushed into the drawing room to tell her and Paul that Meg had disappeared. Jane hadn't liked Elliot's attitude towards young Edna that day and she had no regrets over his retirement, much preferring her new butler, Collins.

Becoming aware that Edna was still there, awaiting any further instructions, she turned to the girl. 'You can let us know when lunch is ready to serve.'

'Yes, Madam,' Edna said, and curtsied.

Meg spoke for the first time. 'Hello, Edna, how are you?'

The maid blushed and curtsied again. 'Very well, thank you, Miss Meg,' Edna replied, and smiled at the children before she left the room.

'Edna is one of my longest-serving maids,' Jane told them, as she handed round the drinks. 'I've cut down greatly on staff numbers as I didn't need so many when your … your papa,' she stopped, her pleading eyes on Meg, … 'when I was left on my own,' she said, stammering her way to a close.

When Jane sat down with her own sherry, she raised her glass. 'Good health, everyone,' she said, and Ginger returned her good wishes. He took Meg's hand and squeezed it, praying that she would give her mother a sign that she was willing to forgive and forget.

Soon afterwards, Collins returned to announce lunch, and the family trooped into the dining room. Ginger was given a seat at one end of the long table, with Jane at the other, and Meg and the children occupied the remaining seats. During their meal, the atmosphere slowly improved, with the children chatting freely to their grandmother, until finally, much to Ginger's relief, Meg joined in the conversation, even if she was only giving one word replies.

'Right,' Jane said, once they'd finished drinking their coffee back in the drawing room, 'would you children like to see your mama's old bedroom?'

'She isn't our mama, she's our mummy,' Adam told her.

Jane chuckled and lifted her hand in a gesture of surrender. 'Of course she is, how silly of me.' She ruffled his fair hair and they left the room, with the other three children trailing behind them.

Ginger took Meg's hand when they were alone. 'I know how difficult this is for you, but the children are so pleased to have found a grandma.'

'I know,' she murmured, looking into his eyes, 'and I am trying, really I am. It's just so hard to behave as though nothing had happened.'

'It is, but it's important to put the past behind you. For all our sakes, but especially the children.' He drew her into his arms and they sat quietly until the door burst open and the excited children raced in.

'We've seen everything,' Gordon told them, the words exploding out of him.

Jane smiled as she followed them in. 'Yes, they've had the grand tour of the house and now they want to explore the grounds.'

'You come with us, Daddy,' Sarah said, taking Ginger's hand and pulling him up from the settee.

'Yes, you go with them Ben, and Meg and I can have a chat,' Jane suggested, as they all headed towards the door.

Jane sat down where Ginger had been. 'I'm glad you felt able to visit me, Meg,' she said. 'It can't have been easy and I applaud you for doing so.'

'It's Ben you have to thank for that, he was the one who persuaded me it was the correct thing to do.'

Jane's eyes filled. 'Yes, he's a good man and an excellent husband and father.' She sighed deeply and looked down at her hands.

'If only you hadn't treated him so badly when we married, or even got in touch with us afterwards, this estrangement needn't have happened.'

Jane laid her hand on her daughter's arm. When Meg didn't draw away, she spoke again. 'I'm so sad about that. I should have been stronger and stood up to your papa, but you know how stubborn he was.' She stopped for a moment. 'Actually, you get your stubbornness from him.' She was pleased to see a smile hover around her daughter's mouth.

Meg leaned closer to her mother, enjoying the scent of lavender that she always wore. 'I was also terrified of disobeying his orders so I shouldn't have judged you so harshly,' she whispered, and the dam of grief burst inside her, and soon her tears flowed freely.

Jane put her arm around Meg's shaking shoulders, and used her own handkerchief to wipe away the tears. 'Shall we let bygones be bygones and start again, my darling?'

'Yes, please,' Meg said, and leaned against her mother's shoulder.

They sat together for a few minutes until, using her stick, Jane got to her feet. 'I'll ring for some tea,' she said, and pulled the cord at the side of the fireplace. By the time the family arrived back, mother and daughter had finished their tea and were chatting happily.

CHAPTER THIRTY-SIX
Lily Turns Nineteen
September 1880

'Are you looking forward to your party next weekend?' Jane asked Lily, while they were sitting together in the Ripponlea gardens on Sunday afternoon. The sculptured face of the nymph on the fountain was veiled by the water which cascaded over it, the tinkling sound adding to the peaceful atmosphere.

'I am, Grandma.' Lily stroked the velvet-soft petals of the pink rose she'd found on the path. 'I'll have my school friends with me again, I haven't seen them since we left school back in May.' Her friends were all now working and she herself assisted the teacher at Dubbo school. 'You'll come to my party, won't you?'

'Try and keep me away.' Jane delighted in all of Meg's children, but Lily was her favourite. Since her reconciliation with the family four years ago, she'd had Lily to stay most weekends, and Jane so looked forward to these visits. It was like having Meg back again, the young Meg, who'd been so close to her mama. She leaned towards Lily and kissed her on the cheek. 'I can't believe you're almost nineteen, a young lady.'

'I love coming here to Ripponlea,' Lily said, edging closer to her grandmother. 'I hated to think of you being here all alone, before … before …' She stumbled to a stop and Jane helped her out.

'You mean before your mummy and I patched up our differences. I was very lonely then, but the last few years have been wonderful. Much better to be one big family, isn't it?'

Lily nodded. 'What was Grandpa like?' she asked. 'I know you've shown me his photograph, with his big bushy moustache, but what was he really like?'

'He was a fine, upstanding man, well-respected in the community. He and I loved your mummy dearly. She was our only child, and as I had miscarried two children before she was born, she was precious, a real gift from God. Your grandpa wanted her to marry well into a wealthy family. I agreed with him at the time, but realised later that we should not have tried to force our beloved daughter into a marriage without love.' She took Lily's hand and squeezed it. 'Your daddy is a very fine gentleman, who has been an excellent husband and father, and most importantly of all, he and your mummy have made a real love match.'

Lily smiled at her grandmother. 'I'm glad you like Daddy. It's important to me as I love him so very much.'

'And that's as it should be,' Jane said, giving her a cuddle. 'How is your picture of the house coming on?'

Lily had painted the front of the house, encircled by the wisteria, a few times during the years she'd visited Ripponlea, but her latest attempt was her favourite. The picture was on her easel in one of the turret rooms, away from prying eyes, until she felt ready to show it to others. 'I think I've managed to capture its beauty at last.'

'That's wonderful. I look forward to seeing it once you are ready.' Jane took her lace-edged hankie out of her pocket and wiped her damp brow. 'Will we pick roses for the dining room table?'

'Good idea.' Lily jumped to her feet and picked up the wicker basket lying on the gravel at her grandmother's feet. She took the secateurs out of the basket, and set to work.

*

The following Saturday afternoon, Lily rushed to open the door to Jane. 'Happy birthday, Lily,' her grandmother called to her, as the Ripponlea coachman helped her down from the carriage. She held her arms out to Lily and, after they'd hugged, she handed her a beautifully wrapped gift.

'Thank you, Grandma.' Lily was overjoyed with the set of oil paints she'd been hoping to use for her artwork. 'They're just what I wanted,' she told Jane, hugging her again. 'It's seemed a long week waiting for my birthday to arrive.'

'And your last one as a teenager,' Jane reminded her, as Ginger hurried out of the house and took her overnight bag from the coachman. She'd been invited to stay overnight at Deepdene, and would return home tomorrow.'

That evening Lily was buzzing with excitement. Towards seven o'clock, when the party was due to begin, she stayed near the front door, ready to greet her guests as they arrived. She ran her fingers down the velvet material of her new lilac dress, which had already been well admired by her family members. Her fingers drifted over to trace their way around the stones in the necklace she was wearing.

'I'm so proud of you, my darling,' Meg had told her. 'I'd like you to wear this necklace tonight,' she'd said, holding the jewellery against the dress.

Looking at her reflection in the mirror, Lily could see how well the purple-coloured stones matched her outfit. 'But Mummy, this is your favourite necklace, the one that Daddy bought you.'

'It is, and that's why I want you to wear it tonight, Lily. It's special because he gave it to me just after you were born, my darling, and I think it's appropriate that you wear it at your party tonight.'

Lily's excitement intensified when she heard a carriage draw up outside and saw, through the coloured-glass panel on the door, two figures approach.

She opened the door to her ex-classmates, Rose Brennan and Grace Williams. 'Great to see you both,' she said and showed her friends into the front reception room where the party was to be held.

'Happy birthday, Lily,' they said, and handed her their gifts.

The two girls sat together on the cream two-seater sofa in front of the bay window, while Lily poured them a glass of fruit punch from the crystal bowl sitting on the sideboard. Rose spread her red skirt out over her legs and pulled down the lacy sleeve of her blouse where it had ridden up. Beside her, Grace looked striking in her frock, made from a brown and green checked material. At the moment, they had the room to themselves, so the three girls could exchange news. Rose was receiving a good training in the accountant's office where she'd been employed since leaving school and Grace seemed very happy working as a waitress in a hotel in Dubbo. She soon had the other two laughing uproariously, about the antics of some of the hotel guests she'd come across.

Lily was in the process of telling her friends about how happy she was working as assistant teacher in Dubbo school, when the doorbell sounded again. 'Excuse me,' she said.

'Come in,' she said to Uncle Olly and Aunt Vicky, who were standing on the doormat, with Herbert and Frances in front of them.'I'm so glad you could come, it wouldn't be the same without my family from Wattle Trees.' From an early age, Lily had looked on Uncle Olly's family as kin, and she knew her parents felt the same.

She introduced the folks from Wattle Trees to Rose and Grace. Shortly afterwards Meg, Ginger, Jane and the other children came in to join the party. Lily was kept busy going back and forward to the front door, each time the bell sounded, and was delighted to see her school friends again. By the time all the guests had arrived, including the adults and the younger children, there were twenty four people crushed into the front room. Lily was a wonderful hostess, making sure that everyone was enjoying him or herself.

*

Jane was sitting quietly in the family room next morning, listening to the birds chirping on the gums outside, when Lily came in, looking fresh as a daisy after her late night. The only other member of the household who was up was

Anna, and they could hear her in the kitchen laying out the crockery and cutlery for breakfast.

'Have you recovered from all the excitement, Lily?' Jane slid along the sofa to make room for her granddaughter beside her.

Lily's smile stretched from ear to ear. 'It was great to chat to my old schoolfriends and I was happy that Uncle Olly and the family could be here too. Did you sleep well, Grandma?' she asked.

Jane shrugged. 'As well as I ever do, darling. When you get to my age you don't sleep as soundly as when you were younger. Still, I don't rush around as much as I did back then, so the sleep I get does me well.'

Lily laid her head on Jane's shoulder. 'I'm glad you were able to be at my party, Grandma, and next weekend I can come to Ripponlea again.'

'Of course you can, Lily, and I'm so happy that Ripponlea means as much to you as it does to me. I want the house to stay in the family when I'm gone.'

Lily lifted her head, her eyes wide as she stared at Jane. 'But Grandma, you're not ill, are you? Please tell me you're in good health.'

Jane smiled and squeezed Lily's hand. 'I'm perfectly well, darling, I'm simply looking to the future. I plan to be here for a long time yet,' she said, laughing to help remove the worry that was creasing her beloved Lily's face. 'Anyway,' she added, cupping Lily's face between her own open hands, 'I must keep well, for us to travel to Wimbledon as I promised you.' Lily had developed her love of tennis from the games she'd played against her grandmother on the Ripponlea courts.

A moment later they heard footsteps descending the stairs. Ginger came into the family room, looking rested after his night's sleep, and the conversation changed.

CHAPTER THIRTY-SEVEN
A New Family Member
November 1880

Meg steered the twins, their eyes tightly shut, into the family room. She guided them to a place in front of the fireplace, and said, 'Sarah and Adam, you may now open your eyes.'

They stared at a wicker basket on Daddy's lap and held their breath as he raised the top, a fraction at a time, until a little black head appeared, the eyes peeping over the rim. Yelling with delight, they raced one another across the room, scrambling to be first to view their new puppy.

Sarah threw herself down at her father's feet and tenderly stroked the shiny head of the German Shepherd puppy, bending down further to kiss his nose. 'A puppy at last,' Adam said, unable to believe their good fortune. Once he realised he wasn't dreaming, he joined his sister on the floor and between them they lifted the puppy out of the basket, taking it in turns to hold and cuddle him.

Sarah looked at each of her parents in turn. 'Thank you, thank you,' she said, her eyes shining with joy. 'I love him already.' The puppy threw his tiny paws on to her shoulder and licked her cheek.

'He's so-oo beautiful.' Adam took the puppy from Sarah and played with his floppy pink-lined ears.

Ginger smiled as he witnessed their reaction. 'You'll need to give him a name.'

Sarah clapped her hands. 'I know. He's a black dog, so we'll call him Blackie.'

'But he's got brown paws and some brown patches on his face,' Adam protested. 'I like Prince better.'

'Yes, that name suits him,' Lily threw into the mix, 'he looks like a little prince.'

'Let's put it to the vote,' Ginger suggested. 'Who's in

favour of calling him Blackie?'

Sarah, Meg and Gordon all put up their hands.

'And raise your hand if you prefer Prince,' he said, putting up his own hand, followed by Lily and Adam.

Meg chuckled. 'What will we do now?'

'We get a casting vote.' Ginger opened the door and called to Anna in the kitchen. 'Anna, could you join us for a moment, please?' When she came in, he said, 'Anna, we need your help in naming the puppy. Which do you like better, Prince or Blackie?'

Anna looked at the puppy held in Sarah's arms, and stroked his head. 'Prince,' she said, with no hesitation.

'Then, Prince it is,' Ginger said.

'He's only eight weeks old, so he has a lot to learn,' Meg told the children, 'but he has been trained to go outside to wee. By the way,' she said, looking especially at the twins, 'he has a bed in the kitchen so no sleeping in your beds, that isn't hygienic. Is that clear?'

The twins nodded. 'And we can take him for long walks,' Adam said.

But Ginger shook his head. 'He's only a baby, Adam, so he won't need long walks just yet, although you can take him out into the garden with you. Right now,' he said, lifting Prince into his folded arms, 'I think he will be needing something to eat.' He walked off to the kitchen, trailed by Sarah and Adam.

Meg laughed and threw her arms around Lily and Gordon. 'Oh dear, we're going to have such disruption in the house with a puppy to look after, but it's worth it to see the excitement on their faces.'

*

Later that evening, when Anna and the children were in bed and Prince had been settled down in the kitchen, a blanket laid over him for warmth, Meg and Ginger sat together in the family room. 'Ben, wasn't the twins' joy at seeing Prince a sight to behold?' Meg said, lifting her head for a moment from the knitting pattern she was studying.

'Mmm,' Ginger murmured, with his eyes on The Sydney Herald. After a few moments, he raised his head and looked at her. 'Sorry Meg, what did you say?'

She laughed and shook her head. 'I knew you hadn't heard a word I was saying. What is it that's so interesting in the paper?'

'Ned Kelly was hanged today in Melbourne jail,' he told her, holding up the newspaper with the outlaw's picture at the top of the page. 'The jury was unanimous about his guilt and it's reported that the death sentence was carried out this morning.'

'I remember the Victorian police capturing him, along with some of his gang members, a few months ago,' she said. 'But even though he's committed lots of crimes, I can't help feeling sorry for him. I don't think he had a good start in life.'

'There are many of our fellow Australians who feel that way about him, in fact, some look on him as a hero.'

Yawning widely, Meg folded her pattern and put it into her work basket. 'I'm off to bed, Ben, I can hardly keep my eyes open.'

'I'll just finish reading the news, then I'll be up myself.'

CHAPTER THIRTY-EIGHT
A Household Mourns
April 1882

Tragedy struck while the countryside was ablaze with spectacular autumn colours. It was the kind of day when nothing bad should be allowed to mar its beauty.

Instead Lily sat beside the bed in Orange County Hospital. She held the cold, still hand, trying to warm it in her own. Encased in her wall of concrete sadness, she found her mind going back a few hours to the sight of the Headmaster coming into the classroom where she was teaching.

'Lily, there's someone to see you in my office, I'll take over the lesson.' Mr Murdoch's voice was low enough not to be overheard by the pupils. She gave him a brief nod and left the room, aware of her pupils' eyes following her.

She walked into Mr Murdoch's office and gasped when she saw her father standing at the window, looking out over the playground. He'd never disturbed her at work before and, when he turned round, the colour had drained from his face. Without speaking, he held out his arms to her. Folding her into his embrace, he stroked her hair and kissed her forehead, like he used to do when she fell in the garden as a child.

'Daddy, what's wrong?' Lily's voice was little more than a whisper, and she felt as though her heart had stopped.

'Darling, it's Grandma.' Feeling her body tense up, he held her closer. 'It's alright, sweetheart, she's alive but has been badly injured, and is asking for you.'

Lily slumped down into the Headmaster's chair for a moment, her head swimming, as she tried to take in what he'd told her. 'Can you take me to Ripponlea now, Daddy?'

But Ginger shook his head. 'She's in hospital, Lily.

Collect your coat and bag from the staff room and we can go to see her.'

'What happened?' Lily asked, when they were halfway to Orange.

He glanced round to look at her for a second, then turned his eyes back to the road ahead. 'Grandma and Edna were out walking. They came out from a country track, and were crossing the highway, when a carriage came towards them, driving too fast. Grandma was slightly ahead of Edna, and walked straight into the path of a horse. Edna tried to pull her back but, although Grandma escaped being trodden on by the horse, she fell under one of the carriage wheels.'

'Is Edna with Grandma now?' Lily asked. Last year Grandma had appointed the girl as her personal maid and companion, and the two had become almost inseparable.

But Ginger shook his head. 'Edna was distraught by the time help was summoned, and she was driven back to Ripponlea, while Grandma was taken straight to Orange County.'

'So Grandma is on her own?'

'It's alright, sweetheart, she's sleeping. When I arrived at the hospital, she was awake and asked for you but then she lost consciousness. The staff are looking after her really well.'

When they got to the hospital, Lily and Ginger sat at Jane's bedside for hours, praying that she would waken up and speak to them. Later in the day, Meg arrived to sit with her mama, while Ginger returned to Deepdene.

'Oh, Mummy, I hope Grandma isn't going to die,' a weeping Lily said, comforted by her mother's arm draped across her shoulder.

'Shh,' Meg soothed, her own tears brimming over, 'don't think like that, my darling. Grandma is a strong woman and she'll pull through,' Meg whispered, keen to keep Lily's hopes up.

They sat for a while in silence, the only sound the

ticking of the clock on the window ledge. Eventually Lily spoke again. 'I love spending time with Grandma,' she murmured, her eyes brightening at the thought. 'Next to Deepdene, Ripponlea is my favourite place to be. It must have been a wonderful home for you to grow up in.'

Meg drew her daughter's head down into the crook of her neck and stroked Lily's soft cheek. 'It was, and I know Mama is always pleased to have you there with her.'

'I love hearing about all the places she's visited.'

'And I think you've inherited her love of painting and tennis. She was always sad that I wasn't interested in either of these pastimes.'

Lily smiled. 'Yes, Grandma has always encouraged me with my art, and she said we'll travel to London one day to view the art galleries and also to watch the tennis at Wimbledon.' That thought made her sob once more, and she blew her nose loudly. 'While we're in London, she's also promised to take me to visit some of the Royal palaces and The Houses of Parliament.'

'She certainly will, she's a staunch Royalist. Remember how distressed she was last month about the attempted assassination of Queen Victoria in Windsor?'

'Yes, that was horrible, thank goodness the Queen wasn't harmed. I hope they lock up the man who tried to shoot her.' Lily stopped speaking when she thought she felt her grandmother's fingers move, but when nothing further occurred, she knew it was wishful thinking on her part.

*

Ten days later, with a steady drizzle adding to the gloom of the occasion, the family left Deepdene in sombre mood. Even Prince seemed downcast with his tail drooping, having picked up the vibes from the family. As they trooped out to the waiting carriages, the dog lay down in his basket, gazing at them with sad eyes.

Adam bent down to fondle their pet. 'You'll look after things here for us, won't you boy?' he murmured, and

Prince gave his hand a comforting lick.

The carriages were draped in black, and the horses wore black feathers on their heads. On arrival in Orange, they gathered with other mourners at Ripponlea. Jane had lost her battle for life, and today was to be laid beside Paul in the cemetery at Ripponlea.

Lily had been so consumed by grief over her beloved Grandma's passing that Ginger had been unsure if she'd be able to attend the funeral. He and Meg had decided they'd stay close to her during the burial.

When the farewells were over, the line of mourners snaked its way out of the cemetery, led by the close family members. After refreshments in the house, the mourners departed Ripponlea, leaving only the immediate family there. Then Ginger, still wearing his black suit and tie, ushered his wife and children into the drawing room, where Mr Fenton, the Stanley family lawyer, sat behind the writing desk, with papers laid out in front of him. Meg returned the lawyer's nod, having known him since childhood, and a few pleasantries passed between them.

When Mr Fenton read out Jane's Last Will and Testament, it transpired that she'd left the entire estate of Ripponlea, house and grounds, to Lily. It said in the Will that she wanted the house to be kept in the family and she knew that Lily loved Ripponlea.

The room remained hushed, with Lily sitting upright in her chair, hands clasped together on her lap. She played with the lace along the cuff of her black dress, and glanced at her father for confirmation that her ears hadn't deceived her. Ginger nodded. It was then that Lily recalled Grandma telling her two years ago her wish that, when she died, she wanted Ripponlea to stay in the care of the family. But neither of them had expected her death would happen so soon.

Mr Fenton went on to tell the family that Jane had left her other assets, a sizeable amount in money and investments, to be shared among her other grandchildren,

Gordon, Sarah and Adam. It went on to say that she hoped Gordon and Adam would join their father in Aussie Crafts and that Sarah would, when she was older, move in with Lily at Ripponlea. Jane had also been generous to her loyal staff and, when all the bequests and other business was completed, the lawyer took his leave, instructing Lily to meet with him the following week to discuss the future of Ripponlea.

CHAPTER THIRTY-NINE
A New School Takes Shape
November, 1882

The foreman stood in the middle of the former drawing room. 'We can erect a stage over there,' he said, pointing to the far end of the room. 'Tomorrow I'll collect the plans from the surveyor.'

'Good. The work needs to be completed for the school opening in February.'

'When you've agreed to the plans, my men will start immediately.'

Once the workmen left, Lily stood at the bay window, notebook and pencil in her hands, staring out over the flower beds. She hoped the budget would stretch to retaining the gardeners, who had been so loyal to her grandmother, but she'd be guided by Mr Fenton. How wonderful that Daddy and Uncle Olly had agreed to put up some capital to help with the renovations.

Grandma's Will had stated that Lily was to reach her majority before taking over Ripponlea, so ideas of converting it into a school had to be shelved until after her birthday. Hiring the best workers had taken longer than anticipated, but she had no doubt Grandma would have approved of the house becoming a place of learning. Uncle Olly's daughter, Frances, had agreed to leave her work as a governess to join Lily in the new venture.

Lily was determined the school would not only be for the daughters of the rich, and she hoped to set up some scholarships for children from poorer backgrounds. In memory of her grandparents, she intended to call the school, Stanley Grammar School for Girls, although the building would still be known as Ripponlea.

Seeing her father's carriage emerge from the tree-lined driveway, she waved as he got down from his seat and hurried to open the front door.

'So, how are things progressing?' he asked, striding into the entrance hall. Although Lily had kept him abreast of her plans, it was some time since he'd been here.

She led the way into the drawing room. 'This will be the assembly hall, large enough to accommodate all the pupils at one time.'

'Will you have the seating set out in rows?'

'Yes, on either side of the room, with an aisle down the middle. The seats will face towards the stage.'

'Will you keep the fireplace?'

'I think so. In winter it would be more comfortable for the pupils to sit in a warm room. I'll show you where the classrooms will be,' she said, as they moved into the old family dining room. 'This will be divided into two rooms, one for age group 10-12 and the other for 13-15-year-olds. Both doors lead on to the entrance hallway, so it's only a matter of erecting a wall in the middle of the room.'

'Good, and what about the senior pupils?'

'Grandpa Stanley's old study is to be converted into a classroom for the senior pupils, the 16-18-year-olds. His library upstairs will remain as it is and the pupils will have access to all his books and, of course, any suitable books I decide to purchase.'

While his daughter was speaking, Ginger's thoughts went back to his last contact with Paul Stanley, which had taken place in the library. He recalled clearly being sent packing for daring to declare his love for Meg, the action leading him and Meg to marry in secret.

'Daddy,' Lily's voice cut into his thoughts. 'Are you alright? You look miles away.'

'Sorry Darling.'

'I've employed a young lady, Betsy Grant, who resides locally and won't need to live in. She has very good qualifications, and she, Frances and I will share the teaching duties. Betsy will teach the most junior pupils, I will be in charge of the middle age range, leaving Frances to educate the senior pupils.'

They moved into the hallway and Lily pointed upstairs. 'On the floor above, we have plans for eight bedrooms, to accommodate the pupils who board, two in each room. Frances and I will each have a bedroom further along the corridor, so we can keep a check on the pupils. The bedrooms on the top floor are for the domestic staff, just as they were when Ripponlea was a family home.'

Lily latched on to her father's arm. 'Come and see where the school dining room will be.' They made their way downstairs to the basement, and walked into the massive kitchen, with its stone floor and long sturdy table running almost the length of the room. There were large ovens lining one wall, and beside them the huge open fireplace housed a spit. The cupboards on the opposite wall stored the provisions and nearer the kitchen door there were sinks for washing up. Copper pots and pans hung on hooks on the remaining unused sections of wall. 'The kitchen will stay as it is,' she told him, 'although I'll have the bars removed from the windows.'

'Yes, that would make it brighter for the staff working here,' he agreed, 'and what about a cook?'

'Mrs Bradley, who's been the cook at Ripponlea since Grandpa was alive, has agreed to stay on.' As she was speaking, she ushered him through a connecting door, into what had been the butler's office. She touched one of the thick walls. 'This will be demolished, so that this room and the adjoining housekeeper's office will become one. We'll have two long tables, one on either side of the room, with bench seating for the pupils. At the far end of the room there'll be a smaller table, sitting on a dais, where Frances, Betsy and I will dine.'

He laughed. 'To keep an eye on the pupils.'

'Correct. The kitchen being so near will help with the serving of meals. And at the opposite end of the corridor, there will be a gymnasium for the pupils and also an art studio.'

'What will happen to James' old cottage?'

'That's where the pupils will learn cookery and housewifery. All the essentials are there.'

'Lily, you've thought of everything, it's sure to be a success.' They linked arms and climbed the stairs again. In the hallway, Ginger took out his timepiece. 'Now, if there's nothing further you want to do here, I suggest we leave and be home in time for dinner.'

Lily smiled. 'I can feel pangs of hunger at the thought.' She collected her belongings from the drawing room and they headed towards the front door.

CHAPTER FORTY
Gordon Falls in Love
December 1882

'When will Frieda join us?' Meg asked, passing Gordon the cranberry sauce. Despite the heat, following the British tradition, the family still tucked into roast turkey and all the trimmings on Christmas day.

'Her dad will bring her after their family meal,' Gordon replied, while he spooned the sauce on to the side of his plate.

'Why are we eating turkey and not goose?' As she was speaking, Sarah's paper hat slipped off her head and she caught it just before it landed in the gravy dish.

'We could have had goose, but turkeys are bigger to serve our large family,' her mother told her. 'Why are you asking?'

Sarah shrugged. 'My schoolfriend, Amelia, said her mother was cooking a goose this Christmas.'

'They probably have a smaller family than we do,' Ginger suggested. While he was speaking, he leaned across the table to pour Gordon another glass of wine. Adam, sitting next to Gordon, looked up at his father in anticipation, but Ginger shook his head and refilled Anna's glass before replacing the bottle on to the table.

'So will Frieda's family have a hot meal, or will they stick to cold foods?' Lily asked, keen to hear more about this girl who'd captured her brother's heart.

'Not sure,' he said, 'but they'll have a lighter meal than they had yesterday. German people celebrate Christmas on 24th December rather than today.'

'Do they open their gifts on Christmas Eve?' Sarah wanted to know.

Gordon nodded. 'I think so, but you can ask Frieda when she gets here.' It was only three months ago that he'd met Frieda Steinberg at a farmers' ball in Dubbo, but he'd fallen in love with her before the evening was over.

Adam looked up from feeding titbits to Prince, lying at his feet under the table. 'Do you think you'll marry Frieda?' he asked his brother.

To spare Gordon's blushes, Meg jumped in. 'What a question, Adam. It's too early for talk of marriage, Gordon hardly knows the girl yet.' She blushed as she caught Ginger's glance, recalling how quickly they'd fallen in love. 'Have you all had enough, before I clear the dishes away and bring the dessert?'

Sarah clapped her hands when the delicious desserts were brought to the table.

Later that afternoon, when Gordon heard the sound of wheels driving over the stony path, he hurried to the front door. By the time Frieda had climbed down from her father's wagon, he was standing outside on the path.

Gordon knew that Karl Steinberg was a dairy farmer, although he'd never met the man. 'Would your father like to come in and meet my family?' he asked Frieda, giving a wave to the man sitting up on the wagon.

'Oh no, that isn't my father,' Frieda told him, 'he's my brother, Jorg. But he needs to return home now, as the cows are due for milking. My father will come and take me home again at 9 o'clock.'

In the family room, Adam was in the process of doing a charade of a book title, with other family members shouting out their suggestions. They fell silent when they saw Frieda. Meg stood up at once and walked over to the pretty blue-eyed girl, with her long blonde hair worn in plaits. 'Lovely to meet you, Frieda, and welcome to our home.'

'Thank you, Mrs Harker,' Frieda replied politely, giving her hostess a quick curtsey.

'You're dress is so pretty,' Lily said, 'is that your national costume?'

'My mother made it for me. It's in the style of the

Bavarian national dress.'

Taking up Meg's invitation to sit beside Lily on the sofa, Frieda smiled her thanks to Ginger, when he held out a glass of wine to her. 'What part of Germany do you come from?' he asked.

'I was born in the south of Germany, close to the Austrian border. But my family have lived in Australia already twelve years.'

Meg laughed. 'So you're almost an Australian now,' she said, noticing the quaint way her guest said she'd been already twelve years in the country. Straight away, she found herself to warming to Frieda.

The evening flew by, with lots of laughter and song, and before they knew it, Frieda's father had arrived to take her home.

'Come and join us again soon,' Meg invited, as the girl took her leave of them.

CHAPTER FORTY-ONE
The Opening of Stanley Grammar School
February 1883

February arrived hot and humid. At Ripponlea Lily bought mesh fly screens. These had become popular in recent years and allowed windows and doors to be opened to let in air but keep out insects.

Lily's heart was pounding when she welcomed her first two boarders, Janet Baxter and Molly Archer, but she tried to curb her nerves as she smiled at them. The girls, who were juniors, arrived at the same time, and both were accompanied by their parents. The sense of anxiety the adults felt about leaving their daughters at a new school was palpable, and Lily understood their concern. 'I'll arrange for you to be served with tea, while I show Janet and Molly upstairs to their rooms.' She pulled on the cord at the side of the marble fireplace as she was speaking, and then invited the adults to sit at a table for four that was laid out for afternoon tea, which included scones and cakes.

A smile passed between the two boarders. Janet, tall for her age, had straw-coloured hair. Molly was a couple of inches shorter than Janet, and her inky black hair was plaited. Lily consulted her room list. 'You two girls will be sharing a bedroom. Bring your cases and we can go upstairs now.' When Janet hesitated, Lily gave her a reassuring smile. 'Once you've unpacked, you can say goodbye to your parents before they leave.'

As they left, Edna, who'd stayed on as a school orderly, brought in a tea tray.

Lily showed the girls into their room, which overlooked the rose garden. 'I used to sit out there beside the fountain with my grandmother when she lived here,' she told them.

The bedroom walls were painted pale green, with darker green, heavily-embossed curtains draped on either side of the window. Two single beds were placed against the opposite wall, and a kerosene lamp sat on the bedside table between the beds. A wardrobe and a tallboy stood against the remaining two walls, and close to the window was a desk and chair for each girl, to afford as much light as possible while they were doing their homework or writing a letter home.

'This is a lovely room,' Molly said, as she looked around.

'I like it too,' Janet agreed.

'Good.' Lily had been keen that each pupil, although sharing a bedroom, would have her own space. 'Now, if you quickly unpack, I'll show you and your parents over the school when they've finished their tea. In no time you'll be at home with us.' The girls' animated chatter followed her as she closed the door behind her.

By the time Janet and Molly, along with their parents, had been given a tour of the school and grounds, more boarders had arrived. Frances and Lily were kept busy all afternoon, as was Edna. By the time the boarders were all settled into their rooms, cook had dinner ready, which she and Edna served in the school dining room.

*

Next morning, the boarders had finished breakfast and were sitting in the Assembly Hall when Lily opened the front door to Annie Tracy, the first day pupil to arrive. Leaving Annie on the front path, Mr Tracy raised his cap to Lily, before turning to make his way back down the drive.

'Welcome to the school,' she said, smiling at the slightly-built 13-year-old, who'd struck Lily as a girl with a bright and enquiring mind when her parents had brought her to see over the school a few weeks ago.

'Thank you, Miss.' Annie dropped a little curtsy, and blushed shyly. She'd been delighted about the offer of a scholarship place, as her parents wouldn't have been able to pay for her education.

Putting a tick against Annie's name on the attendance register, Lily said, 'Annie, if you follow Miss Jenkins into the Assembly Hall, you'll come into my classroom when assembly is over.' The doorbell rang as she finished speaking, and she hurried away to welcome another day pupil.

CHAPTER FORTY-TWO
Gordon's Wedding
August 1884

'Catch,' Ginger called, and threw the ball as far as he could. Prince streaked across the open grassland in pursuit of the ball, which he found wedged between two sturdy tree trunks. He barked loudly a few times, before clawing at it with his large paws until the ball finally came loose. Picking it up in his huge teeth, he loped back to Ginger, dropped the ball at his feet and wagged his thick ropelike tail with gusto.

'Good boy,' Ginger praised him, and threw the ball again. As Prince bounded off to retrieve it, he marvelled at how tall the dog had grown in the four years they'd had him. When he came to a banking of stones further along the track, Ginger sat down. In his head, he rehearsed his speech for Gordon and Frieda's wedding tomorrow. 'Here, boy,' he called to Prince, who'd begun to forage in some nearby bushes. Next minute Ginger felt a wet nose on the side of his neck, and the dog sat down beside him, tongue hanging out and panting.

With his arm lying loosely around Prince's warm, pulsating back, Ginger stared at the swirls of water in the fast flowing river below him, the sun's rays casting flashes of gold across its surface. Contentment washed over him, thinking of his life here in Dubbo. The town sat on the banks of this mighty river, the Macquarie, named after the last Governor of New South Wales. Ginger felt an affinity to Lachlan Macquarie, a fellow Scot, and a man who'd been known to support freed convicts.

On their walk back to Deepdene, Ginger dropped in at Wattle Trees. Jess barked a welcome and next minute the two dogs were rolling around on the grass in a frenzy of excitement. Olly emerged from the hayloft and waved to

Ginger. As he got nearer, Prince left Jess and bounded over to Olly.

'Hello boy, how you've grown,' he said, bending down to stroke Prince's thick gleaming coat. The dog jumped up, with his paws on Olly's shoulders. 'You're so much taller than Jess, aren't you?'

Ginger laughed. 'He'd be useless as a sheepdog though. Instead of rounding the flock up as Jess does, this fella would cause havoc.'

Olly threw an arm round Ginger's shoulder. 'Great to see you, mate. Come and have a beer, help to calm you before tomorrow's wedding,' he said, and they walked towards the farmhouse, with the two dogs at their heels.

*

That evening, Gordon celebrated the ending of his bachelorhood in The Sheep's Head pub in Dubbo with his friends, and he was singing loudly and out of key on his return home to Deepdene. Having been awakened by the noise, Ginger grabbed hold of his son as he stood, swaying precariously, at the top of the stairs. He helped the lad into his bedroom, and got him into bed. Gordon was snoring soundly before Ginger left the room.

'Wass the time?' Meg asked sleepily, as Ginger slid back under the sheets beside her.

'It's early, Meg, go back to sleep,' he whispered into the darkness, feeling for her hand and giving it a squeeze. He didn't feel any anger towards his son, aware that his friends would have been plying him with celebratory pints and, being unused to so much alcohol, it would have gone straight to Gordon's head.

Despite taking some time to drift back to sleep, Ginger rose early. He was downstairs in his dressing gown and slippers when Gordon joined him, looking remarkably sober.

'How's the head?'

Gordon smiled shamefacedly. 'Bad. But it's my own fault.'

'Oh, well, it isn't every day you marry. Sit down, Son, and I'll pour you a glass of soda water. Best thing for a hangover,' he threw over his shoulder, as he went into the kitchen. On the rare occasions that he and Olly had drunk too much, he'd always found soda water settled his stomach.

'Here you are.' He kept his voice low as he handed over the glass of fizzing liquid. 'And try and eat a good breakfast, Son, better to get some food inside you before you leave for the church.' Then, leaving Gordon to nurse his sore head, he went upstairs to wash before breakfast.

*

Tom drove the family to Dubbo's Lutheran Church. Gordon and Adam made themselves comfortable on the bench seat next to Tom, and Ginger sat in the carriage with the ladies.

'Will Maud come with Olly and the family?' Meg asked.

Tom glanced round. 'Yes, she was putting on her hat when I was leaving.'

'Autumn's almost here,' Meg announced, as she viewed the changing colours. Sarah pointed to a tree they were passing. 'There's a beautiful one.'

'A claret ash, they grow to quite a height.'

Tom guided the horses through the lychgate and on up the path to the church. Gordon came round to his mother's side of the carriage to help her down. As Meg took her son's hand, she caught her breath at how like Ben he was. Although he'd always resembled his father, the similarity had become more obvious as he'd reached manhood. He had inherited Ben's thick, red hair and the same shaped nose and striking greeny/grey eyes. Unlike Ben, Gordon didn't have a beard but he sported a jaunty handlebar moustache.

Meg walked towards the church door, holding up her long skirt to avoid catching her foot in the hem. A black cat, sunning itself on the church window ledge, opened one eye and looked at her with a pained expression at being disturbed from its slumbers. She tried to recall what her mama had told her about black cats and bridal couples; was it good or bad luck they brought? But she kept her thoughts to herself.

Gordon and Adam went on ahead of the rest of the family, to stand in front of the altar and await the arrival of the bride. The others followed them down the aisle, the pews on either side packed full of guests, and took their seats at the front of the church. Meg turned round to say hello to Maud, sitting in the pew behind them, then her glance stole across the aisle, and she smiled at Heidi Steinberg and Jorg.

Soon afterwards the organist began to play Wagner's Wedding March and Pastor Neumann led Frieda down the aisle on her father's arm. Lily kept Freida's long, white satin train in her sights, fearing to tread on it, as she followed behind the bride. A hairband of fresh flowers matched her deep cerise bridesmaid's gown. Once they drew level with Gordon and Adam, Freida let go of her father's arm and stood beside her bridegroom. Karl Steinberg slipped into the pew next to his wife and Lily took her place beside Freida.

After the ceremony, they returned to Greenacres, the Steinberg's farm. Ginger always felt the name ill-suited a farm in the sun-baked colony of New South Wales, where the grass was the colour of straw for much of the year.

Their meal finished, Karl Steinberg pushed back his chair and got to his feet to address the company. His eyes were moist as he spoke movingly about the joy his daughter had brought to him and his wife, and he turned to Gordon, seeking his promise to take good care of her. Gordon's speech came next and he assured the proud father that his daughter would be well treated. As best man, Adam congratulated the bride and bridesmaid on how beautiful they looked and at the end of his speech he raised his wine glass and wished 'health and good fortune to Gordon and Freida'. With a lot of scraping of seats, the guests stood up and toasted the happy couple.

Finally it was Ginger's turn, and he had a lump in his throat when he started to speak. 'Ladies and Gentlemen, it gives me great pleasure to welcome Freida into our family. Indeed, she has been one of us since the first time she visited Deepdene, and she and my daughter, Lily, have become like sisters. I have no doubt that Gordon and Freida will love and support one another in the years ahead, and together face whatever ups and downs life brings them.

Since Gordon left school, he has been my right hand man in the family business and I'm delighted he has agreed to take over the running of our shops in Victoria. When he and Frieda return from their honeymoon in Queensland, they will move into their beautiful home in Melbourne. Of course they will be greatly missed, but we wish them well in their new life together.' Turning to smile at his son and daughter-in-law, he said, 'I should warn you, don't think you'll get rid of us as we'll be visiting you at every opportunity.'

He sat down again to a tumultuous round of applause.

CHAPTER FORTY-THREE
New Term at Ripponlea
February 1885

The screams wakened Lily. She sprang out of bed and threw open her door, colliding with Frances, whose sleep had also been disturbed. They followed the sound to the bedroom occupied by Janet and Molly.

Molly was already at her friend's bedside, trying to shake her awake. 'Janet, wake up, you've had a bad dream,' she said, then stood back when Lily and Frances came in.

By this time Janet's eyes were opened, and she was sobbing. 'It's alright, you're safe in your bed at Ripponlea.' Lily helped Janet to sit up and Frances lit the kerosene lamp, flooding the room with soft light.

'Go back to bed, Molly, in case you catch cold,' Lily said in a soft voice to her young pupil. Molly and Janet had become firm friends and you rarely saw one without the other. They worked hard at their lessons and Lily had high hopes for their future careers. These girls were particularly dear to her, probably because they'd been the first to arrive when the school opened two years ago.

Lily sat on the edge of Janet's bed, with her arm around the girl, until her sobs ceased and she grew calmer.

'Something in your dream frightened you,' Lily said, 'do you want to tell us about it?' It was only two weeks into the new school year, but already she'd noticed that Janet had seemed a bit tense. This hadn't affected her school work, but Lily hoped the nightmare wouldn't be repeated.

Janet was shaking her head. 'No, Miss Harker, I don't remember what it was about, a jumble of things that didn't make sense. I'm fine now.'

Lily and Frances chatted quietly to Janet until she began to yawn. 'Right, try and get some sleep,' Lily whispered, noticing Molly's eyes were already closed. 'In another couple of hours it'll be daylight.' She put out the lamp, plunging the room into darkness once more.

'Thank goodness no-one else wakened,' Frances whispered to Lily, as they tiptoed back to bed, hopeful of snatching at least another two hours' sleep.

*

A few days later Frances went into the library after dinner, where she found Lily smiling as she read a letter she'd received in the morning post but only now had time to read it.

'Good news?'

'Yes, it's from Frieda.' Gordon and Frieda were well settled into Melbourne life by now and happy in their home in St Kilda. 'Read it for yourself,' she said, handing the letter to Frances.

18th February, 1885

My Dear Lily

Thank you for your last letter. Your time spent at Deepdene during the summer break sounds excellent and it was kind of you to visit my family at Greenacres while you were there.

I have some happy news for you, Lily. You are going to be an aunt. Gordon and I are expecting our first baby in August. We are overjoyed about this and Gordon has begun to carve a crib. We both hope that you will agree to be our child's Godmother.

You'll be back at Ripponlea by now and it would be a joy to greet your pupils again. The schools in Melbourne resumed last week so the town has been quieter during the day. Gordon and I are hoping you'll visit us during your next holiday break. We've at last got the decoration of our house completed. Our rose bower in the side garden traps the sunshine, and we have wisteria growing around the front door. St Kilda is a beautiful spot for us, with the beach on our doorstep.

Gordon is kept busy going between the two shops in Melbourne and the newly opened one in Ballarat. The manager in the Ballarat store is efficient and hard-working, which means Gordon doesn't have to be on hand constantly. The larger shop in Melbourne has a tearoom upstairs, modelled on the one in Sydney. The tearoom has been well received by the customers.

I will stop now, my dearest Lily, as I don't have any more news, at least none as exciting as what I've told you at the start of this letter.

Please write again soon.

Much love from us both,

Frieda

xx

'An aunt, how exciting,' Frances said, handing back the letter.

'I can scarcely believe it.' Lily's eyes sparkled at the thought.

'I'm so happy for you and the parents-to-be.'

'Sorry if I've held you back from whatever you were looking for.'

'I was hoping to find a book on psychology in your grandfather's collection. Ruth Gillies has expressed an interest in the subject.' Ruth had been top girl in Frances' class last year and both she and Lily were keen to help with her studies.

Lily looked at the books lining the shelves behind her. 'There is one I recall, written by an eminent psychologist. Mackie I think, or is it McNair?' she deliberated as she went to the section in the far corner.

*

'Please read from the top of page 26, Annie?' Lily said a week later, when her pupils were studying Shakespeare's Othello. Her prediction that Annie Tracy would earn her scholarship had proved correct and the girl showed great understanding of the Bard's work.

After the reading, Lily looked around the class. 'Now, girls, I want you to write down what, in your opinion, Desdemona is feeling in the part we have just read.' A hush came over the room, with only the occasional squeal of the chalk going across their slates.

There was a knock at the door, and Edna came into the classroom. 'Excuse me, Miss Harker,' Edna said, keeping her voice low, 'Mrs Baxter is here to speak to you about Janet.'

'Thanks, Edna, please give her a seat in the office and I'll be with her directly.' Yesterday Lily had sent Edna to Mrs Baxter's home with a letter, asking her and her husband to come to the school to discuss their daughter's recent nightmares.

After Edna left, Lily spoke to her students. 'I have to leave the room for a short time, girls, so please continue with your exercise, and once you are finished, I'd like you to begin reading quietly from where we stopped.'

'Yes, Miss Harker,' the pupils said in unison.

Mrs Baxter was sitting in the school office, her hands tightly clenched and resting on her lap, when Lily got there. 'On your own? Was Mr Baxter unable to accompany you?'

'He couldn't.' Mrs Baxter's voice was hardly audible and her eyes cast down to the floor. When she looked up her face was deathly white and she seemed about to faint.

'Are you unwell, Mrs Baxter? Would you like some water?'

The woman nodded and Lily went off to the kitchen to fetch a drink.

'Thank you.' Mrs Baxter took the glass from Lily and had a long swallow. The water seemed to revive her. 'You wanted to speak to me about Janet. Is she alright?'

'No, Mrs Baxter. She's been having nightmares fairly regularly since she returned from the summer break. I'm concerned if it continues it will affect her work. I wondered if something had happened during the holiday to bring on these bad dreams.'

Mrs Baxter's face was soon awash with tears, which she wiped away with her handkerchief. 'It's been a stressful time for Janet and me recently … you see … my husband has left us. He's … he's … he's gone away with another woman,' she finished in a rush.

'Oh dear, that could account for Janet's nightmares.'

'It could, because her father and I often had rows, which usually ended up with him being violent.' Mrs Baxter pushed her hair away to let Lily see the angry bruising on her neck. 'Poor Janet saw things a young girl shouldn't. But he's agreed to pay the school fees so that Janet can remain at Ripponlea.'

'I'm glad to hear that Janet will be able to continue here with us, as she's an excellent student, and I'm sure she's perfectly capable of becoming a teacher herself when she's older.'

This praise for her daughter caused Mrs Baxter to smile for the first time.

'I'm glad you've explained things to me, Mrs Baxter, as it will help me to deal with Janet's bad dreams when they occur. Understandably, she didn't want to say anything to me about her father. Would you like me to bring Janet from her class so you and she could have a chat?'

Mrs Baxter let out a sigh of relief. 'That's most kind, Miss Harker, I'm sure it would help both of us.'

'I'll ask Edna to give you both a cup of tea and a biscuit while you chat. Please try to make it clear to Janet that she can remain here at the school and go home to you at holiday periods. I take it she will still see her father from time to time?'

'Yes, he's promised to take her out now and again, although I've said I don't want her meeting that woman.' For the first time there was a tinge of bitterness when Mrs Baxter spoke.

Lily asked Edna to arrange the tea tray, then went into Becky Grant's classroom and quietly explained the situation to her. Becky looked over at Janet, sitting in the front row. 'Janet, could you go with Miss Harker? You're excused from the rest of the lesson.'

Janet got up at once and followed Lily out into the hallway.

Lily smiled at her. 'It's alright, Janet, you aren't in any trouble. Your mother's in my office and would like a chat with you, that's all.'

After escorting Janet into the office, she returned to her own class to continue the lesson.

CHAPTER FORTY-FOUR
The Twins Turn Fifteen
October 1885

'How's my favourite girl, then?' Olly asked, when Sarah opened the door to him.

'Uncle Olly,' she screamed in delight. 'Come in, it's great to see you,' she said, as though she hadn't seen him in years instead of only two weeks ago.

'I've never known the house to be so quiet,' he said, when they walked into the empty family room. Usually Deepdene rang with conversation and laughter, all the family buzzing about.

Sarah pushed the duster she'd been using into her apron pocket. 'Mummy's working in the garden, and Adam is helping her. Anna's gone to the market, but Daddy's in his den if you want to go through.'

'Come and join me, Olly,' Ginger called out from across the hallway, having heard his friend's voice.

Olly winked at Sarah and disappeared into the den, a large sparsely-furnished room overlooking the back garden. He was hit by the rich aroma of wood from the panelled walls. A sturdy work bench stood against one wall and in front of the window, with the daylight streaming in behind him, Ginger sat at his desk with a spread of files and papers littering its top. Without any fancy ornaments or decorations, this was definitely a man's domain, where Ginger could go when he wanted some peace and quiet from the noisy household.

He swung round in his chair and stood up. 'Will you join me in a beer?'

'Sure will, I'm parched.'

Olly was standing beside the bench admiring the carvings being worked on when Ginger returned with two bottles of beer. Taking the bottle Ginger held out to him,

Olly sat down in the only armchair in the den. 'Great place to escape to,' he said, and raised the bottle to his lips.

Ginger nodded and returned to his seat beside the desk. 'Yep, much as I love my family, sometimes I have to come in here for a little solitude. With Lily at Ripponlea and Gordon in Melbourne, it only leaves the twins with Meg and me but it still gets noisy at times.'

'How're Gordon and Frieda doing in St Kilda?'

'They're enjoying life in Melbourne and we're waiting to receive word any day now about the new arrival. Heidi's gone to stay with them. I think Frieda will be happy to have her mother's help when the baby comes. So, how are things at Wattle Trees?'

Olly swallowed the last of his beer, belching in appreciation. He stretched over and put the empty bottle at the side of his chair. 'Going fine, it was great to be drought-free last summer and, with the amount of rain we've had during the winter months, the reservoirs and water tanks are full.'

'It's good that Herbert chose a career in farming,' Ginger said, savouring the last few dregs of his beer.

'Yep, he and I make a good team. Herbert's got more modern ideas from his agricultural classes which he passes on to me. Helps to keep our methods up to date. I left him chopping down some trees when I came into Dubbo to stock up on sheep dip.'

Olly leaned back in the chair and stretched out his sun-bronzed legs.

'Glad you dropped by while you're in town. Another beer?'

'Good plan,' Olly said, and when Ginger returned with the bottles, Prince came trailing in after him. For such a large dog, he padded about very gently.

'Hello, boy.' Olly fondled the dog's ears, sticking up in German Shepherd fashion. 'Hard to remember you getting him as a pup, when he could sit in the palm of your hand, and now he's the size of a small pony.'

'Yep, that was five years ago. We bought him as a gift for the twins' tenth birthday.' Prince stood with his head to one side and stared at Ginger for a few minutes, then went over and licked his hand.

When he was leaving, Olly said goodbye to Sarah, who was in the kitchen making scones. She stopped for a moment and held up her floury hands. 'Uncle Olly, will you and Aunt Vicky come on Sunday for our birthday tea?' She and Adam always had a joint party for their birthdays and this one, their fifteenth, was no exception.

'Of course we will, Sarah, we wouldn't miss it, and Herbert will come with us.'

Sarah's heart did somersaults at the mention of Herbert's name. 'It's good it falls on a weekend so that Lily and Frances can be here too. Pity Gordon and Frieda can't travel at the moment, but maybe their baby will be born on our birthday.'

Olly smiled at her obvious excitement about both events, and he gave her a wave as he climbed aboard his wagon.

*

By Saturday, Sarah's excitement was at fever pitch. She talked non-stop all morning, until around noon Ginger took himself off to the den in search of some peace for an hour or two. Lily and Frances were due to arrive from Ripponlea around one o'clock and Ginger was looking forward to seeing his elder daughter again. He and Lily shared a wonderful relationship, and could sit for hours chatting about everything and anything. He was proud of Lily's success at the school and was keen to hear how things were going there.

An hour later he looked up when he heard the door open, and beamed at Lily when she came into the den, looking pretty as a picture in her blue dress.

'Hello, Daddy.'

'My precious girl.' Ginger's smile widened as he got up from his chair and held out his arms. He and Lily had enjoyed a closeness from the day and hour she was born. He often wondered if being born so early and surviving had made her all the more special.

Lily went into his arms, her eyes sparkling as she looked up at her beloved father.

'Is everything well at Ripponlea?' he asked.

'It is. My day pupil, Annie Tracy, performed well in her recent examinations.'

'Excellent, Lily. You've always had high hopes for her, haven't you?'

'Yes, I'm sure she'll go far in whatever career she chooses. What are you doing?'

He lifted up the papers he'd been writing on and handed them to her. 'I was working on some new ideas for the business.'

They were deep in discussion about the future of Aussie Crafts when Meg put her head round the door. 'Lily, Adam's wondering which bushes you want cuttings from for the Ripponlea gardens?'

'The magnolia and the bush with the red leaves, I can't remember its name.' With a smile to her father, Lily followed her mother out into the garden.

Just before four o'clock, Meg called up to the twins. 'Sarah, Adam, Uncle Olly and Aunt Vicky are here.'

Sarah raced downstairs, with Adam close on her heels, to find their guests in the kitchen, chatting with Meg. Sarah smiled sweetly at Herbert, his light-coloured shorts and loose cotton shirt showing off his deep bronzed legs and arms. From childhood, she'd secretly worshipped him, and now knew for certain that she loved him. She had butterflies in her stomach every time he came near her. Herbert, at 25, still treated her like a young sister but she longed for him to see her as a grown woman.

'Happy Birthday.' Aunt Vicky gave both her and Adam a gift.

'And these are from Tom and me,' Maud said, handing over more gifts.

'Come and have a seat while the twins open their presents,' Meg said, and she ushered them all into the family room. Sarah was delighted with her new red blouse and the brush, comb and mirror set, as Adam was to receive a new cricket bat and a pair of hand-knitted socks.

Half an hour later Anna called everyone out into the garden, where a table with all sorts of goodies on it, awaited them. With lots of chatter and laughter, they cleared the plates and drank the twins' health. Sarah kept stealing glances at Herbert, imagining herself in his arms, but it annoyed her that he constantly looked across the table at Lily, speaking to her at every opportunity. She couldn't understand what he liked about her sister; Lily was such a bore and all she talked about was that stupid school of hers.

The meal ended with a birthday cake, baked by Anna, with both Sarah and Adam's names written in icing on the top. After sampling the cake, folk began to drift back indoors again. It was then that Herbert noticed Lily was missing from the party. He spotted her blue dress at the bottom of the garden, and walked down to where she was sitting on the swing beneath its canopy. The memory flooded back of how he'd often sat on it with her and Gordon when they were young.

'May I?' he asked, pointing to the spare seat beside her.

'Of course,' she said, and moved over to make room for him.

As he and Lily swung to and fro, Herbert's heart was full. He'd loved Lily since they were children and had decided today that he was going to propose marriage. They'd always enjoyed one another's company, but she'd never given him reason to believe she was in love with him. By now, with his heart beating faster every time he saw her, he felt he had to know if she'd agree to be his wife.

Only Sarah saw Herbert leave, and she followed him from a distance, planning to make it appear that she'd met him in the garden by chance. She would tell him she'd found it stuffy indoors and came outside for air. She walked around the side of the glasshouse and drew up sharply when she caught sight of Lily and Herbert sitting together on the swing under the peach trees. She knelt down behind the magnolia bushes, close enough to hear what they were saying. She knew she shouldn't eavesdrop, but was desperate to know what was going on.

Whatever Herbert had just said, Sarah was certain that Lily was weeping. Her sister's voice, soft though it was, reached Sarah clearly in the still evening air. 'Oh, Herbert, I'm so sorry but I can't.' There was a gentle concern on Lily's face as she continued to explain. 'Believe me, I am fond of you, and will always value your friendship, but …'

'But you don't love me enough to be my wife,' he finished for her. His voice broke up, and he dropped his eyes to the ground.

From her place of shelter, Sarah felt empty inside, and knew she'd just witnessed her darling Herbert propose to Lily.

Lily spoke again, her tone imploring Herbert to understand her refusal. 'It isn't that I don't care for you, I don't want to marry anyone. I love being a teacher and I want to commit my life to that.' She reached out and touched his hand. 'But I will be your friend forever.'

Herbert remained silent for a moment or two, then slowly pulled his hand away. 'I can't pretend I'm not disappointed, Lily, but I respect your honesty and hope you don't hate me for asking you.'

'I could never hate you,' she whispered, brushing her hand down his cheek. 'I'm flattered to be asked, but I can't lie to you. Please say we can always be friends.'

'Of course,' he replied, trying to smile through his misery. 'You go back to the house, Lily, and I'll come in soon.'

Sarah crept further behind the bush as Lily walked up the path. She felt the leaves on the bush shaking as her sister passed by and she gave a sigh of relief when Lily moved on, unaware of her presence. But she couldn't move from her hiding place, in case Herbert saw her and knew she'd been spying on him and Lily. He let out a cry like a wounded animal and she could see his shoulders shake with grief. She had to fight the impulse to run to him and throw her arms around him. Her legs were beginning to cramp by the time he got off the swing and went indoors.

Sarah stood up but stayed in the garden for some time after he'd gone. Her sadness was mixed with anger when she thought how unfair it was. Here she was yearning to be his, while her sister had turned down his proposal of marriage. If only he'd asked me instead of Lily, she thought.

There and then she made a vow that when she was older she'd try to get Herbert to notice her as a woman and not a child. Some day she hoped he'd ask her the same question he'd asked Lily tonight, and she wouldn't refuse him.

CHAPTER FORTY-FIVE
Lily Goes to Melbourne
January 1887

Ginger and Lily ate breakfast well before dawn, while the rest of the family were still sleeping. Lily had warned him that she didn't want any fuss before her journey, so he'd crept out of bed, careful not to wake Meg.

He knew Lily couldn't wait to be with Gordon, Freida and Karl but had insisted that he and Tom would accompany her on the first 250 miles to Sydney, where she would board the train. They were planning two overnight stops, first at a hostelry in Orange, and the second night would be spent at one close to Sydney Central Railway Station.

'Lily, you must be very careful when you're in the company of strangers,' Ginger said, as he spread butter on his toast.

'Of course I will, Daddy.'

'It's such a long way for you to go on your own.' Despite his business commitments, he'd offered to accompany her all the way to Melbourne, but she'd pooh-poohed that idea.

She stifled a yawn. 'I'll go and finish my packing, as Tom will be here soon.'

*

'You're making good speed,' Ginger said from his seat beside Lily in the family carriage. They'd felt rested after their stay in the hostelry in Orange last night.

'The roads aren't as busy as I expected,' Tom replied, glancing round from his seat behind Clarence and Rusty. They'd replaced Matt and Norm, who'd been put out to pasture at Wattle Trees and lived until they were thirty.

Ginger took Lily's gloved-hand in his. 'You will be careful on tomorrow's train journey, Darling, won't you?'

'I will, Daddy,' she said, patting his hand, 'and don't worry, I'll be fine.'

'I know that the Simpsons in Goulburn will look after you.' He loosened his grip, but worry was still etched on his face.

Lily relished this adventure, keen to see her Godson, Karl. Gordon and Frieda had brought him to Dubbo a few weeks after his birth, to be christened in the Lutheran church. Lily was thrilled to be Godmother to Karl, who'd smiled and gurgled all through the service. That was fifteen months ago and she couldn't wait to see him again.

She put up her parasol against the strong sun and Ginger closed his eyes and dozed, wakening up when they were driving through Sydney town.

Lily couldn't believe the amount of carriages and pedestrians. The place teemed with people, some carrying shopping bags, others with dogs on the lead or holding their children's hands. She admired the magnificent buildings the town boasted, some business premises and others private homes. The houses were fronted with well-tended gardens, many with a verandah around the property.

After another overnight rest, they made their way to the train station. When the carriage came to a halt outside Sydney Central Railway Station, Ginger jumped down and helped Lily out of the carriage.

'Have a good time, lass,' Tom called to her.

They purchased her ticket, and Ginger waited with her on the platform until they heard the train whistle nearing the station. Thick grey smoke belched from the engine funnel, and there was a ringing screech of brakes as the train slowed down in front of them. Painted along the train body, underneath the carriage windows, were the words NEW SOUTH WALES RAILWAYS, with a picture of an emu and a kangaroo beside them.

Ginger carried her brown leather Gladstone bag and her trunk on to the train. He lifted the trunk up on to the luggage rack, and placed the bag on the seat beside her. 'Don't try to bring that trunk down yourself, Darling, ask the Conductor for his help.' She nodded to keep him happy, although was fully prepared to struggle with it herself. 'I think you'd better get off the train now, Daddy, as it's almost time to leave,' she suggested, glad that their farewell wasn't going to be extended. He opened his arms wide and she stretched up to kiss him, his beard as ever tickling her cheek.

Back on the platform, Ginger spoke to her through the open carriage window. 'Remember everything I've told you, Lily.'

'I will, Daddy.' Her words were drowned out when the train whistle blew. Smoke floated back from the funnel and, when the guard waved his green flag, she felt the train moving.

*

Lily laid her luggage at her feet when she got to the reception desk in the Wodonga hostelry. She'd had a comfortable sleep in the hostelry in Goulburn and, as her father had predicted, the Simpsons had been very kind to her. The change of trains in Albury had gone smoothly, and she'd arrived safely here in Wodonga. Albury and Wodonga were very close, around 4 miles apart, with Albury on the New South Wales side of the Border and Wodonga on the Victorian side.

She'd enjoyed watching the scenery flash past the compartment window, but by now was feeling weary and needed to sleep.

'Can I help you, Madam?' the man on the other side of the counter asked.

'Good afternoon Mr Wallace. My father, Ben Harker, recommended your inn to me, and I hoped to get a room tonight.'

'You're Mr Harker's daughter. And a fine man he is. Now, let me see,' he said, and checked his room plan. 'I can give you Room 15 on the upper floor.'

Once she'd signed the register, he gave her the room key.

'I'll have your luggage brought to your bedroom, Miss Harker, and will send up a supper tray. Breakfast will be served from 7 am.'

'Thank you. I want to travel to Melbourne tomorrow so could you please hire a carriage for my journey?'

'No problem, Miss Harker. I know the very man. You leave it to me.'

*

'Make yourself comfortable, Miss. We have a long journey ahead.' The driver, who'd come recommended by Mr Wallace, handed Lily a rug to spread over her knees.

'How far exactly is it from here to Melbourne?'

'Approximately 200 miles. We'll stop occasionally to change horses and you can have something to eat and drink at an inn while I'm doing that,' he called over his shoulder, then flicked the reins and the horses set off at a canter.

Darkness was descending as they approached Melbourne but it was still very warm and she wore only a short-sleeved dress.

The driver glanced back at Lily. 'It was Flinders Street Railway Station you said, Miss, wasn't it?'

'Yes, please. My brother will be awaiting me there.' Gordon would have calculated how many hours it would take to drive the 200 miles from Wodonga, and she knew he'd be waiting outside the station well before her expected time of arrival.

At Flinders Street, with the help of the gas lights, she saw Gordon standing on the stairway outside the station. Once the horses became stationary, the driver helped her down from the carriage, then laid her luggage on the pavement. She thanked him and slipped a few shillings into his hand as a tip.

'Thank you, Miss,' he said, raising his cap.

Gordon appeared at her side and kissed her. 'Welcome to Melbourne, Lily, I've got the carriage sitting round the corner,' he told her. He picked up her trunk and would have taken the Gladstone bag in his other hand, but she insisted on carrying it herself. They walked round the corner, Lily taking his arm. 'How are Karl and Frieda?'

'Both well. Karl is asleep but you'll see him in the morning. Frieda will have supper ready when we get home. This is Horace and Blondie' he said, when they reached his carriage. In the glow coming from the gas street lanterns, one horse looked black and the other cream. She stroked their noses and Blondie nuzzled her arm.

Lily slept soundly that night, and when she awakened the house was quiet. She drew on her dressing gown and followed the soft hum of voices to the kitchen, where Gordon was enjoying his bacon, eggs and sausages, while Frieda fed Karl his porridge. There was as much on his face as in his mouth, because he insisted on trying to take the spoon to feed himself. 'What a mess you're making, Master Karl,' his mother rebuked him, wiping his face clean with a flannel.

She looked up and smiled. 'Good morning, Lily, did you have a restful sleep?'

Lily was used by now to her sister-in-law's pronunciation of have, which sounded like haf. 'I did thanks. I was tired after my journey.'

'You were exhausted.' Gordon carried a chair over to the table for her. 'What would you like for breakfast?'

'Finish yours while it's hot. I'm in no rush.' She leaned forward to speak to her Godson, sitting in the high chair Gordon had carved for him. 'And how are you, Karl; my, how you've grown since I last saw you.'

The baby's blue eyes studied her face, but he was too intent on filling his tummy to return her smile. 'He'll be happy to play with you once he's finished eating,' Frieda told her, as she rubbed Karl's back to help him break wind. 'He eats so quickly that he often gives himself indigestion.'

'He's definitely inherited his blue eyes from you, Frieda,'

Lily said, glancing round at Gordon's dark brown ones.

Frieda smiled. 'Karl has Steinberg eyes. Bacon and eggs alright for you?' she asked, and seeing Lily nod, moved over to the stove. Lily, who was usually in charge of others, was enjoying being fussed over.

She lifted Karl out of his chair, and held him on her lap, amusing him with his rattle while her breakfast was being prepared.

'Would you like to visit the Botanic Gardens today?' Frieda asked Lily, while she was eating.

Lily swallowed before she replied. 'How lovely. As you know I'm a keen gardener, so will appreciate seeing all the blooms on display. 'Do you visit the gardens often?'

'We go most weekends when Gordon isn't working. The grounds are spacious, with ponds and fountains and picnic areas.'

'We could take a picnic today,' Gordon suggested.

'Good idea.' Frieda sat the baby down on his play mat and stood up. 'I'll go and arrange that before I dress Karl.'

'Do you want me to help you?' Lily offered, before swallowing her last piece of buttered toast.

'No, you play with Karl. It's good to let him get to know you.'

Lily laid down her used cutlery and wiped her fingers on the snow white napkin. Then she picked up Karl's blue fluffy ball. She dropped it gently between his legs and he laughed heartily. He tried unsuccessfully to throw it back to her, and she continued to retrieve the ball and drop it back at his feet, much to his amusement. 'When did the gardens first open?' she asked Gordon, who was sitting nearby watching them play.

'It's been opened for some time now, around forty years or so.' Frieda came into the kitchen at that moment with the picnic basket and, aware of what a good memory she had for dates, he asked, 'Frieda, when did the Botanic Gardens first open?'

'It opened in 1846,' she said, without hesitation.

*

'Look at the scarecrow, Karl,' Lily said, as they stopped in front of the straw man, positioned in the middle of the vegetable display garden. 'He's there to chase away the birdies when they try to eat all the lettuce and beans.'

'Bi .. dis,' the little boy tried to say.

'Yes, that's correct, birdies,' she repeated.

Frieda knelt down at the side of the perambulator and smiled at her son. She pointed to the scarecrow's hat, a large brown floppy one. 'See, mein Schatz, he's got a sun hat on, just like yours,' she said, and pulled Karl's hat further over his forehead.

Lily smiled, noticing how Frieda always reverted to German when using endearments. The straw man's green trousers were torn and patched in places and his puny arms poked out of the sleeves of his red and white gingham shirt. She chuckled as she watched little Karl open his arms wide at his sides, imitating the scarecrow.

'Let's find a place to enjoy our picnic.' Frieda suggested.

They chose a spot in the rose gardens, where they laid their blanket on the grass. The scent of the flowers wafted over them as they ate.

'Will we let Lily see the glasshouse?' Gordon asked Frieda, when they were gathering the plates and cups into the picnic hamper again.

Frieda nodded. 'You'll see blooms and cacti from all over the world. You like the glasshouse, don't you, mein Schatz?' she said to Karl, tickling his tummy. The infant laughed, showing off the two teeth on his lower gum.

Lily looked in awe at the array of giant orchids in the glasshouse, blues, yellows, pinks and purples all mingling into a wall of colour. On their walk around the glasshouse, she admired the other exotic plants and flowers on display, and wrote down the names of her particular favourites, hoping to buy similar for the Ripponlea gardens. At Frieda's suggestion, they rested on a bench, bookended by

Italian marble statues, on one side Venus, the goddess of love and on the other Minerva, the goddess of wisdom. The atmosphere in the glasshouse was one of peace, with the melodic sound of water running in the nearby fountain.

'You're lucky to have a place like this so near home,' Lily said to Gordon.

'Yes, we love our life in St Kilda. Karl likes it here too,' he said, running his fingers down the infant's chubby arm. Karl's response was to yawn widely and rub his eyes.

'I think it's time you went home to bed, young man.' Frieda put her son into his perambulator and, by the time they'd walked back home, he was sound asleep.

*

Frieda rang the bell to let the driver know they wanted off at the next stop. When the tram drew to a halt, she carried Karl off the vehicle, with Lily following behind.

'That was so exciting, my first ever tram journey.' Lily watched the number 4 tram head off towards Flinders Street. Trams had been running in Melbourne since 1885 but this was the first time she'd had the chance to try it out.

'We're going to miss you when you leave tomorrow,' Frieda said, when they were walking along St Kilda Road. She and Lily each held one of Karl's hands, and he shrieked with delight every time they swung him up into the air.

'I'll be sorry to go, but I have work to do before the pupils return from their holiday.'

At the beach Lily removed her shoes and stockings, enjoying the feel of the warm sand trickling between her toes. They sat down, with the dunes behind them. From here they could hear the roar of the frothy white waves crashing in on the shoreline.

Lily drew Karl into her arms and cuddled him. 'Let's make sandcastles,' she said, and picked up his red bucket and spade. He followed her down the beach to where the sand was damp. She helped him fill the bucket with sand, then turn it upside down and use the spade to release the sandcastle. Karl giggled with delight and jumped on the castle to demolish it, then asked her to build it again.

Frieda smiled as she watched them. 'He'll have you do that all day.'

'And I'd be happy to do it all day, wouldn't I, little man?

Karl gurgled with delight and threw his sand-smeared hands round Lily's neck.

CHAPTER FORTY-SIX
Anna Reveals a Secret
May 1888

Meg and Sarah had gone to the mid-week Dubbo market and Adam was at Aussie Crafts with Ginger. Anna's visitor arrived at the usual time of eleven o'clock. On the Thursdays he could get away, he was always prompt. When she opened the door, he scooped her into his arms and they clung together for a few minutes. Then, pushing his straw-coloured hair back from his face, he followed her into the kitchen.

'I've made your favourite shortbread,' she said, and stood back to let him carry the tray out to the glasshouse. They always sat in there, where no-one would disturb them.

Anna stayed for a while in the glasshouse after he'd left, savouring the time they'd spent together, before going indoors to dust the furniture in the family room. She froze in the doorway when she saw the chaos. 'No,' she cried out, staring at the drawers pulled out of the sideboard, their contents strewn around the floor. The silver cabinet had been raided, with many items missing. She wrung her hands. The burglary had happened while they'd been in the glasshouse; the thief must have been hiding somewhere in the garden, and watched them leave the house.

While she was trying to think what to do, she heard footsteps outside on the gravel path, and rushed back to the kitchen to find a weapon to use against the intruder.

'I'm back to collect some papers I …' Ginger was saying as he came in, but stopped when he saw Anna, holding aloft a heavy frying pan, tears pouring down her face.

'Anna, what's happened?' He took the frying pan from

her shaking hands and put it down on the table. He followed her into the ransacked room, where the door of the silver cabinet was hanging open and spaces on the shelves revealed that many items were missing. 'Are you hurt?' he asked her.

Anna shook her head, sniffing back the tears. 'No, but it's my fault a thief broke in. You see, I was in the glasshouse …'

But Ginger stopped her mid-sentence. 'I'm sure you weren't to blame, Anna. Don't worry, the police will sort it out for us,' he assured the distraught woman.

'If I'd only come back into the house sooner,' she said, sobbing by now, 'I would have caught him in the act.'

'No, I'm glad you didn't, as you might have been injured, or worse.' He turned to Tom, who'd come in behind them. 'Will you go to the police station and report the crime?'

'Sure, right away, Ben,' Tom replied, and disappeared out to the carriage once more.

Still weeping, Anna made to clear up the mess but Ginger stopped her. 'No, Anna, leave that until after the police have been. The thief might have left his fingerprints somewhere.' He'd read in the papers recently about a Scottish surgeon who'd written a Paper on the possibility of detecting burglars by their fingerprints, although he wasn't sure if the police had taken up the idea yet. Still, better to leave the crime scene as it is meantime, in case they have, he thought.

When Meg and Sarah came home, they stood in the middle of the room. 'Oh no,' Meg said, when she saw the state of the room and she sat down beside Anna, whose face was deathly white.

Sarah had gone to make some tea, when there was a knock on the back door and Tom came in with a policeman, who identified himself as Officer Watkins. The policeman questioned Anna as to what had happened, and took a note that the thief may have struck while she was in the glasshouse.

'How long were you out of the house?' he asked.

Anna chewed her fingernail for a moment, then shrugged. 'I'm not sure, maybe about half an hour,' she ventured, choking back her tears.

Watkins duly jotted that down, then turned to Ginger. 'By the time your man here got to the station,' he said, nodding towards Tom, 'we'd already had a report of a man being spotted bolting along Dubbo High Street, carrying a heavy sack. A few people gave chase but he escaped into the market crowds. Can you tell me what is missing, Mr Harker?'

'I'm not sure about the drawers,' Ginger told him, 'but I can already see that two silver salvers and two silver candlesticks are missing from the cabinet.' He moved over to where Meg was sitting and laid his hands on her shoulders, aware of how upset she'd be as these pieces had been wedding gifts from Olly and Vicky.

Watkins wrote this information in his book. 'If you can check later, Sir, once my men have left, you can give me a note of anything else that has been stolen.' The officer closed his notebook as he was speaking. 'I take it you had the silver insured, Sir?

'Yes, with the Australian Unity. I've had my home and business premises insured with them since the 1850s.'

Watkins put his notebook into his uniform pocket. 'One last thing, Mr Harker, can you think of anyone who might have stolen from you?'

'No, Officer, I can't.'

'Not even anyone who may hold a grudge against you?'

'No-one.'

'I'll get off then, and we'll do our best to bring the burglar to justice.'

'What about fingerprints?' Ginger asked. 'I read that the idea has been suggested to the Metropolitan police in London by some Scottish surgeon.'

'I know about that, Sir. But so far, the police

departments haven't used it. I'm sure it will come into force soon though, as it would help us catch more criminals.'

When Watkins left, Sarah made some tea they sat down around the fire to drink it. She'd begun to gather up the cups, when she suddenly said, 'Daddy, you told the policeman that no-one had a grudge against you, but what about the man you thought might have started the fire in Orange?'

Ginger tried to think who she was referring to, then he nodded. 'Of course, Ted Jackson, I'd forgotten about him but I can't see him being the guilty party. After all, that fire was almost twenty years ago, he might not even still be alive.'

'I think it's someone who saw his chance and took it,' Tom suggested.

Ginger turned to Anna. 'It's occurred to me that you told the policeman you were in the glasshouse for about half an hour. What were you doing all that time?'

Anna's face reddened. 'I … I …. I had a visitor and we had tea in there.'

'But why not here in the house?' Ginger's voice was soft and kind.

Anna's blushes increased, then she said, 'Well you see … I … I didn't want anyone to see him.'

Sarah burst out laughing. 'Anna, have you been meeting a man in secret?'

'Don't be unkind, Sarah,' Meg said sharply, 'of course Anna hasn't been doing any such thing.' She glanced over at Anna for confirmation of this.

But Anna sat looking down at her lap, her fingers tightly knotted and drained white. Finally, knowing she had no option but to explain, she began to speak. 'Steve from Wattle Trees was here to visit me. He comes every Thursday,' and she added, 'he didn't commit the burglary, as he was with me in the glasshouse.'

Ginger shook his head. 'Steve Black? Of course he

didn't steal from us. But, Anna, why did he come to see you, and why all the secrecy?'

Anna wriggled in her seat, trying to feel more comfortable. 'Because he's my son,' she said at last, her voice barely audible.

Meg gave a start, and looked at Anna in disbelief. 'But how can he be your son, Anna? You've never married.'

Everyone stared at Anna and, after a few minutes, the taut balloon of silence was burst by her sobs. When she finally spoke, her words were interspersed with bouts of weeping. 'No,' she agreed, 'I wasn't married, because … because … Steve's father already had a wife,' she finished, her words tumbling out in a rush.

Meg moved over and sat beside Anna, putting an arm on her shoulder. 'Who was he? You won't be in any trouble,' she said, her voice a whisper.

Anna's eyes dropped to the floor. 'It'd rather not say. Anyway, he's dead now.'

Sarah brought Anna a glass of water. After a few sips, she looked at the concerned faces turned towards her. With her hands clenched into a tight ball, she said, 'Meg, it's time I told you the truth. I've remained silent all these years because I didn't want to upset you.'

'Upset me? What on earth do you mean, Anna?'

'Steve's father was the late Mr Paul Stanley.'

Meg had a sharp intake of breath, and would have fainted, if Ginger hadn't held her in his arms. He sat beside her on the sofa, and held her hand.

'My father,' Meg said, her voice a strangled whisper. 'Steve is Papa's son?'

'I'm sorry, Meg, I didn't encourage Mr Stanley's attentions, but he … he … forced himself on me.' Anna began to sob again and blew her nose loudly into her handkerchief.

'Take your time, Anna,' Ginger said.

'When I told him I was with child, he refused to recognise the baby as his, and said he had no option but to dismiss me. I think he was afraid your mama would find out about my pregnancy and connect it to him. At the time you were ten, Meg, and I was lady's maid to your mama. He instructed me to say that I was going to work up north with my cousin for a few months. I had to obey your papa. As one of ten siblings, I knew my parents couldn't help me with a baby.'

'Did he look after you, Anna?' Meg asked, her face like parchment.

'Yes, he gave me some money, and arranged a place in Sydney, where he paid for me to be looked after and have a midwife to deliver my child. After the birth, your papa paid for Steve to be brought up in a children's home, where I was allowed to visit him regularly. I didn't give the baby my surname of Forsyth but used Black, which was my mother's maiden surname.' Lost in memories, she fell silent again, and pulled her fingers through her hair.

'Did my mama suspect anything?' Meg asked, wiping her eyes with her handkerchief.

'No.'

'And Steve?'

'Yes, my Steve's always known he was my son, but he didn't know who his father was until recently.'

Ginger helped Meg to her feet. 'Let's get you to bed, my dearest,' he said, adding, 'Anna, you get some sleep too, you've had a terrible shock. No, leave the clearing up to Sarah and me,' he said, when she started to protest.

*

After dinner Meg went into the kitchen where Anna was washing the dishes. 'I'm so very sorry Anna for the things you have suffered because of my father,' she said, 'he was very strict with me and I know Mama was afraid of his temper, but I never suspected him of behaving so badly towards his servants. I wish I could make amends for what he did to you.'

'You've already done so, Meg. You and Ben gave me a roof over my head when your papa dismissed me at the time of your marriage. I've never been happier than here at Deepdene. I kept it secret that Steve was my son so as not to make it awkward for you.'

Meg smiled for the first time since she'd returned to find the policeman in the house. 'It occurred to me when I was lying in bed earlier that Steve is my half-brother. I always wanted to have a brother or sister, and now I have one.'

'I was always pleased to think you were related, even though I couldn't tell you.'

Meg moved closer and kissed Anna's cheek. 'I'm glad it's no longer a secret, and you know Steve is welcome to come here anytime without the need of secrecy.'

Anna took off her apron, which she folded and put into the kitchen drawer. 'That means a lot to me. He's a good lad, you know.'

'I do know,' Meg said, as she headed back to the family room. She turned round in the doorway. 'And you should be very proud of the man he has become.'

CHAPTER FORTY-SEVEN
Sarah's Confession
November 1888

Ginger looked up from the memoire he was writing when Sarah poked her head round the door. 'Are you busy, Daddy?'

He laid his pen down beside the inkwell and pushed the jotter aside. 'Never too busy to speak to my children,' he said, taking off his spectacles.

'I wanted to tell you a secret.'

He sat back in his chair and folded his arms.

'Daddy, I'm in love.'

'In love?'

'I've loved Herbert since I was a young child. I didn't think he'd ever love me back, but last night at the party at Wattle Trees, he told me of his love when we were dancing together.' She stopped to catch her breath, eagerly awaiting her father's response.

Giving himself time to digest this, Ginger lifted his spectacles and huffed on the lenses, then polished them. 'And does this mean we are going to hear wedding bells?'

'We both hope so, Daddy. Herbert means to come and ask for your permission, but you will agree won't you? I'd die if you didn't.'

Ginger smiled. 'Of course I won't say no to you marrying Herbert. After all, I've known the lad all his life and Uncle Olly is like a brother to me.'

She bent down and caught him in a strangle-hold hug. 'Daddy, thank you, thank you.'

Ginger gently pushed her away and looked at her with a slight frown. 'There's only one thing that bothers me.'

'What's that?' The momentary fear in her eyes masked her current joy.

Ginger rolled his pen between his fingers. 'Although

Lily hasn't confided in me, I've always suspected that Herbert loved her.'

She tried to interrupt, but he stopped her. 'No, Sarah, hear me out. I was sure they'd marry one day, and I wonder if he has proposed to her and she refused him, as she's so dedicated to her pupils. I would hate for you to be hurt if you are second best in Herbert's heart. Are you sure he truly loves you for yourself?'

Sarah dropped down on to the floor, with her arms resting across her father's knee. 'I am, Daddy, and I know we will be happy together.' She dropped her gaze for a moment, then raised her eyes to his. 'I have to confess, Daddy, that I too was sure Herbert and Lily would marry and, on the day of my fifteenth birthday, I eavesdropped on them in the garden, when Herbert asked her to marry him and she turned him down. Oh, Daddy, I know it was cruel of me, but I was glad because I loved him by then.'

'Well, who am I to stand in the way of true love? Can I tell Mummy your secret?'

'Yes, but only Mummy, until Herbert has called to see you.'

Their conversation was interrupted when Meg walked into the study, her eyes gleaming with excitement. 'The postman has just delivered this telegram from Melbourne,' she said, handing it to Ginger. He read it over, then smiled. 'We have a new family member. Frieda has been safely delivered of a daughter. A sister for Karl, who is to be named Annabelle.'

His wife and daughter gave a whoop of joy.

'How exciting.' Meg kissed both Ginger and Sarah in turn. 'Annabelle Harker has a lovely ring to it,' she said, and hurried away to give Anna the good news.

CHAPTER FORTY-EIGHT
A Double Celebration
January 1890

'It's exciting to think that by this time tomorrow the twins will both have made their wedding vows,' Maud said, as she and Anna were putting the finishing touches to the cakes.

'Mmm.' Anna's reply was short as she concentrated on writing Adam and Kitty on her cake. Maud had decorated the one for Sarah and Herbert.

'What about the meats you've cooked?' Maud asked.

Anna carried the icing bag and cutlery she'd been using over to the sink, where she washed her hands. 'The meats are at Deepdene in the cold cupboard. Tom will bring them here tomorrow morning, along with the desserts I'll make first thing.'

'Yes, I'm going to prepare mine early on too, before I get dressed for the weddings.' Maud clapped her hands. 'It's good to have a double celebration, so it is.'

'Especially as the twins were always together, growing up. It's fitting that they tie the knot at the same time.'

Wattle Trees had been chosen as the preferred venue for the occasion because of the vast area surrounding the farmhouse in which to lay out the buffet tables. It was also where Herbert had lived all his life, and it was about to become Sarah's home too. Adam and his fiancée, Kitty Thom, would make their home with Meg and Ginger, as there was more room at Deepdene than in Kitty's parents' house.

As she helped Maud fetch the best china out of the cabinet, Anna said, 'Sarah's happy to live at Wattle Trees, as she's always been fond of Olly and Vicky.'

'And they adore her.' Maud chuckled. 'She'll order everyone around, myself included.'

Tom came into the kitchen. 'I'm ready to start my deliveries so if you're finished here, Anna, I can drive you back to Deepdene.'

'Thanks, Tom,' she said, taking off her apron.

*

'How pretty you look in your pink dress,' Sarah said to 14-month-old Annabelle, when the womenfolk were dressing at Deepdene.

'Me, too,' said Karl.

'Yes, you're so handsome, Karl,' Lily told her 3-year-old Godson.

He smiled happily and fiddled with his bow-tie.

Lily was bridesmaid to Sarah, and Kitty had her sister, Theresa. Kitty's parents had arrived at Deepdene a short time ago and would accompany Meg and Ginger to the church.

'I wonder how things are at Wattle Trees right now,' Lily said, to no-one in particular, as she fastened Sarah's pendant for her.

Sarah giggled. 'No doubt as chaotic as here.' The men of the party were dressing at the farm, with Gordon acting as best man to Adam, while Steve had been delighted to accept Herbert's invitation to be his best man. Steve had always been treated as family at Wattle Trees, but even more so since the revelation that he was Anna's son and Meg's stepbrother.

*

'How wonderful to see our children settled and happy,' Ginger said to Meg, as they were getting into bed that night. The bed springs creaked as he turned himself round to look at his beloved wife.

A frown creased Meg's face. 'All except Lily. I worry about her being on her own.'

Ginger kissed her. 'We don't need to worry about Lily. She's independent and married to her work. She'll receive great joy from watching her nieces and nephews grow and, with our extended family, she'll never be lonely.'

Meg looked into his eyes, their greenish shade shining in the candlelight, and smiled. 'I hope you're right, Ben, you usually are. Goodnight, Darling,' she whispered, her lips brushing against his cheek. Then she yawned widely and blew out their bedside candle, plunging the room into darkness.

CHAPTER FORTY-NINE
Ginger Retires
October 1892

'How do you think Ben will take to being a gentleman of leisure?' Anna asked Meg, as they were preparing for tonight's party.

Meg took the pastry cases out of the oven and began to spoon jam into them. 'I expect he'll keep busy helping Adam and Gordon when staff members are sick or on holiday. Look at Tom, who retired as delivery driver last year, yet he still insists on driving Ben around wherever he needs to go.' She laughed. 'Not that Maud complains, she says it gets him out from under her feet.'

Anna lifted her eyes from the mountain of potato peelings piled up in front of her. 'It'll be good for Ben and Tom to relax more after all their hard work.'

'Yes, and it's great to know that Gordon and Adam will look after the business Ben built up over the years.'

'You must be proud of how much Ben has achieved.' Anna dropped the last potato she'd peeled into the largest of their heavy iron pots. 'Do you think I've peeled enough for such a large crowd?'

Meg peered into the pot. 'I think so. Whatever happens, no-one will starve. Vicky tells me she is going to make a few different dishes with their spring lamb.' Meg dried her spoons and started to fill the apple and rhubarb tarts. 'I'm hoping Ben and I will be able to spend some time in Melbourne with Gordon and Frieda and the children this summer.'

'Yes, you've missed out on Karl and Annabelle's childhood so far.' Karl was now a 7-year-old schoolboy and little Annabelle was three years younger. 'Where are the family today?' she asked, as she fetched the ham and beef out of the larder. Gordon had arranged things at work, to allow them to be here for his father's retirement party.

'They're spending today with Frieda's family, and they'll come back to Deepdene in time for the party.'

'I think these cuts are cold enough now to slice,' Anna said, taking the carving knife and fork from the kitchen drawer. She was sharpening the knife ready to begin carving, when Prince came into the kitchen, and lapped up some water from his bowl. Then he padded over to the table and raised his nose, sniffing at the meats.

Anna looked across the table at Meg and smiled. 'I'll make a bargain with you, boy,' she said to the German Shepherd, 'I'll give you the first slice of meat I cut and afterwards you've to go and lie down.' The dog stared up at her, salivating, then dived to catch the slice of beef she threw down on the floor. He gobbled it up and, when no more was coming his way, he slouched over to the corner and lay down beside his water bowl, his eyes firmly on the cuts of meat.

'Will I start making the trifles?' Meg asked. Although she was the lady of the house, she always deferred to Anna in matters of catering.

'Yes please, Meg. I think we're well ahead of schedule. When do we expect Lily to arrive?'

'She should be here around three o'clock,' Meg replied, as she cut up the sponges to line the trifle dishes. 'I was worried she wouldn't be able to join us. It's so kind of Frances and Betsy to keep things going at the school in her absence. Betsy is going to live in tonight while Lily is here with us.'

'Yes, it would have been a pity if she'd been the only member of the family not able to attend her father's retirement party. Especially as they've always been so close.' Anna stopped speaking, when they heard the carriage come up the driveway.

'That'll be Ben and Tom back from Wattle Trees, no doubt with some of the food Vicky's been preparing,' Meg said, as she went to open the door for them.

*

'Can you wipe the ice cream off Clara's dress?' Sarah asked Herbert that evening, when the family were sitting round the table, sampling the delicious desserts. From her place across the table from her husband and their 2-year-old daughter, Sarah had seen Clara drop a large blob of ice cream down the bodice of her party dress. When 1-year-old Larry began to cry, Sarah bounced him up and down on her knee, in an attempt to soothe him.

'Looks like he's teething, if all the dribbles are anything to go by,' Meg said to her younger daughter. Sarah and Herbert had been delighted to become parents but, with two children born just one year apart, Meg and Vicky both offered to help look after them as often as they could.

As Meg was speaking, she caught sight of the yearning look on Kitty's face. She knew her daughter-in-law was desperately wanting to have a baby and she and Adam were both disappointed that up to now they hadn't been blessed by a child. It saddened Meg greatly that this was the case and she'd prayed hard for their attempts to be successful soon. What it was like for Kitty to see Sarah with Clara and Larry, Meg could only guess.

When Olly asked Meg something, she turned to reply, and her sad thoughts about Adam and Kitty were pushed aside meantime.

*

'It's been great to have all the family together tonight,' Ginger said in their bedroom after the party. 'Apart from Frances, everyone from the Harker and Jenkins families was here.'

Meg stepped out of her dress and dropped it on to the chair beside the bed. 'It was good of Frances to stay at Ripponlea and let Lily enjoy your party.'

'I can't believe what a lot of work you've all put in to make my retirement so special, including you ladies who've been working in the kitchen for the past few days. Here, let me help you,' he said, when he saw Meg struggle to unfasten her necklace. He undid it for her and kissed the side of her neck.

'Thanks, Ben,' she said, and put the necklace into its box in the dressing table drawer. 'Yes, it was a wonderful evening, and you deserve it after all the years you've worked to support me and the children. It was lovely that we could do something for you for a change.' Undoing the studs in her corset, she let out a sigh as it dropped off her shoulders. She pulled her cotton nightdress over her head, before sitting in front of the dressing table mirror to brush her long hair.

Ginger got into bed and watched Meg's magnificent hair cascading over her shoulders as she brushed. 'Did I tell you the silver shares have risen sharply over the past few months?' Despite his substantial losses in the Bendigo gold mines back in '67, nine years ago he'd decided to buy shares in the Broken Hill silver mine. Two years later he and his fellow shareholders had registered themselves as the Broken Hill Proprietary Company, which was doing very well.

Meg laid her brush down and turned to face him. 'No you didn't, but that's good news. Will you become more involved in the mine now that you've retired from Aussie Crafts?' she asked, as she got into bed and snuggled up beside him.

Ginger stroked her arm. 'I think I might. As you know, my name was put forward at the last shareholders' meeting to replace George Armstrong as President. Poor George is so frail by now that it's getting too much for him. Not that I need to earn any money,' he added. Although Ginger had handed over the business to Gordon and Adam, he and Meg would still get a living from any profits Aussie Crafts made.

She chuckled. 'Much as I would like you to stop working and have more rest, I don't suppose I can expect you to do that. I'm sure you'll work until you drop.'

Ginger smiled and kissed her. 'You know me too well, Meg. And anyway it stops me from getting under your feet.' She heard him chuckling as he blew out the bedside lamp.

CHAPTER FIFTY
Ginger's Great Sorrow
December 1895

Meg put her head round the study door. 'We're off to the market. Is there anything you need?' A pile of papers from the silver mine lay unattended on the desk. Ben sat each day and stared into space, and today was no exception.

Every Thursday she and Kitty went to Dubbo market and when Ben wasn't involved in meetings, he'd go with them and have a beer in one of the taverns while the ladies browsed around the stalls. But these outings had ended nine months' ago when Tom suffered a heart attack. It had happened at Wattle Trees and he'd died in Maud's arms.

Without looking up, Ben shook his head. 'No thanks.'

'Righteo,' she said, keeping her tone bright, a smile covering up the anguish she felt. The spark had gone from Ben's eyes and she was at her wits' end as to how she could help.

Although devastated by Tom's death, Maud appeared to be coping better with his loss. But everyone reacts differently to grief, she thought. 'We won't be long,' she said, and closed the study door behind her.

Bruce awaited them outside. 'Good morning ladies,' he said, and helped them into the carriage. He'd been employed as a delivery driver for Aussie Crafts when Tom retired four years before. As they moved off, Kitty turned to her mother-in-law. 'Poor Dad, I think he's taking Tom's death very hard.'

Meg nodded, fanning herself. 'I've tried everything, but the shock of losing Tom has taken its toll.'

Kitty laid her hand over Meg's, and gave it a reassuring squeeze. 'I'm sure his mood will improve with time.'

'He and Tom had a special relationship,' Meg said, with a catch in her voice, 'they've been friends for almost fifty years, and Ben looked on Tom as a father figure.' None of the family members knew that the two men had been convicts, and she was too loyal to tell them. Ben was writing his memoirs so, after his death, the family would read about his time in the penal colony.

'When do you want me to return?' Bruce asked, when he brought the horses to a halt outside Dubbo Hotel. He planned to make some deliveries for Aussie Crafts while the ladies were at the market.

'Come back in two hours, please, Bruce,' Meg said.

Thursday morning was the main market of the week and it was crowded with shoppers. First of all, they stopped at the haberdasher's.

'Good Morning, Ladies,' Letitia, the stallholder, greeted them, 'and what can I do for you today?'

Meg had known Letitia for years. 'I want some wool, let's see, two hanks of this one,' she said, holding up a pale grey hank, and I'll take two of the navy.' Meg kept the men at both Deepdene and Wattle Trees provided with warm socks and she bought all her wool from Leitita's stall.

Letitia checked the shade numbers on the hanks. She took the money and counted out the change into Meg's palm. 'How's Maud doing?' she asked.

'Bearing up really well,' Meg told her, 'although of course she misses Tom greatly.'

'Yes, he was a true gentleman.' Letitia turned to where Kitty was looking through the box of ribbons. 'How are you getting on there?'

Kitty draped some ribbons over the back of her hand, and looked at Meg. 'Which ones do you think would be best for my new bonnet?'

'Maybe that one and this,' Meg replied, touching a pale blue and a pink ribbon. After all, both these colours are in your best frock.'

'Yes, they will do me well. Thank you,' she said, pulling the ribbons out of the box and handing them over to Letitia.

'Good morning Meg, good morning Kitty,' Hannah Gray said, when she almost collided with them as they left the stall. 'How are you both?' she asked, her eyes fixed on the wool in Meg's basket and the edge of ribbon sticking out of the paper bag Kitty was holding. 'What pretty colours,' she said to Kitty, 'will we be seeing them soon decorating one of your dresses?'

Kitty shook her head. 'Not on my dress, on my bonnet.'

Hannah was known as a local gossip, so they kept their conversation as short as possible, excusing themselves soon afterwards to go to the book stall.

*

Ben didn't enter into the conversation at dinner that evening. When the meal was over, he took himself off to his study and closed the door behind him. Meg made no comment while the others were with her in the family room, but later, when she and Ben had retired for the night, she took the chance to speak to him. 'I'm not saying this to be cruel, Ben. I understand that Tom's death has been a tremendous loss to you, as you and he shared a wonderful friendship over the years, but the rest of us are still here for you.' When he didn't respond, she leaned closer to him and pushed some strands of hair away from his forehead. 'Moping about in your study is doing neither you, nor us, any good.' Then, afraid she'd been too hard on her beloved Ben, she kissed him, brushing her fingertips across his cheek as she did so.

With still no response, she was certain her words had made the situation worse, until his fingers tightened around her hand and she felt his shoulders shake. He began to cry like a baby, all his sadness coming out in choking sobs. Meg held him in her arms, relieved that at last the floodgates had opened.

*

Next morning when Meg wakened, she stretched and yawned, rubbing the sleep from her eyes with the heel of her hand. When she turned round, Ben's side of the bed was empty.

She looked up when he came in, carrying a breakfast tray, with a single red rose in a small vase sitting beside the white china teapot. 'Good morning, my darling,' he said, and smiled at her as he lay the tray down on the bedside table.

She clapped her hands. 'What a lovely surprise to have breakfast in bed.'

He went off to dress and trim his beard, and she'd finished breakfast by the time he returned. 'You look very spruce,' she said, and smiled.

She threw her legs out of bed and hurried over to where he stood at the window. 'How wonderful it is to see you smile again, Ben,' she murmured, and threw her arms around his waist, laying her head against his shoulder. She remained there, silent, for some time, glad that the old Ben had returned to her.

CHAPTER FIFTY-ONE
Olly's Loss
September 1897

'Look at that, he's ready to walk any minute now,' Meg said, her face glowing with pride as she looked at her grandson. The sturdy little chap, called Ben after his grandfather, held on to the table leg, juggling with the notion of letting go.

As they watched, Ben Harker the second let go of the table leg and took two tentative steps, then another two, before losing his balance and dropping down on to the carpet, his bottom protected by the thick napkin he was wearing. His anxious mother hurried over and picked him up. He looked at her, ready to howl, but Meg clapped her hands and said, 'Ben, what a clever boy you are.' The little boy, tufts of red hair covering his head, clapped too and the howl turned to laughter. Spurred on by Meg's praise, he struggled down and took some more steps.

Meg laughed. 'Now he's found his feet, he'll get into everything,' she said, and went off to help Anna prepare dinner. With Anna ageing, she now relied on Meg's assistance.

'So young Ben's taken his first steps, I hear,' Anna said, turning round from the sink where she was washing the breakfast dishes. 'It seems no time since he was a newborn.'

'Yes, I can't believe where the time has gone.' When Kitty and Adam had announced the good news of her pregnancy last June, Meg's heart sang. When the baby was born on New Years' day, she'd been sure he'd help Ben's state of mind. How true this had been; Ben was thrilled that the baby was given his name, and he doted on the little chap.

Ben appeared at that moment carrying a box of

vegetables, plus some apples and early peaches. Winter had been so mild that all the fruit and flowers were ahead this year. The garden supplied the household all year round, thanks to Ben's careful planning. He gave the box to Anna and pulled off his muddy boots. 'How's my little playmate this morning?'

Meg gave him a fond smile. 'Your little playmate has just taken his first steps. He's in the family room with Kitty.'

'Oh, this I must see,' he said, and padded away in his stocking soles to find his namesake.

Meg smiled at Anna when he left. 'Young Ben's raised his grandpa's mood after losing Tom. It's a true saying, when one door closes, another opens.'

*

That afternoon Meg was playing with her grandson when there was a knock on the kitchen door. The clock above the mantelpiece struck four as she lifted the boy and carried him into the kitchen. 'Come in, how nice to see you,' she said and moved back to let Maud in. 'What's the matter?' she asked, when she saw Maud's red-rimmed eyes.

Maud slumped down into a chair, disbelief on her face. 'I've got terrible news for you and Ben,' she said, a waterfall of tears flowing down her cheeks.

It struck Meg at that moment how much Maud had aged since Tom's death.

'Let me get Ben,' she said, and sat the little lad on the rug beside Maud's chair. Through her tears, Maud managed to smile at the youngster, who gurgled with delight at seeing her. When Meg turned round as she left the room, he was holding out his arms for Maud to lift him on to her knee.

Meg crossed the hall, and went into the study, where Ben was writing his memoire. 'Maud's here, something's wrong at Wattle Trees. She hasn't told me yet what's happened, but she's very upset, so it must it must be serious.'

Ginger took off his spectacles and got up from his desk immediately, while Meg called for Anna and Kitty to come downstairs. When Anna saw Maud's distress, she went off to make her a cup of tea. Kitty lifted Ben from Maud's knee, and they all stood silently around Maud's chair. 'Olly, poor Olly,' she said, and stammered to a halt.

Ginger dropped down into the armchair opposite Maud's. 'Has Olly had an accident?' he asked, one hand tugging at his beard while the other rubbed his birthmark.

Maud cast her teary eyes on him, and eventually she spoke. 'No, it's Vicky. Poor Olly is distraught … I don't have words to comfort him … I didn't know what to do and came here.' She stopped speaking abruptly, and massaged her forehead with her fingers.

Looking closer at her, Meg spotted the wrinkles worn into Maud's skin. She perched on the arm of the chair and hugged the older woman to her. 'Is Vicky ill?'

Still weeping, Maud held tightly on to Meg's hand, but she spoke now in a calmer tone. 'She's dead … Vicky's dead … oh, poor Olly.'

During the stunned silence that followed, Anna brought in a cup of tea. 'Drink that Maud, it'll help with shock.'

Meg exhaled deeply, only now becoming aware of how long she'd been holding her breath. It crossed her mind how often Maud had made tea for others who were in crisis. Finally she found her voice. 'Vicky's dead? But she's always so healthy. How did it happen?'

Maud took a sip of her tea, the cup rattling on the saucer as she put it back down on the table. Another drink of tea calmed her further and then she explained the circumstances of Vicky's death. 'She's had a cold and chesty cough for a few days but nothing that we thought staying in bed wouldn't cure. With Sarah there to help me in the kitchen, we managed fine. Then, yesterday, Vicky became worse, feverish and rambling a bit in her speech. Olly sent for the doctor, who said she had pneumonia. He gave her some medicine and said he'd return today.' She stopped for another drink of tea, leaving the others time to take in what she was telling them. 'Early this morning before dawn, I was awakened by a noise and I found Olly trying to rouse Vicky, but it was too late, she'd slipped away in the night.' She halted and stared out at the tall sunflowers lined along the garden fence like guardsmen.

'Poor Olly,' Meg said, a stunned look on her face.

Maud moistened her lips with her tongue. 'He's in a dreadful state and has hardly uttered a word since it happened. I've left Sarah and the children trying to comfort him while I came here.' Her tears surfaced again but she sniffed them back.

Ben remained silent, with a faraway look in his eyes, so Meg took over. 'Maud, when you finish your tea, Ben and I will come to Wattle Trees with you.'

CHAPTER FIFTY-TWO
Adam Goes to War
November 1899

The news came out of the blue during dinner.

'I joined up for the war today,' Adam announced. Beside him at the table Kitty shifted in her seat but continued to encourage young Ben to eat his dinner.

Across the table from Adam, Meg's cutlery clattered on to her dinner plate. She stared in disbelief at her son. Earlier in the day she'd read a report in the paper about the Second Boer War, but hadn't for one moment thought any of her family would be going off to fight.

'How long have you been thinking of doing this, Son?' Ginger understood that young men only saw the glamour of war and not the danger, but his strong hatred of the British Government made him angry that Adam was offering his support to that nation.

Adam laid his cutlery on his empty plate and sat back in his chair, arms crossed in front of him. 'It's been in my mind ever since the war started back in October. I feel it's my duty to serve my country against the Boers.'

Meg could hardly believe her ears. 'But what about Aussie Crafts? Why do you want to go to some far off country and fight in a war that has nothing to do with us here in Australia?' A frown flitted across her face and Anna, sitting next to her, laid a comforting hand on her knee under the table.

'You're prepared to leave Kitty and Ben and go off to war?' Ginger asked.

'I am Dad.' Kitty said nothing, but carried on her struggle to get Ben to eat his mashed potato from a spoon rather than playing in it with his fingers.

'We can't allow the Boers to get the upper hand, and I want to fight for Queen and country.' Adam looked over at his mother. 'Mum, the shops can survive without me while I'm away. Hopefully the war won't last long, and I'll be back before you know it. I've spoken to Gordon and he's agreed to stay and look after the shops in Victoria, while Joe is able to deal with those in New South Wales.'

Ginger sighed. 'There's no point in me trying to dissuade you, Son, since you've already enlisted. Joe is very capable and I can work with him a few days a week to keep things moving smoothly. What Regiment are you joining?'

'I've been assigned to the Scottish Horse Unit. The Recruitment Officer said my experience of riding and shooting will be invaluable. A lot of the fighting will take place on the African veldt.' His voice softened. 'Don't worry, Mum, I'll be fine.'

'When do you have to leave?' Ginger asked.

'I'll be issued with my uniform in the next couple of days. Not sure how soon after that I'll be going.'

'And won't you have to get vaccinations to go to Africa?'

'They offered me a typhoid vaccination but I've refused it. I don't want them pumping anything into me that might do more harm than good.'

'I take it you've told Joe about this plan?' Meg asked, trying to contain her hurt that he had signed up before preparing them beforehand.

'Yes, I mentioned it to Joe shortly after the war started. He said if he'd been younger he'd have enlisted too.'

The conversation moved away from the war and with so many of them living in Deepdene it wasn't until Ginger and Meg were getting ready for bed that they had a chance to further discuss the matter.

'You encouraged Adam in his decision to join the Army,' Meg accused, as she pulled her nightdress over her head.

Ginger stepped into his pyjama trousers. 'Meg, it's natural for a mother to worry about her son going off to war, but he's as much of a man as he'll ever be. He's already signed up, and we can't alter that. Surely you don't want him to go without our blessing?'

'And what about his wife and son? They could be left without a husband and father.'

'Lots of men go off to war and return home safe and sound.' Ginger opened his arms to Meg who, sobbing, laid her head on his shoulder. Gradually her sobs subsided and she said, 'I'm sorry to sound selfish, Ben, but I can't bear the thought of Adam being injured, or …,' she stopped, and her voice melted away, leaving the word unsaid.

Ginger led her towards the warm bed, and he cradled her in his arms before dousing the lamp. 'We have to support him,' he whispered, holding her until she fell into an exhausted sleep.

He was awakened by the sun streaming through the curtains, bathing their bed in light. He'd lain awake for some time after Meg had fallen asleep, worrying about his son fighting out there on the Veldt. War brought not only physical injury but also mental. When he thought how the British Government had treated him, it was hard to reconcile himself to the thought of Adam putting his life in danger to fight alongside British troops.

He rolled on to his side, and admired Meg's beauty that had been undiminished by the years. 'Feeling better?' he asked, when her eyes slowly opened.

'I can't believe Adam is going to war and I'm angry that he didn't discuss it with us before signing up.'

'I'm none too happy myself that he's going, especially to fight for the country that treated me so badly,' he said, through gritted teeth. 'But Meg, we aren't seeing things through a young man's eyes. He thinks it's a great adventure he's going on and we must pray that he comes back to us in one piece, for Kitty and Ben's sakes as well as for ours.'

CHAPTER FIFTY-THREE
A New Century Dawns
January 1900

Stars twinkled down from the night sky, as a large crowd gathered in Dubbo Town Square. Despite a lot of happy chatter, their anticipation was mixed with a dash of uncertainty as to what the 1900s had in store for them. But, in the main, the mood was one of joy.

Members of the Jenkins and Harker families had joined the New Year revellers. With the school closed over the Festive Season, Lily and Frances were both here, and Gordon, Freida and the children had travelled from Melbourne to celebrate the occasion, staying with Freida's parents during their visit. 'The children are so grown up,' Meg murmured to Ben, as she watched 15-year-old Karl and his 12-year-old sister, Annabelle, standing beside their parents, waiting for midnight to strike. 'Karl, Annabelle,' Lawrence's shrill tones called out, as he and his big sister, Clara, skipped over to stand beside their Melbourne cousins. At 9 and 10 respectively, the siblings bristled with excitement at being allowed to stay up and welcome in the twentieth century.

In the darkness Ginger felt for Meg's hand and squeezed it. 'It's wonderful to have the families all together tonight, isn't it Darling?' he whispered in her ear.

Meg's voice was fearful when she replied. 'Except Adam isn't here. We can only pray he is safe.' They hadn't heard anything from Adam since he'd enlisted in November and the reports of the many battles that had taken place frightened Meg. She knew Kitty was equally worried, but when she glanced round at her daughter-in-law, standing at her side, cuddling Ben in her arms, it was too dark to see the sadness on her face.

Meg reached out and gently stroked young Ben's hair,

red like his grandfather's. Despite being surrounded by noise, the 4-year-old was sleeping soundly, as only a young child could.

As the hands on the Town Hall clock crept towards midnight, Ginger's grip tightened on Meg's hand. The countdown began and, as soon as the clock boomed out, the people around them kissed, hugged, cried and wished one another good fortune in 1900.

'Happy New Year, Mummy and Daddy,' Lily said, coming over to hug each parent in turn.

'And to you, my darling,' Ginger said warmly, taking his daughter into his arms. 'I hope Ripponlea continues to prosper in the new century,' he said, raising his voice over the din around them.

'It's wonderful to see how well the pupils are doing, and many of the girls have come back to let us know how successful they have been in finding careers.' She sighed. 'Makes all our efforts worthwhile.'

He released her from his embrace and smiled down at her face, illuminated in the starlight. 'I'm glad you found your vocation, my darling. You're a born teacher.'

Olly came up behind Ginger, and threw his arm around his neck. 'Happy New Year, mate,' he said, holding out his hand.

'And you Olly,' Ginger responded, shaking his friend's hand with gusto. In the three years since Vicky's death, Olly had got on with life as best he could, which is what Vicky would have wanted. Herbert and Sarah and the two children staying with Olly at Wattle Trees had helped to ease him back into a normal existence. As Olly told him once, 'you can't be down for long with boisterous children around.'

Once the crowd had begun to disperse, they all made their way to Wattle Trees where Maud, despite being in her nineties by now, had prepared some food and drink for their return. Ginger helped Olly to fill the glasses, which were handed around the adults, with juice for the children.

'Now I'm almost an adult, can I have some wine, please?' Karl asked Gordon.

Gordon nodded. 'Okay, just this once.'

When everyone's glass was full, Olly raised his. 'A toast to the new century, and to friendship,' he said.

'To friendship and the new century,' Ginger echoed, then looked down at Ben, asleep in his mother's arms, 'and to my grandson's 4th birthday, even if he is sleeping through it.'

Maud drained her sherry glass and laid it down on the table. Then she lifted off the paper serviettes that had been covering the plates of food. 'Please help yourselves,' she told the folk nearest her, 'and I'll make some tea.'

'I'll give you a hand,' Meg said, and followed her into the kitchen.

'I'll help too,' Annabelle called out, racing after them, with Clara at her heels, not wanting to be left out.

CHAPTER FIFTY-FOUR
A Footballer in the Family
March 1901

Kitty waited outside the school gates for Ben. Although not yet five, he'd been accepted into Dubbo primary because he was a tall, well-built lad, already able to read and write.

She prayed there'd be good news about Adam soon. The telegram had said, Private Adam Harker of the Scottish Horse Brigade, missing in action. It had been a sad start to 1901, with the death of Queen Victoria coming so soon after the telegram.

When the school bell rang, the pupils flooded out. Ben's red hair was easy to spot. 'Hello, Mum,' he called, and raced towards her. His satchel was slung across his shoulder by one strap and his knee-length socks had slipped down and were bundled around his ankles.

She made to hug him but he pushed her away. 'Don't Mum, I'm a big boy now,' he said, checking that none of his playmates were watching.

'So, how was school?' Kitty asked.

'Great, Mum, and, guess what, I've been picked for the school football team,' he told her, bouncing his ball in front of him as they walked.

'Well done, Ben, and how did you get on with your sums today?'

He shrugged. 'Fine. Will you tell Daddy about me getting into the football team?'

'Of course I will, the next time I write to him.'

Ben was too intent in kicking his football to notice the frown that spread over her face. He kept up a steady stream of chatter, mainly about how much he liked Mr Brown, the football coach.

'Grandad, I'm in the school football team,' he told

Ginger when they reached Deepdene, racing into the house ahead of Kitty.

'Well done, Ben,' Ginger said, from his armchair at the side of the fireplace.

'Ben, go upstairs and change out of your school clothes, and then you can tell Grandad more about the team.'

Ben made a face, but he obeyed. In a very short time he was back and laid his football on the floor at Ginger's feet. 'Grandad, can we go outside to play? I'll need lots of practice now I'm in the team.'

'And what about your homework?' Kitty asked.

'I can do that later,' Ben called out, as he headed towards the garden.

'We won't stay out for long,' Ginger promised Kitty, and followed his grandson into the garden.

CHAPTER FIFTY-FIVE
The Returning Warrior
July 1901

Adam's return came without warning on a wet winter's afternoon. The sky had been black all morning, with rumbles of thunder, and torrential rain had finally been let loose in the past hour. When he came into the kitchen, he dripped pools of water on to the floor. He looked tired and leaned heavily on his crutches. His left foot was missing.

Kitty rushed over and guided him to the nearest chair. He dropped down into it and she ran her fingers over his face, kissing him tenderly. 'Adam, you're home, what a surprise for Ben when he returns from school.'

He smiled at the mention of his son. 'How is the lad?' he asked, his voice cracking with emotion.

'Bigger and cheekier with every day that passes, but he'll be so glad to see you again.'

'Welcome home, Son.' Meg wrapped her arms around his neck. 'Thank God you've survived, we never gave up hope, even when the telegram arrived that you were missing.'

'I lay low after the battle ended, and later an ambulance took me to a field hospital. I gave the name of my Unit but in the chaos they probably failed to pass it on. They discharged me on medical grounds.'

Meg picked up one of his crutches which had dropped on to the floor and laid it beside its neighbour propped up against the back of the chair.

'I can take over the shop again.' When Meg looked at his injured limb, he said, 'Mum, don't worry, I'm to have an artificial foot made for me, and I'll soon learn to work minus these,' he added, raising his right hand where only his thumb, index finger and pinkie remained.

'But first you must rest and get your strength back,' Kitty told him, as she put the kettle on to boil and make him a hot drink.

'Where's Anna?' he asked.

'Gone to visit her cousin in Orange.'

Adam had washed the grime off his body and was settled in an armchair beside the fire when Ben arrived home. 'Hi, Grandma, guess what I got for my spelling today,' the boy called out, and dropped his satchel on to the floor. He drew himself up abruptly when he saw his father.

'Dad,' he yelled and launched himself on top of his father, arms clinging round his neck, almost strangling him with kisses and hugs. Kitty and Meg smiled at the scene, then Kitty gently removed Ben, with the words, 'Son, let your father breathe.'

*

Dinner that night was a celebration of Adam's safe arrival back. On Ginger's return from helping in the shop, he greeted his son joyfully and listened to his account of the long and scary journey home.

'It's wonderful to have you home, Adam,' Sarah said, as she passed him the dish of pumpkin pie. The family from Wattle Trees had come to Deepdene as soon as Ginger had got word to them of Adam's safe return.

Adam steered the conversation away from the war, as he couldn't talk about the horrors he'd experienced in Africa. With his left hand he slid a piece of pie from the dish. It wobbled about a bit, looking like it might break up, but then it landed squarely the right way up on his plate. He looked across the table at Lily, who was home from Ripponlea during the winter school break. 'And how are things going at the school, Lily?'

'All good thanks. The girls have been working hard so I've no complaints.'

'Recently Lily and Frances have been busy with their meetings,' Meg told him.

'What meetings?' he asked his sister.

'Frances and I have been attending the Women's Suffragette meetings,' Lily explained, as she spooned a portion of mashed potato on to her plate beside the pie. 'We're fighting hard for votes for women. We hope soon New South Wales will bring it in.'

Ginger took a drink from his wine glass. 'South and Western Australia already have the vote, Darling, so I think it's only a matter of time before it's law here too.'

'It can't come quickly enough for me.' Lily turned to her mother. 'Have you let Gordon and the family know of Adam's return?'

'No, Adam just arrived this afternoon but tomorrow morning Daddy is going to send a telegram to Gordon.'

After dinner, they all sat comfortably around the fire, chatting about everything except the war. Earlier, young Ben had asked Adam about the fighting, but now he was sitting cross-legged on the floor, playing cards with his cousins from Wattle Trees.

'Time for bed, Ben,' Kitty said a short time later, and Ben reluctantly said goodnight to the others, and followed her upstairs.

'Your bed is ready too, Adam,' Meg said, noticing how drawn and tired he looked.

'Thanks, Mum. I think I'm ready for a sleep,' he agreed, and swallowed down the last of the generous measure of whisky his father had poured for him. 'Great to be home,' he murmured, and went to bed, hoping he wouldn't have any of the nightmares he'd been suffering.

CHAPTER FIFTY-SIX
Ripponlea School Christmas Fayre
November 1902

Long before the fayre opened at ten o'clock, a crowd had gathered outside the school gates.

'Looks like your fayre is as popular as ever,' Ginger said to Lily, as he and Meg stood with her in the grounds.

'Excuse me,' Frances said, as she squeezed past them carrying a box of Christmas cards. A great deal of creative work was done by the girls in the weeks running up to the fayre, including lavender bags, soap bags, knitted socks and scarfs, embroidered aprons and all manner of Christmas cards and tree decorations. The stalls with their brightly striped canopies were set up on the lawn, each stall manned by two senior pupils. Other girls ran the tearoom set up in the assembly hall, with yet others selling entry tickets.

Lily disappeared into the office for a moment and returned with bags of coins. Surrounded by a buzz of conversation, she went over to check that the stallholders had plenty of loose change in their cash boxes. She was making her way back through the crush, when she heard her name called out.

'Hello Miss Harker,' the voice called again, and she turned to see Janet Baxter and Molly Archer come towards her, wending their way through the mass of people.

'Hello, girls, how nice to see you.' Lily recalled clearly them arriving at the school as her first two boarders. They had excelled in their academic studies and, since they'd left school and taken up posts as governesses, the two girls made a point of attending any event at Ripponlea.

'Just try to keep us away, Miss Harker,' Molly said, showing Lily the lovely knitted gloves and lavender bags she'd purchased.

'You can do away with Miss Harker now and call me Lily,' she said, her eyes twinkling. 'Would you like to come into the tearoom to get out of the hot sun?'

'Oh, yes please,' Janet said, and the two of them followed their old headmistress to the assembly hall, where she showed them to a table at the window overlooking the well-stocked garden.

'Miss Baxter and Miss Archer used to be pupils here,' Lily told the young girl who came over to serve them. She put her arm on the girl's shoulder and said, 'Marjory here is doing well with her studies and she's making her teacher and myself proud.'

'Thank you, Miss Harker,' Marjory said, giving a little curtsey, before turning to ask Janet and Molly if they'd like tea or coffee.

*

'Another successful fayre,' Lily said to her parents, when the three of them finally sat down at a table, to be served by the girls running the tearoom. Meg had been given the job of laundering all the embroidered tea cloths that were now spread across the tables.

'I'm glad you can come home to Dubbo when the school closes,' Meg said, 'you need to relax after all the work you've been doing for the Suffragettes.' All women over 21 in New South Wales had finally been given the vote on 27th August, following the robust campaign by Lily and her friends in the movement.

'Would you like tea or coffee?' a young schoolgirl asked them, stopping at their table, which had plates of delicious-looking cakes and scones on it.

'I'll have tea please,' Meg said to the girl. Lily asked for tea too, and Ginger decided to have coffee.

'I can't wait to register my vote at the next election,' Lily told them, returning to their previous conversation.

'But all your efforts have paid off,' Ginger said, 'it's high time that women were given the vote.'

Lily laughed. 'Well at least Australia is the second

country, after New Zealand, to make it a law. Hopefully the rest of the world will follow.'

'I'm sure they will. I read in the Sydney Herald that the suffragette movement is extending all the time in Great Britain,' Ginger began, then stopped speaking when the young waitress arrived back with their drinks.

*

It was early the next morning that Ginger and Meg's sixth grandchild arrived, a daughter for Adam and Kitty and a sister for young Ben. After a joyous family reunion when Adam arrived home last July, he'd had his artificial foot fitted and was able to return to Aussie Crafts and take some of the weight of the business off Ginger's shoulders. Having the new limb had even allowed Adam to play football once more with his son.

It was back in April that Kitty had broken the news of her second pregnancy. After all the heartache and worry when Adam was missing in action, they were now to be blessed once more by the birth of another child.

Kitty's pregnancy had gone very smoothly and early that morning, shortly after daybreak, the cry of a newborn was heard throughout Deepdene.

'Does she have a name yet?' Meg asked her daughter-in-law, who was sitting up in bed, cradling her baby girl.

'We're going to call her Molly,' Kitty said, 'after my late grandmother.'

'Hello, Molly,' Meg said to her granddaughter, taking the baby's tiny hand and smiling down at her. Ginger joined her at the bedside, and he touched the little mite's other hand. 'Our family is truly blest,' he murmured, as he gazed down at her pretty face and rosebud mouth.

CHAPTER FIFTY-SEVEN
Farewell to a Precious Soul
July 1905

The dismal mid-winter morning added to the desolation the mourners were feeling. The gloomy atmosphere made her death even sadder to the folk who'd loved her. Rain had drizzled down since first light and had only eased slightly in the past half hour. Many local farmers had been crying out for rain during the dry winter so far, and that included the Jenkins family at Wattle Trees.

Maud had endeared herself to many people over her long life of service and caring for others. There had been a party for her 99th birthday earlier in the year and the folks at Wattle Trees had already begun to discuss an even bigger celebration when she reached her century next year. However, Old Father Time had caught up with Maud, and family members took some comfort from the fact that her death had been sudden; she had simply dozed off in her armchair and hadn't wakened up again.

People packed into the pews in Dubbo Church, where the preacher described Maud as being 99-years-old in age but much younger in spirit. Her favourite hymn 'Tell Me the Old Old Story' was sung during the service. On leaving the church, the mourners congregated in Dubbo cemetery for Maud to be interred beside her beloved Tom.

'She was loved by everyone who crossed her path,' Meg whispered to Ben, feeling the crush of people behind them, and facing them, around the grave. Tears rained down Meg's cheeks as she was speaking.

'She was, Meg,' Ginger murmured, and he took her cold hand in his, their arms rubbing together through their raincoats. 'It's wonderful when someone makes such an impact during their lifetime,' he added, thinking back to the welcome Maud had given him when he arrived at

Wattle Trees as a pauper.

They fell silent as the minister began to speak.

After the interment, mourners made their way back to Wattle Trees, where Anna and a couple of the farmhands had been busy preparing food for the wake. 'I need to lay on a good spread for Maud, considering all the times she's done it for others,' Anna had told Meg the day before. Olly attended to the refreshments and Ginger took the mourners' coats and hung them in the cloakroom off the kitchen. Meg, Lily and Sarah handed round plates of food, while Anna served the tea and coffee.

People began to chat about their memories of Maud, smiling over something she'd said or done. Meg said to Lily, 'Maud will never be forgotten as long as we're still alive.'

Gradually the mourners left, until only the folk from Wattle Trees and Deepdene remained. In this spirit of togetherness, they said farewell to their dearest Maud.

CHAPTER FIFTY-EIGHT
War Looms Once More
July 1914

'Do you think there will be a war?' Meg asked Ben, when they were sitting on the sofa beside the fire. The assassination of Archduke Franz Ferdinand two weeks ago had stunned the world and brought the likelihood of war closer.

'I hope not,' he said. 'At least we don't have to worry about the boys; Adam wouldn't be able to fight because of his injuries in the Boer war, and Gordon would be too old to enlist. Come to think of it, so would Adam.'

'But what about our grandsons, Ben, they're the right age.'

'Hopefully this time Australia won't become involved in what's going on in Europe,' he whispered, cocooning her in his arms. They sat like that until the embers of the fire died away and they headed off to bed.

*

The prospect of losing their grandsons to the threatened war still hung over Meg and Ginger when Olly arrived at Deepdene a few days later with happy news.

'The baby's arrived, he was born two hours ago,' he told them, his eyes gleaming with happiness.

'What's his name?' Meg asked, the sparkle in her eyes matching Olly's.

'They're calling him Oliver after me. What do you think of that?'

Ginger slapped him on the back. 'Oliver Jenkins the second, excellent.'

'What a joy for Sarah and Herbert,' Meg said.

'Sarah would hardly let Margo hold her own child.' She and Herbert suffered the loss of their daughter, Clara, from fever back in 1908 so, when Larry and Margo announced they were expecting a child, the news had given them a huge lift.

'The last couple of years have brought a lot of new life to both families,' Ginger said, staring out at the garden, where the trees were at the mercy of a stiff breeze. 'What with Dolly being born to Annabelle and Luke recently and Karl's two children before that.'

'Yes we have indeed been blessed,' Meg agreed. 'And Dolly's birth helped to comfort us after Anna died. Will you have a cuppa?' she asked Olly.

'No, something stronger is called for to celebrate the news,' Ginger said, going to collect the glasses from the cabinet.

CHAPTER FIFTY-NINE
Goodbye to Karl
April 1915

Platform 15 at Melbourne's Flinders Street station was packed, people squeezing in to any niche in the crowd that they could find. Meg pulled her coat collar up against the fierce autumn wind charging across the station platform. She shivered when some raindrops splashed down on her from a hole in the roof. The farmers can't complain about lack of rain this autumn was her wry thought as she stood there beside Ben. It wasn't only the weather that chilled her, but also the departure of her oldest grandson, Karl, to fight at Gallipoli.

As Ben's grip on her hand tightened, she tried desperately to smile. They'd travelled to Melbourne to see Karl leave and now, with Gordon, Frieda and Annabelle, they huddled together on the station platform, waiting for the troop train to arrive. Lily had come too, to be there when her beloved Godson left his native soil. The gas lights flickered, giving the place a ghostly glow and reflecting the feeling of sending loved ones to war and possible death.

Karl held 2-year-old Meg in his arms, her face leaning against his cheek. His spare arm stretched down so he could run his fingers through 3-year-old Ben's red hair, as the boy clutched on tightly to his father's Army great coat. Like his fellow recruits, Karl proudly wore the uniform of the Australian Imperial Forces known, because of their bravery in previous wars, as shock troops.

'Oops,' Karl said, when Meg grabbed his digger hat and knocked it back. He swept it off and held it above his daughter's head, which raised a laugh from family members. When Ben began to complain that he too wanted to wear it, Karl held the hat on his son's head for a few moments before replacing it on to his own head.

As their farewell drew nearer, Meg tried to remain upbeat, although her body felt weighed down with grief. She glanced round at Ben senior's face and saw her own thoughts mirrored there. Meg stood on one side of him and Lily on the other.

When the troop train arrived, the goodbyes were quick. Karl hugged each of his family members, and kissed his two children. Then he threw his arms around his wife, Alice, who clung to him until he gently pulled away and joined his fellow soldiers who were piling on to the train.

A moment later the whistle blew, the guard waved his green flag and the huge wheels began to move forward. Karl and some other fellows hung out of the compartment window and waved until the train built up speed and followed a bend in the line, taking their beloved faces out of view.

CHAPTER SIXTY
A Death and Two Enlistments
October 1916

When Ben arrived home from Wattle Trees, Meg knew immediately that he had bad news to deliver. He'd been in high spirits when he'd gone to visit Olly a couple of hours ago, but now he looked tired and despondent.

'What's wrong, Ben?' she asked, helping him out of his overcoat. Until a few years ago, Ben had never worn a coat, summer or winter, but he felt the cold more these days. At the age of 89, his fresh complexion and energetic behaviour belied his age, and Meg had high hopes of him living for a long time yet.

He hung his walking sick on its hook behind the back door, and pulled out a kitchen chair. Sitting down, he raked his fingers through his hair, which he still had in abundance, though the red had turned to silver years ago. 'Olly tells me Larry has signed up.'

Meg gasped. 'That's going to be hard on Margo.' At 2-years-old Oliver was quite a handful.

'She'll get support from Sarah and Herbert, and don't forget Olly's also very good at amusing the lad. He really dotes on the boy and plays with him every chance he gets.'

'True,' she said, sitting down across the table from him, 'but Olly's the same age as you, Ben, so he isn't going to be able to play football with young Oliver.'

'No,' he agreed, 'but Herbert will. After all, he's only in his fifties and still fit.'

'But he and Sarah have the farm to run,' she pointed out.

'He'll be able to do both. It's good Herbert employed more farm hands last year with Larry going away and Steve running his own farm.'

Meg smiled at the mention of her half-brother. If only

Anna had lived to witness her son buying a farm. She and Ben were fond of Steve's wife, Janet, who came to Deepdene as often as work on the farm allowed.

'When does Larry leave?'

'When he gets his uniform, Olly thinks within the week.'

'It's hard to see him go. And coming so soon after Luke enlisted.' Luke Aster, Gordon's son-in-law, had also joined up, leaving Annabelle to look after 2-year–old Dolly. Meg was sad to think how many children were being separated from their fathers due to this cruel war in Europe.

*

'Visitors from Wattle Trees,' Meg called to Ginger next morning, as she ushered Margo and young Oliver into the family room.

Margo held out a paper bag to her son and helped him hand it over to Meg. 'Plums from our trees,' he told her, obviously having rehearsed the words earlier.

'Thank you so much,' Meg responded, smiling down at the 2-year-old. 'Your speech has come on a treat, hasn't it?'

Oliver stared at her, not understanding a word, then turned his attention to Ginger, who came into the room from his study across the hallway.

'Well, if it isn't Oliver Jenkins the second,' he said.

'Me not Oliver, me Olly,' the boy protested, tapping his chest with his hand.

The three adults burst out laughing at the sight of this little mite giving his great-grandfather a telling off.

'I'll go and make some tea. Would you like milk or juice, Olly?' she asked the boy, emphasising the last word.

'Milk.'

Margo frowned. 'Milk what?'

'Milk please.' Olly gave Meg a smile that would have melted the coldest of hearts.

After Margo and Olly left, Ginger returned to his study to continue writing his memoir, while Meg went off to change their bedsheets. If she got them washed and out on the line, they'd dry quickly on such a warm day.

In the study, Ginger twirled his pen around in his fingers. His last entry had been the day before they'd said farewell to Karl on his way to Gallipoli, almost eighteen months ago. Painful though it was to write about that event, he forced himself to do so. Recently Ginger had become more aware of his age, and was keen to keep his memoir up to date. Sometimes he wondered why he was writing it, as he wasn't sure anyone would want to hear his life story. But Meg had assured him it would be of great interest to future generations of their family. With that thought in mind, he dipped his pen into the inkwell and started to write.

An hour later, Meg was rolling out her scone mixture when there was a knock on the kitchen door. When she opened it, the postman said 'g'day, Mrs Harker,' and handed her a telegram. She thanked him, her heart sinking when she saw it was from Melbourne.

She went into the study, where the silence was broken by the scratching sound of Ben's pen moving across the page. She laid the telegram down in front of Ben, and perched on the arm of his chair. He opened the envelope and they both read the words, then clung together as they tried to take it in.

MELBOURNE TELEGRAPH OFFICE, 14th OCTOBER, 1916

SAD NEWS. KARL DEAD, DYSENTERY. BURIED IN GALLIPOLI.

GORDON.

Meg spoke first, her voice caught with tears, and still clutching at Ben. 'Last year when Karl was hospitalised due to shell shock, I prayed he'd be invalided out and brought home. Now, thanks to dysentery, he is to lie in a foreign field, far away from home.'

Ginger dropped his head into his hands and when he looked up, tears glistened. 'Karl will be surrounded by his dead comrades. And when all this carnage ends, we can go to Italy and lay flowers on his grave.' He stood up and took her hand. 'Let's go into the garden.'

They walked outside, arm in arm, to find some peace amongst the flowers and shrubs.

CHAPTER SIXTY-ONE

The War Finally Ends

December 1918

Ginger sat at his desk, still trying to take in that the war had finally ceased. After four long years of fighting, with massive losses experienced on both sides, the signing of the Armistice last month had been emotional for everyone. It had been called the war to end all wars and he fervently prayed that would be the case.

His eyes welled up at the thought of Larry, killed last year in the Battle of Passchendaele. Like Karl he too was buried in Flanders. He closed his eyes for a moment of reflection. They'd now lost two family members to this war and were praying that Luke would return to them, safe and sound. They hadn't heard news of him for some time. Little Dolly had now passed her fourth birthday and she asked Annabelle every day when her daddy would be coming home.

Meg popped her head around the study door. 'Ben, I'm going over to the community hall to help with the arrangements for next week, will you be alright until I get back?' She'd noticed a decline in his health recently, with some breathlessness, and didn't like to leave him for too long at a time.

'Of course, Meg, I'm going to add a bit more to my memoir. You go and help the other ladies get everything ready for our returning heroes,' he said, smiling at her. 'Let me know if I can do anything to help.'

'I think we've enough helpers right now.'

They were planning to decorate the hall with banners this afternoon and make out a list of the food to be prepared to welcome home the men returning from the Front.

She stood in front of the mirror to put her hat on, pushing her hat pin in near the back. 'I'm off then,' she called to Ben. On her short walk to the hall, her thoughts swivelled between Luke and Ben; her concern for Luke's safe return on the one hand and her nagging worry about Ben's health on the other.

CHAPTER SIXTY-TWO

The End of an Era

April 1919

Meg sat in front of the mirror, her own bleak face staring back at her. After a few seconds the picture changed and superimposed on her image was that of the man she'd loved and cherished for almost sixty years. Through good times and bad, they'd supported one another. She winked at his image, almost expecting him to return her wink. To Meg, he'd looked as handsome with his silver hair in recent years as he'd done with the red of earlier times. She found it hard to imagine going on without her life's companion, yet for the sake of the family she was determined to do so.

A glance at the clock forced her to move. The family members would be gathering soon and she wasn't even dressed yet. Her black taffeta dress rustled as she stepped into it and pushed her arms down through its long sleeves. Her fingers trembled as she fastened the buttons on the front bodice, but she steeled herself to get through the day.

Meg was fixing the pin into her hat when she heard her daughter's feet on the stair treads. 'Need any help?' Lily asked, as she entered her parents' bedroom. 'I had hoped to get here sooner but the carriage driver had to stop when his horse became lame.'

Mother and daughter fell into a tight hug. When Meg finally released her grip, she staggered back, her eyes glistening with unshed tears.

'Careful, Mummy,' Lily said, moving behind Meg to steady her. 'You look so dignified,' she added, taking in her mother's dress and hat.

'I needed to be properly turned out for Daddy, it's what he would have expected.'

Despite the sadness etched on Lily's face, she gave a brief smile. 'He will be so proud of you,' she assured her parent. 'Where is Daddy?'

'Come with me,' Meg said, and lead the way downstairs into the front reception room. It hadn't been used much in recent years, but was more spacious than the family room, and could easily accommodate the large crowd of mourners expected to attend the wake later.

Ben's coffin, with a brass plaque on the top, sat on a long trestle table in the centre of the room. A candlestick sat on either side of the casket, and the flames flickered now and again in the soft spring breeze coming through the open window. Lily stood at the foot of the coffin and wept quietly; she bent and laid her head against it, drawing her fingers slowly down its wooden slats.

Meg gently stroked her hair. 'We weren't allowed to leave it open, Lily, because Daddy died of the 'flu.' The epidemic of Spanish 'flu, which had swept across the world following the war, had overtaken Ben. At first the doctor thought he'd pull through, but in the end he'd succumbed to the weakness and fever.

Lily and Meg were comforting one another when Gordon and Frieda joined them. They'd travelled from Melbourne and planned to stay at Deepdene with Meg for a few days after the funeral. Gordon hugged his mother and sister. 'I have some good news for you both. Annabelle has had a telegram to say that Luke is safe and will be coming home soon.' They were discussing the wonderful news when Adam and his family arrived at the same time as the folks from Wattle Trees, headed by Olly, looking his age today.

Ten minutes later they heard the sound of hooves outside, accompanied by the jingling of harnesses and, holding on to Gordon's arm, Meg led the way outside.

The groom was trying to quieten the lead horses, who were a bit restless, causing their black plumes to wave about with the motion. The coffin was placed in that first carriage, with family members sitting in the ones behind it for the short drive to Dubbo Church. Despite the rain that had been falling all morning, the streets were lined on either side with silent townspeople; shopkeepers, innkeepers, tradesmen, lawmen and so on, all wishing to pay their respects to Ben.

The pews inside were packed as Gordon led Meg down to the front. As a body, the congregation stood when the coffin was carried into the church. There was a shuffling of feet as people sat down again, then silence descended and the Minister began to speak.

We gather here today with heavy hearts to mourn the death of our friend and brother, Ben Harker. Our thoughts are with Meg and other family members in the loss of their beloved husband, father, grandfather and great-grandfather. The residents of Dubbo will also miss such a highly respected member of their Community. Ben helped so many people in this town and elsewhere, usually in private, seeking no glory for himself. A more honest and sincere gentleman would be hard to find.

But, in addition to mourning, today we also celebrate his long life. Starting from humble beginnings in Scotland, Ben came to Australia at the age of 21. He was employed at Wattle Trees farm, working with Larry and Olly Jenkins, who became his lifelong friends. While working on the farm, Ben discovered he had a gift for wood carving. Encouraged by Larry, he started his own business, selling his work initially from a stall in Dubbo market, before opening his first shop, Aussie Crafts.

In later years his business expanded into other States. Aussie Crafts still operates in Australia, with Ben's sons, Gordon and Adam, now in charge. But up until Ben's recent death he retained an interest in the stores and visited them as often as he could.

After his retiral from the business, Ben continued to work on various Committees. He was a Director of the Broken Hill Silver Mine and constantly fought for improvements in workers' conditions and pay. Ben was a Freemason and a member of the Order of Oddfellows.

But despite his dedication to his business, it took second place to Meg and the children for Ben. He enjoyed being a father, grandfather and great-grandfather. Ben married Meg Stanley near the beginning of his career and together they loved and supported one another during the good times and the bad, having the delight of seeing their family expand. Ben was overjoyed when his daughter, Sarah, wed Herbert Jenkins, cementing even further the closeness between the folk at Wattle Trees and Deepdene. Ben was proud of his eldest child, Lily, who inherited her grandparents' mansion house, Ripponlea, and turned it into a school for girls. Lily has made a great success of running the school and she tells me she has no plans to retire anytime soon.

And now, in tribute to Ben's remarkable life and the legacy he has left behind him, we will sing his favourite hymn, 'Will Your Anchor Hold?' Meg tells me that Ben's mother taught him this hymn back in Scotland, and he always enjoyed singing it.

The organist started up the music and the congregation got to their feet, their hearts full as they sang.

And so it was that our beloved Ben Harker was laid to rest in Dubbo cemetery. The rain had finally stopped when the mourners came out of the church and on the journey to the cemetery Meg saw a magnificent rainbow from the carriage window. Tears flowed as she stared at the gorgeous colours, but they were tears of joy, that her beloved Ben had fought the good fight and was now safe in his next life, where they would meet again one day.

Kitchener Crescent, Longniddry, Scotland
March 2020

When Brenda went into the kitchen, the roast beef was sizzling away in the oven. Turning the temperature gauge down a notch, she listened to Classic FM while she prepared the veggies. The kitchen looked over the side garden where clumps of daffodils were already in bloom.

Before she and Harry bought this house, it had been in the same family since the 1920s, and had the feeling of being loved and cherished down the generations. The previous owner told them there had been a black-leaded range in the kitchen and a fold-down bed right here where she was standing. From a photograph taken in the 1930s the house hadn't changed much. A hedge encompassed the property, with the same white painted gates, a front and a side one, and the green front door remained.

She and Harry had built an extension at the back of the house to include a dining room and bathroom. The original upstairs bathroom had been turned into an en suite for their bedroom.

Hearing the front door open, she hurried into the hallway.

'Hello, Aunt Kate,' she greeted her elderly relative, a few months short of her 90th birthday and immaculate as ever in her twin set and pearls. She'd invited Aunt Kate today because of the threat of lockdown due to the Coronavirus that had affected the whole world.

Hanging her walking stick over the wing of the armchair, Aunt Kate sank into its cushioned depths. 'I'm looking forward to hearing more about this Archie fellow.'

'I've been in email contact with Emma Ford from Melbourne. She's a descendent of Archie's and came over last summer to trace the Speirs' grave here in Longniddry.'

'Was it she who put his name on the stone?'

'Yes.'

'And how did she get in touch with you, Brenda?'

'As you know I've been trying to trace Archie. On the website, I found the name Archie Speirs on the passenger list of a convict ship, the Waverley, sent to Tasmania in 1847. I posted a message on Facebook, giving my maiden name of Brenda Speirs, and asking for information on an ancestor who might have been transported to Australia back in the 1840s. Emma emailed me the following day to confirm that Archie was her ancestor and that she and I were therefore related.'

'Beats me how you can get all that information from a total stranger.'

Harry laughed. 'Technology, Aunt Kate. It's wonderful.'

'Lunch is ready, so let's eat first before I tell you the rest.'

'Tell me more about Archie,' her aunt said, once they were back in the living room.

Laying the family tree on Aunt Kate's knee, Brenda pointed to one of the names on it. 'James Speirs, your great-grandfather, born in 1860.'

'I think he died some years before I was born,' Aunt Kate said, dipping a ginger nut into her tea.

'That's right, in 1922, eight years before your birth. One thing puzzles me. He had four children; Hugh, your grandfather, was killed in 1918. Lizzie died when she was 11, but the remaining two sons were both called James. How could that be?'

'When did they die?'

'The first James died in 1889 when he was 2-years-old. The second James died in 1916 fighting on the Somme.'

'I think I can help you there,' Aunt Kate said, 'in those days if a child died in infancy, it was common practice to give the same name to the next born in that gender.'

'That's weird,' Harry chipped in.

Aunt Kate shrugged. 'I suppose it was just the custom at the time.'

'It's confusing with the names James and Hugh featuring so often down the generations,' Brenda said.

'I've given up trying to work out who's who.' Harry picked up The Sunday Post and began to read it.

Aunt Kate looked again at the family tree. 'Was Archie an uncle or cousin to one of our earlier ancestors?'

'I thought that at first, but Emma was able to tell me that Archie was the illegitimate son of your great-great-great-grandfather. See, here at the top of the tree, James Speirs, born in 1798. He was a butcher, and started the Speirs' family business.'

'I knew that butchering was in the family, and we always had the best of meat in our house. So that first James was a naughty boy, was he?'

'He was married but he seduced one of his young female assistants. Jenny Thom was her name.'

'Tell me more.' Aunt Kate was fascinated by the story.

'When Jenny later told James she was pregnant, he gave her a sum of money and sent her on her way.'

'The cad. How did the woman in Australia discover this?'

'A couple of years ago Emma was clearing out her grandparents' house and found an old jotter. Inside was a memoir written by her ancestor, Ben Harker, who wrote that he'd been born Archie Speirs. Emma read that Ben was born in Edinburgh and his mother was Jenny Thom. She'd given him the surname Speirs and left him a letter after she died telling him who his father was. He always wanted to confront James Speirs but never did. Jenny took casual jobs to allow her to work and look after Archie at the same time. This way she kept them out of the workhouse. She also taught him to read, write and count, something that very few poor kids could do in those days.'

'So what happened to his mother?'

'She died from consumption, or tuberculosis as we

know it, when Archie was 12. He was left to fend for himself, sleeping on the streets most of the time and stealing to feed himself. It was for stealing food in Glasgow that he was transported to Australia.'

Aunt Kate gasped. 'Just for stealing food because he was starving?'

'Just for that.'

'What a sad tale.'

'Well, at least Archie's story has a happy ending. He was transported to Tasmania where he slaved in a coal mine, until he escaped from the penal colony. In his memoir, he tells that he changed his name to Ben Harker because he'd become a fugitive being hunted by the police. He describes going to the mainland and walking from Victoria across the State border into New South Wales, where he spent the remainder of his life.'

'What did he work at?'

'He worked on a sheep farm for a few years and later took up wood carving and opened a shop. In fact, he opened lots of shops all over New South Wales and his Empire eventually extended into Victoria and other Australian States. He became a very wealthy man and, by all accounts, enjoyed a happy family life.'

'Did he live to an old age?'

'Yes, he died of Spanish 'flu in April, 1919, at the age of 92. Emma sent me a copy of his obituary in The Sydney Herald. It mentioned him being well-respected and trusted in his hometown of Dubbo.'

'And what happened to his shops when he died?'

'They were taken over by his two sons, then passed on to their children and the business is still flourishing today, with shops all over the country. Emma's father was a director in the company.'

'All that achieved by a convict.'

'Yes, and a convict ancestor of ours. Although he died over a century ago, I feel very close to him.'

'Are there many family members left?'

'There's Emma and one other Harker cousin, Ben Harker the 4th. He's married with a baby son, Ben Harker the 5th and it will be up to this baby to keep the Harker name going. The Speirs surname will die out and it's only the made up one of Harker that will go on.'

'It's nice to know that Archie is included in his family circle at last,' Aunt Kate said.

Seeing her great aunt look tired, Brenda got up. 'I think we're needing another cuppa.'

Aunt Kate's wizened hand caught hold of hers. 'Thanks Brenda, you've done a great job, lass. Now the mystery about Archie is solved, I can die happy.'

'Well don't go yet, not till I've made you a cup of tea.'

Aunt Kate's laughter followed Brenda into the kitchen.

The End

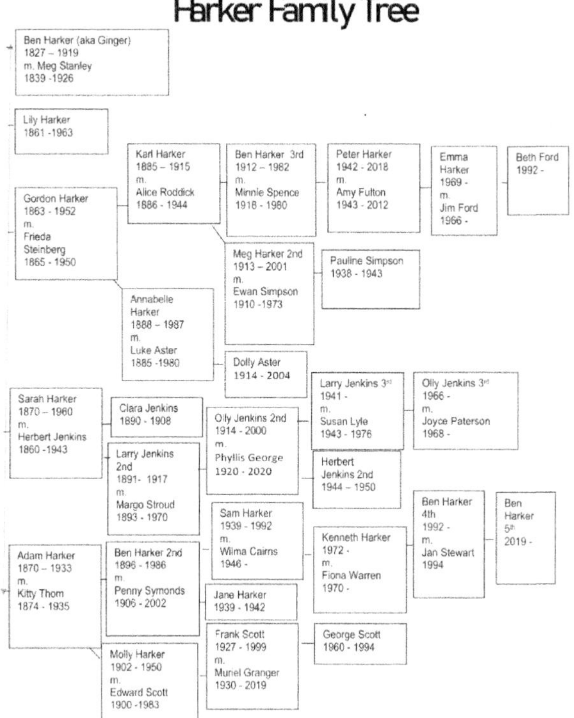
Harker Family Tree
Ben Harker (aka Ginger) 1827 – 1919 m. Meg Stanley 1839 -1926
Lily Harker 1861 -1963
Gordon Harker 1863 - 1952 m. Frieda Steinberg 1865 - 1950
Karl Harker 1885 – 1915 m. Alice Roddick 1886 - 1944
Ben Harker 3rd 1912 – 1982 m. Minnie Spence 1918 - 1980
Peter Harker 1942 - 2018 m. Amy Fulton 1943 - 2012
Emma Harker 1969 - m. Jim Ford 1966 -
Beth Ford 1992 -
Meg Harker 2nd 1913 – 2001 m. Ewan Simpson 1910 -1973
Pauline Simpson 1938 - 1943
Annabelle Harker 1888 – 1987 m. Luke Aster 1885 -1980
Dolly Aster 1914 - 2004
Sarah Harker 1870 – 1960 m. Herbert Jenkins 1860 -1943
Clara Jenkins 1890 - 1908
Larry Jenkins 2nd 1891- 1917 m. Margo Stroud 1893 - 1970
Olly Jenkins 2nd 1914 - 2000 m. Phyllis George 1920 - 2020
Larry Jenkins 3rd 1941 - m. Susan Lyle 1943 - 1976
Olly Jenkins 3rd 1966 - m. Joyce Paterson 1968 -
Herbert Jenkins 2nd 1944 – 1950
Adam Harker 1870 – 1933 m. Kitty Thom 1874 - 1935
Ben Harker 2nd 1896 - 1986 m Penny Symonds 1906 - 2002
Sam Harker 1939 - 1992 m. Wilma Cairns 1946 -
Kenneth Harker 1972 - m. Fiona Warren 1970 -
Ben Harker 4th 1992 - m. Jan Stewart 1994
Ben Harker 5th 2019 -
Jane Harker 1939 - 1942
Molly Harker 1902 - 1950 m. Edward Scott 1900 -1983
Frank Scott 1927 - 1999 m. Muriel Granger 1930 - 2019
George Scott 1960 - 1994

ABOUT THE AUTHOR

Having enjoyed writing since childhood, it wasn't until I retired from full-time employment with the NHS that I began to work at the craft seriously. I write in many genres but my greatest love is the novel. My four previous novels have all been published by Author Way.

Although I'm a romantic at heart, the books aren't purely love stories. My characters face challenges and often grapple with major issues, some of which readers may have experienced in their own lives.

My first three books are set in the 20th century and Rutherglen in South Lanarkshire features in all of them, with two of the books having parts in Australia. As a Ruglonian the town means a lot to me, but I've also worked and spent holidays in the Antipodes, both Australia and New Zealand. I adore the countries and their people, so I enjoy setting my scenes there.

I had a change with the fourth book 'Who Were You?' and set the story in New Zealand. Another change was that the story takes place in the 21st century. Although not a sequel, there is a connection with an earlier book, but you will need to read the novels to find out what that is!! Published in February 2020, I held a book signing in Rutherglen Library ten days prior to the first Coronavirus lockdown. How's that for good timing! The book has been well received and I'm delighted that so many readers enjoyed the story.

This inspired me, during the lockdowns and restrictions over the past two years, to write my fifth book 'Ginger'. As I have a male main character this time and the story is set in the 19th century, it has been both challenging and satisfying to do a lot of research into the period. The story takes place in Australia, beginning in 1847 on a convict ship and finishing just after the end of World War I.

Printed in Great Britain
by Amazon